Martha Rogers, with her winsom[e]
immediately pulls readers into the 1898 setting of small-town
Prairie Grove, Kansas. In moments we are immersed in the
lives of ex-con Clayton Barlow, his family and friends, and the
townfolk who are understandably wary of him. The story car-
ries us into the approaching holidays with passion and purpose,
keeping us eagerly engaged right up to the satisfying ending.
—KATHI MACIAS
AUTHOR OF *THE DELIVERER* AND *UNEXPECTED CHRISTMAS HERO*

I love Christmas novels. With *Christmas at Holly Hill* Martha
has given us a story about Christmas right before the turn of the
twentieth century. The characters and plotline kept me turning
pages. And I loved the way she tied it to her first Realms release,
Becoming Lucy. I highly recommend this wonderful read.
—LENA NELSON DOOLEY
AUTHOR OF *MAGGIE'S JOURNEY*, *MARY'S BLESSING*, AND THE SOON
TO BE RELEASED *CATHERINE'S PURSUIT*, AS WELL AS
THE WILL ROGERS MEDALLION AWARD WINNER *LOVE FINDS
YOU IN GOLDEN, NEW MEXICO*

Once again author Martha Rogers pulled me into her story
on page one and held me captive until I finished the book.
Christmas at Holly Hill is filled with emotion from characters
I cared about in a setting that seemed so real I felt as though I
was actually there. This is why Martha Rogers has a permanent
spot on my bookshelf.
—DEBBY MAYNE
AUTHOR OF *WAITING FOR A VIEW* AND
THE UPCOMING CLASS REUNION SERIES

Christmas at Holly Hill is a story about second chances. It's a
charming tale of starting over and finding love instead of hatred

and resentment. It will pull at your heartstrings, engage you, and leave you filling as satisfied as a fine Christmas dinner. Kudos to Martha Rogers for a job well done.

—VICKIE McDONOUGH
AWARD-WINNING AUTHOR OF TWENTY-FIVE HISTORICAL BOOKS
AND NOVELLAS

A WINDS ACROSS
THE PRAIRIE
HOLIDAY NOVEL

Christmas at HOLLY HILL

MARTHA ROGERS

REALMS

Most Charisma House Book Group products are available at special quantity discounts for bulk purchase for sales promotions, premiums, fund-raising, and educational needs. For details, write Charisma House Book Group, 600 Rinehart Road, Lake Mary, Florida 32746, or telephone (407) 333-0600.

CHRISTMAS AT HOLLY HILL by Martha Rogers
Published by Realms
Charisma Media/Charisma House Book Group
600 Rinehart Road
Lake Mary, Florida 32746
www.charismahouse.com

Cover design by Bill Johnson

Visit the author's website at www.marthawrogers.com.

Library of Congress Cataloging-in-Publication Data:
Rogers, Martha, 1936-
 Christmas at Holly Hill / Martha Rogers. -- 1st ed.
    p. cm.
 ISBN 978-1-61638-837-9 (trade paper) -- ISBN 978-1-61638-838-6 (e-book)
 1. Ex-convicts--Fiction. 2. Christmas stories. I. Title.
PS3618.O4655C47 2012
813'.6--dc23
                                    2012018020

First edition

12 13 14 15 16 — 9 8 7 6 5 4 3 2 1
Printed in the United States of America

In memory of my mother, Dorothy Mae Miller Stead,
who loved Christmas and gave so much of her time
making sure others had a very happy Christmas

Acknowledgments

With gratitude to:

Nineteenth-century writers loop and their willingness to answer questions

My First Place Friends, Barbara Amy and her mother, Theda, who brainstormed with me at lunch one day at Round Top and gave me the idea for this story

Carole Lewis and Pat Lewis, for always believing in me and praying with me about my writing

Tamela Hancock Murray, my extraordinary agent who keeps me plugging away

Lori Vanden Bosch, for giving my stories just the right extra *oomph* to make them so much better

All the staff at Charisma, for believing in me and my books

And most importantly, Rex, the love of my life, for always being available for whatever I need and supporting me in all my endeavors

And I will restore to you the years that the locust hath eaten.... And ye shall eat in plenty, and be satisfied, and praise the name of the LORD your God, that hath dealt wondrously with you; and my people will never be ashamed.

—JOEL 2:25–26

Chapter 1

Prairie Grove, Kansas, October 1898

HOME FOR THANKSGIVING and Christmas! Clay's heart pumped blood through his veins at a frantic pace. After serving five years for his part in a bank robbery, he'd be home for his two favorite holidays. The question looming in his soul was whether he'd be welcomed by anyone other than his parents.

The train hissed and steamed its way into the station with a blast of the whistle as Clay peered through the window. When the cars came to a screeching stop, he remained in his seat, fear gripping his heart. The conductor stopped in the aisle.

"Son, this is your stop. Time to get off."

Clay willed himself to stand and make his way down the aisle. No one would be here to greet him since no one knew he'd be on the train. He'd planned it all as a surprise, especially for his mother. He stepped to the platform, gripping the handle of the small bag containing all his worldly possessions. Around him the trees wore their best fall colors in welcome, and as Clay made his way to the street in front of the depot, he drank in the sight he'd seen only in his dreams for the past five years.

The good citizens of Prairie Grove moved about on their way to one place or another, oblivious to his presence. The livery still stood close to the station with the post office nearby, and right next to it a new addition announced itself in gold letters. The telegraph office was now the Prairie Grove Telephone and Telegraph center. His hometown had grown more than he realized.

He spotted the hotel and the Red Garter Saloon a few blocks away, then he breathed deeply of the fresh smell of baking bread drifting from the bakery next to his father's store. The green and yellow letters on the sign hanging in front welcomed customers to Barlow's General Store, still the only mercantile in town. A slight breeze sent the sign swinging with a creak he heard from his position near the depot. Dust whirls danced across the street where he'd once played with other boys his age.

By Christmas those streets would most likely be filled with snow, and snowball fights would be the game of the day at the school. His days at the red clapboard schoolhouse had been some of the happiest of life. He viewed the bell tower of the school at the end of the street and could almost hear the sound of it clanging in his memory.

Doubt lodged in Clay's throat, but he kept walking to the store. When he stepped through the door, it could well have been ten years ago when he helped Pa. He inhaled the familiar smells of coal oil, fresh ground coffee, fabric dye, and peppermint candy. Nothing had changed.

Then he spotted his ma. He observed her for a minute or two, savoring the sight of her graying hair and slight frame. She didn't move as fast as she once had, and she stopped to catch her breath after placing some items on a shelf.

From the corner of his eye he saw his father coming from the storeroom. A good five inches shorter than Clay, Pa's sturdy frame handled the box in his arms with ease. He turned to set the box on the counter, and Clay cringed the moment his father recognized him. The meeting he both dreaded and anticipated had come.

Pa didn't move from behind the counter. He simply stared for what seemed an eternity but in reality amounted to only seconds. His words barely reached Clay's ears. "Son, you've come home."

At Clay's nod his father stepped around the counter and called to Ma. "Cora, our boy is home."

A can clattered to the floor, and his mother turned with hands to her mouth. She hurried toward him and hugged him. "Thank You, Lord, for bringing him home safe." Tears glistened in her eyes. "I've waited and waited for this moment to come." She reached up and placed her hands on each side of his face then kissed his cheeks.

Heat rose in his face, but Ma's arms and kisses were the welcome he'd hoped for in the past few days of travel. His arms went around her thin frame. She'd lost a good deal of weight since the last time he'd seen her, and that bothered him more than his earlier observations.

He glanced up at his father. His graying hair had thinned

some, and his eyes held both a welcome and uncertainty. Gaining Pa's trust would take time.

His parents stood in front of him and shook their heads. Pa wrapped his arm around Ma. "We've waited a long time for this day. Thank God you made it home."

Clay didn't know what God had to do with anything, since it had been Pa who had turned Clay over to the authorities five years ago. The road back would be long and hard, but then that's no more than he'd expected.

Ma grabbed his hands. "Are you planning on staying here in Prairie Grove with us? You're not going to get mixed up with those...those...thieves again, are you?"

Before Clay could answer, Pa added his own sentiments. "If you do decide to stay, I expect you to stay away from them. If you don't, you won't be welcome here."

Clay stiffened but kept his voice neutral. "I understand, Pa, but I'm not going to get mixed up with Karl's gang again. I would like to stay as long as you'll have me."

Or until the townspeople ran him off. Two older women in the corner eyed him and whispered between themselves. The prodigal had returned, but not everyone welcomed him. He nodded to the ladies, who immediately turned their backs. So much for the town's greeting.

"Of course we want you to live here with us," Ma said, not even seeming to notice the ladies. "Now let's go upstairs and get you settled in. I know you're hungry. You always were, and I have supper almost ready." She held onto his arm and led him to the stairway up to the living quarters above the store.

A voice calling his name stopped him at the bottom. He nodded for his mother to go on up and turned to find an old friend, Jimmy Shanks, grinning from ear to ear. "It is you, Clay Barlow." The blond-headed young man reached out to grasp Clay's hand.

"Yeah, it's me. I decided to come home, Jimmy." He grasped the outstretched hand and blinked at the strength in the grasp.

"It's James now, and I'm married to Grace Ann Higgins."

Clay had to chuckle at that revelation. Grace Ann had run away from Jimmy every time he'd tried to get close.

"So, you finally got Grace Ann's attention. I'm glad since you always liked her."

"You'll have to come out to the house for dinner some night so we can catch up on old times."

"I'll think on that, Jimmy…James." Not much to catch up on from his side since he'd been behind prison bars for five years. "And you'd better check with Grace Ann. She might not cotton to having an ex-con at her dinner table."

James blinked. "Don't you worry none about that; we'll always be friends." He stepped back and picked up his purchase. "Had to pick up some coal oil. With the days getting shorter, we need more of it."

Clay walked with him to the door and stepped outside with James, who shook Clay's hand once again. "I'm so glad you're home. This is one Christmas your parents will be glad to celebrate." With a grin and a salute he stepped down to the street and mounted his horse. "See you around, Clay."

If he'd stayed good friends with Jimmy instead of getting mixed up with Karl, things would have been much different. Still, the warm welcome from his old friend and the greeting from his parents lightened the load in Clay's heart.

If Pa would have him, Clay wanted to work again in the

store. Being locked up with bad food, hard cots, little sunshine, and no privacy motivated him to stay out of trouble. He'd had a lot of time to think in prison, and one thing remained sure and steadfast. Clayton Barlow would not end up behind bars ever again.

Merry Warner stepped onto the boardwalk up the street from the school where she taught. The wonderful aroma of cinnamon stopped her in front of the bakery. Cinnamon buns for breakfast in the morning would make up for her being late this afternoon. She hurried up to the counter where Mr. Brooks placed fresh pies into the case. On second thought, two pecan pies for supper tonight would be even better.

She grinned at the baker, who reminded her of the pictures she'd seen of Santa Claus, right down to the white beard and rosy cheeks. "I'll have two of those pecan pies. I'm sure Mama will appreciate them for supper tonight."

"Good choice, Miss Warner. We had a good crop of pecans this year, so Mrs. Brooks is busy with recipes using the nuts." Mr. Brooks placed each pie in a paper bag then tied the top closed with string. "There, that should make them easier to carry."

She plunked several coins onto the counter and picked up her purchase. "I hope she makes some of that pumpkin bread for the holidays."

Mr. Brooks laughed. "Oh, she will. I'm sure of that. You have a nice evening now, and tell your ma I said hello."

Merry nodded and hurried out to be on her way. She stopped short when she spotted a man standing in front of the general store next door. A gasp escaped her lips, and her heart skipped a beat. He looked just like Clay Barlow, but Clay was in prison. Surely she would have heard if he had come home.

He turned, and his gaze locked with hers. Recognition shot through her with streaks of delight that dissipated almost as soon as they began. No one but Clay had eyes so dark a brown that they penetrated to her very soul.

How could Clay be out of prison already? Then she counted and realized five years had indeed passed since he'd gone away. When Grandma Collins had said she needed Mama and Papa to come back and take care of the orphanage at Holly Hill, Merry's heart had been torn apart. She loved Barton Creek and wanted to stay there, but the memory of her years in Prairie Grove beckoned for her to return. One of those memories included Clay Barlow and the schoolgirl crush she'd had on him before he got involved with Karl Laramie's gang.

Shoving aside her misgivings, she gave in to her delight and ran up to hug Clay. "Clay Barlow, it's been too many years." Heat filled her face, and she jumped back. She was no longer a sixteen-year-old girl but a young woman who should practice better manners befitting her age.

Clay's eyes opened wide in surprise. "Merry?"

"Yes. We moved back to Holly Hill last summer after Grandpa died. I'm so glad you're home."

"I'm glad to be here too." He stepped back. "It...it's nice to see you. I...I..." His voice trailed off, and he glanced over her shoulder. Without another word he bolted through the door to the store.

Merry stood with her mouth agape. How rude. Then she

turned and saw three women staring at her with disapproval written all over them. Mrs. Pennyfeather, wife of the school superintendent, shook her head and frowned.

Heat rose in Merry's face again. They'd seen her greeting Clay. No sense in trying to apologize. Mrs. Pennyfeather wouldn't listen anyway. Merry gathered up her pies and fled up the hill toward Holly Hill Home for Children. Along the way her thoughts whirled. She had never expected to see Clay again, figuring that he'd be too ashamed to come back to his hometown. What could his return mean?

She burst through the door then closed it and braced herself against the smooth wood. Her heart pounded not only from the long walk but also from seeing Clay again.

Imogene and Eileen raced over to grab her around the waist. The blonde-haired ten-year-old-twins wore matching blue-and-white striped dresses with white pinafores over them.

Eileen eyed the bags in Merry's hands. "You went by the bakery. What did you bring?" She reached for one of the bags.

Merry held it high. "Not until after supper. Then we'll have pecan pie."

Imogene jumped up and down, her pigtails bouncing on her shoulders. "That's my favorite. Oh, I love you, Merry." The young girl wrapped her arms about Merry's waist again.

Emmaline appeared with a stack of silverware in her hands. "It's about time you got here. Mama Warner could use your help."

Merry set the pie bags on a table near the door and unwound Imogene's arms. "I'm sorry I'm late. I stayed at the school to prepare the lessons for tomorrow. Did you know we have ten different varieties of trees around our school building?"

Emmaline shook her head. "No, and I don't care right now. Are you going to help me or not?"

"Yes, I'm on my way." Merry removed her shawl and bonnet then hung them on a hook by the door in the entry hall. She picked up the pies and made her way to the kitchen. Emmaline plunked the silverware onto the table behind Merry. At thirteen Emmaline had begun to rebel against doing so many chores around the home, but Mama could usually get her to cooperate.

Merry sighed and pushed open the swinging door into the kitchen. She kissed her mother's plump cheek. "Sorry I'm late. I got detained at school."

Mama ladled stew into bowls and set them on a tray. "I figured as much. Check the cornbread for me. Supper's about ready."

Grandma Collins opened up the bakery sacks. "Pecan pie—now that's going to make for a good dessert. Thank you, Merry."

"I figured since I was so late coming home, I might as well contribute something to the meal." Merry opened the oven door and removed two pans of cornbread. She set them on the counter and reached up to the shelf to grab a plate for serving it. She turned one pan onto the counter then cut it into squares and arranged them on the plate.

"Mama, did you know Clay Barlow came home?"

The ladle stopped, dripping stew back into the pot. Mama stood still for a few seconds, as did Grandma. "No, I didn't. Has it been five years already?" She shook her head. "Such promise that boy had before he got into so much trouble. Where did you see him?"

"Outside the store. I'm…I'm afraid I made a spectacle of myself. I ran up and hugged him because I was so glad to see him back. The problem is, Mrs. Pennyfeather and her friends saw the whole thing. They weren't too happy about it either."

Mama laid the spoon aside and reached over to pat Merry's shoulder. "I'm sure they'll get over it. How did he seem?"

"I don't know. Embarrassed to see me, I guess. He didn't say much."

Mama nodded sagely. "It's been seven years since we moved away from Holly Hill and went to Barton Creek. You were only sixteen when you thought you were so in love with him. Being in prison changes a man, so he won't be that same boy you liked so much back then."

"I know, Mama. It just seems strange that he would be released and come home not long after we moved back home."

Grandma shook her head. "I don't know what happened to that boy. I always liked him. Maybe he's learned his lesson and will make something of himself yet."

Papa chose that minute to swing open the back door and enter the kitchen with Henry and Kenny. The boys' arms were filled with logs for the fire. Papa planted a kiss on Mama's forehead then motioned to the boys, who had unloaded their wood into the bin near the stove. "Let's get washed up and have some of Mama's stew."

Merry finished piling the cornbread onto a plate and headed to the dining room with it. More talk with Mama and Grandma about Clay would have to wait until they were alone.

She settled in for dinner with her family. Although none of the children were actually her brothers or sisters, every one of them held that place in her heart after the few months she'd been back here with them. Emmaline and Henry had lived at the orphanage the longest, with Kenny and Robert next, but those two had been babies when her family had left. The rest were new to her, but she'd grown to love them quickly. Each one had their own tale of tragedy and loss.

Papa stood behind his chair and bowed his head to ask the blessing on the meal. Papa never varied his blessing, using the one his pa had taught him growing up. Merry only half listened to the familiar words until Papa took a new turn. "And Father, we ask thy blessings on young Clay Barlow. Guide him on the right path now that he's served his time and come home. May we act and think kindly toward him. Amen."

Merry swallowed hard and blinked her eyes. She lifted her gaze to her father's and saw understanding in their blue depths. Around her the others clamored to know who Clay was and why Papa prayed for him. She bit her lip and bowed her head. No man or boy had claimed her heart like Clay. From the encounter this afternoon, she realized he still possessed a piece of it, and she had no idea what to do with that revelation.

Chapter 2

CLAY OPENED HIS eyes, unsure of his surroundings. Then his gaze landed on the familiar wallpaper and curtains of his old room. Home. He'd come home and slept in his own bed. He sniffed the air, and instead of rotting bed rolls and the rancid odor of unwashed men, the scent of fresh, sun-dried linens filled his nose. He savored the moment and vowed once again to never do anything that would send him back to prison.

The reception by his parents yesterday had been more than he'd hoped for. Where his faith had weakened and almost disappeared, theirs had grown stronger. Ma's letters during his imprisonment had given him encouragement, but they had done nothing to lessen the pain of betrayal. Even the letter from Pa explaining once again his reason for turning Clay into the sheriff had not helped until the past few months as freedom drew closer. Ma loved him no matter what, but Pa's reception meant only that he'd accept Clay back, but with reservations.

Besides his parents and James, one other person welcomed him back with open arms. He chuckled at her enthusiasm and how Merry had literally opened her arms and hugged him. Merry had been the last person he'd expected to see, but there she was.

He hadn't seen her since her family moved to Oklahoma, but in that time she hadn't changed much, only grown prettier. Ma said she was the new schoolmarm in town since the former one married this past summer and moved away. Merry as a schoolteacher. If he remembered correctly, she always did like to tell others what to do and how to do it. He'd been smitten with her once, but then he'd made friends with Karl Laramie, the biggest mistake of his life. After that, everything took a downhill turn that ended with Clay in prison and the Laramie gang running free.

Clay shoved back the covers. He harbored no hopes of ever being more than an ex-convict to her.

Clay shivered in the cool morning air as he washed up and dressed. The aroma of frying bacon drifted into his room, and his mouth watered in anticipation of the meal Ma would serve this morning. How he'd missed those hearty breakfasts these past years. Lukewarm coffee, occasional watery eggs, and hard biscuits had been the fare during prison. He stuffed his shirt into his pants and headed to the kitchen.

He kissed his ma's cheek. "Sure smells good in here. I've dreamed of eating your scrambled eggs and biscuits." He towered over her petite frame and wrapped an arm around her waist.

She tilted her head up to beam at him. "I'm so thankful you're home. Pa and I never stopped praying for you."

"Thank you." Not that they had helped shorten the

sentence. He'd still served five hard years. He rubbed his hands together. "Anything you want me to do?"

"No, just sit down and enjoy."

Steps sounded on the stairway, and Pa appeared in the doorway. "Good morning, son." He held a can aloft. "Just brought up some peaches to go along with breakfast." He set the tin on the counter then sat at the table.

Clay joined him, and Ma filled their cups with hot coffee. He savored the rich aroma of fresh-brewed coffee. Just the thing for a cold day.

Pa said nothing but eyed Clay over the brim of his cup. The wary look stabbed at Clay's heart. If he couldn't regain Pa's respect and trust, there'd be no point in staying in Prairie Grove.

Pa set his cup down as Ma placed steaming platters of scrambled eggs and bacon on the table. She followed it with a basket of hot biscuits, a mound of fresh butter, and the bowl of canned peaches. Clay's taste buds watered just looking at the array.

Ma sat down and grasped his hand, as did Pa, who then spoke a blessing over the meal. The squeeze his mother gave his hand after the prayer reaffirmed her pleasure at having him home.

After helping himself to the eggs and bacon, Pa turned his gaze to Clay. "Son, you said you want to stay around Prairie Grove awhile. If you mean that, and you want to start living right, then you can help me in the store. It would mean your ma wouldn't have to work so hard."

Clay swallowed a bite of egg. Even if he'd considered leaving and striking out on his own, one look at Ma's frail frame reminded him where his duty lay. "I think I'd like that, Pa. Maybe Ma will have more time to do some of that baking I remember."

"Now, I'd planned to do that anyway. You always had your hand in the cookie jar, so I may as well start keeping it filled again." A touch of red warmed her cheeks and gave more color to her pale face.

Pa's mouth set in a firm line. "Since you're willing to stay, let's get started today. Soon as we finish here, we'll go down and open up. I'll show you the few changes I've made since you were home last. It's time to order and get ready for the big Christmas season ahead."

Clay nodded, relieved at his father's offer. Even if the others in town shunned him, he'd have his parents' support, or at least Ma's. He'd earn Pa's, and that was most important to him now. Although he had questioned the reasoning behind Pa's betrayal five years ago, Clay had finally accepted it as proof of his father's integrity and longed to regain his trust.

"A lot of people will be in town tomorrow picking up their supplies for the coming week. Some of them won't be too happy to see you back home, but then we have many new folks who don't know about what happened back then. And it appears you still have a few friends from school." Pa sipped his coffee and peered over the edge of his cup at Clay.

"Yes, I saw James yesterday, but he's married now and will be too busy for much else." The same was probably true of the others, but Miss Warner remained single, although that wouldn't do him much good. That she hadn't married by now meant only she was very selective or that young men didn't recognize how good she was.

Twenty minutes later he turned the sign on the door to let people know the store had opened. He stepped out onto the boardwalk to set the barrel of brooms in place and spotted Merry Warner. A grin formed as he watched her march her young charges down the street.

He counted four girls and five boys trailing after her. They must be the ones now living at Holly Hill orphanage. She'd lived at Holly Hill with her mother and brother while her father served as a federal marshal. He shook his head at the irony. Her father had been the one who had escorted Clay to prison. Mr. Warner most likely wouldn't trust him now, and that gave him even more reason to steer clear of Merry and her family.

He remembered her first day at school all those years ago. She'd been very shy at first, but after he and Jimmy had pulled her pigtails and teased her, she had stood up to them with her hands on her hips. He could almost hear her voice now as she informed them that she'd tell her big brother about them if they didn't leave her alone. That hadn't scared either one of them, but Clay admired her spunk and left her alone after that. Besides, he didn't really like the idea of tangling with Zach Warner.

Merry stopped near the store to help the last little boy in line with his book bag. He didn't look to be more than six years old, and the bag weighed him down. Merry's voice drifted over to him.

"Teddy, if you didn't carry so many books home with you, you wouldn't have trouble toting them back to school."

The little boy shifted the bag and peered up at her. "Aw, Merry...I mean Miss Warner, you know how I like to read."

"Yes, and it's an admirable quality." She reached into the bag. "Here, let me carry a few for you." She tucked two books under her arm and turned back to the others. Her gaze swept across the street and straight at him.

This time a brief smile lit her face before she proceeded up the street to the schoolhouse. His heart jumped and he couldn't breathe. What a beautiful young woman she'd become, and if her behavior just now was any indication, she'd become a very caring one too. He continued to watch her until she reached the school a few blocks away and disappeared inside.

Pa spoke behind Clay. "Pretty little thing, isn't she? The children all seem to love her from what I've heard from parents."

Clay swallowed hard before answering. "I can understand why. How long did you say they've been in town?"

"Just since summer. They'd been back to visit a few times since they left, but Mr. Collins passed away last spring, and Mrs. Collins needed her daughter's help with the home. They have nine children there now."

"Is her pa still a marshal?" They'd have to meet sometime, but Clay didn't look forward to it and would avoid the man as long as possible.

Pa shook his head. "No, he retired so he could help his wife and Mrs. Collins with the home. He didn't want to leave them alone in the times he'd need to be away. Can't say that I blame him for that."

No matter if Mr. Warner was no longer a lawman, he was

still Merry's father and a man with whom he didn't want to tangle. He shook off his images of Merry and headed back into the store. Time to get busy and quit thinking about the schoolmarm.

Merry's cheeks still burned from the heat that infused them when she realized Clay had been watching her and the children. Would they be able to be friends again? The only way to find that out would be to talk to him, but then he might run away again, and that would hurt more than not knowing. She sighed then stepped up to the bell rope and pulled it to signal the beginning of the school day.

Twenty boys and girls ranging in age from six to fourteen marched into the building, each one giving her a smile and a greeting. She'd only have eleven students if the ones from the home didn't attend, but a number of school-age children lived in the outlying areas and didn't come to school. She'd spent two months trying to persuade the parents to allow them to attend, but with no laws saying they had to, her efforts failed. Hope came with the number of younger than school-age children now in town. With them she'd have plenty of students in the future.

She rapped on the desk with a ruler and greeted her students with a smile and her usual words. "Good morning, boys and girls."

In unison they responded, "Good morning, Miss Warner."

Merry picked up a spelling book. "All of you in the lower grades get out your spelling books and slates. Write your words on the slates and study them while I work with the upper grades on our history lesson."

The younger ones answered with a "Yes, ma'am" and went to work. Her oldest student, Bert Norris, would have his fifteenth birthday in January. He was also the largest in size and could be a handful when she didn't keep a watchful eye on him. He raised his hand now. "Yes, Bert."

"Miss Warner, why do we have to study all this boring history stuff?"

Merry smiled. "It's so we can learn from the things that have happened in our country."

"You mean how to have wars and stuff?"

"No, of course not, Bert. Whatever gave you that idea?"

"Well, it seems to me that's what we've studied the most. The French and Indian War, the Revolutionary War, the War of 1812, and then the War Between the States, and that war going on right now."

"That may be true, but each of those wars helped shape our country. The war going on right now is the Spanish-American War." Best not get started down that trail. "Now, let's open our books and continue our reading about President Monroe and his doctrine of 1823. Can one of you tell me the purpose of the doctrine?"

As the students recited what they'd read and offered their ideas, Merry listened with interest and a few comments, but her thoughts continued to return to Clay Barlow. This afternoon she'd stop in at the general store to speak with Mrs. Barlow about the fabric for new shirts for Henry, who grew faster than they could keep him outfitted. If Clay was there, she could talk with him about being back home.

Before she realized it, the morning passed and the children dismissed for lunch. She sauntered out to the school yard and sat on the steps to devour the biscuit and ham Mama prepared this morning. The crisp fall air held a hint of the colder weather to come, but it remained pleasant enough to be outdoors.

The children had divided themselves as usual between the boys and girls, but as soon as they'd finished eating, the boys would think of some way to torment the girls. Clay and Jimmy Shanks had made her life miserable when she started school here, but Clay had stopped when she fussed at him and threatened to tell her brother. Then she'd missed his teasing. For ten more years she'd longed for his attention, but she never got more than a smile or a nod. Finally, when they were both sixteen, he'd asked her to the church social. He'd even stolen a kiss behind the church, and she could have died and gone to heaven.

Her fingers touched her lips now at the memory of that moment. Not long after that time her parents had picked up and moved to Barton Creek, but she never forgot that kiss. Even when she studied in teacher's college, she remembered and thought about Clay Barlow. When she learned the news of his arrest and sentencing, her heart had broken. Clay was a good person, but he'd made some bad choices.

A student's voice startled her from her reverie. Merry blinked. "What was that?"

Emmaline stood at the bottom of the steps with hands on her hips. "I said, are we going to have classes this afternoon? We've already been outside almost forty-five minutes."

Merry jumped up and grabbed the bell rope. "Of course. I just thought I'd give you a few extra minutes of play."

Emmaline rolled her eyes toward the sky and shook her head. The others came running and clambered into the room and to their desks. In the next week or so it would be time to practice the Thanksgiving program in the afternoons. Then before they could rest, they had to prepare for the Christmas play.

One thing she loved about Prairie Grove was the way it celebrated Christmas. She had been in a few of the Christmas programs back in her school days, and she looked forward to directing it this year.

The afternoon dragged on until finally Merry glanced at the clock on the wall and announced school was dismissed for the day.

"Emmaline, wait a minute, please. Will you make sure the children get safely home? I have a stop to make at Barlow's store to buy fabric. I won't be late again, I promise."

The girl pursed her lips and frowned. "I will, but I don't want to do your jobs again this evening." She turned with a flounce of her skirts and marched up the aisle and outside.

Merry stayed behind for a few minutes, not only to gather her belongings but also to garner the courage she needed to speak to Clay. If he shunned her, she would be embarrassed all over again. But if he acted friendly, what would come next? She tied the ribbons of her bonnet firmly under her chin then picked up her shawl. *Lord, give me the words I need to say, and give me the courage to say them.*

She sat back in her chair with a thud. What in the world was she thinking? Clay had been in prison. How could she make friends with an ex-convict? Then she remembered her father's prayer from the evening before. He had asked that people be kind to Clay. Offering her friendship would be one way to be kind. But until he proved his past was truly behind him and that he would be an upstanding citizen, and a man of God, that's all she could offer.

Shadows of leaves from the oak and elm trees outside the window danced across her desk and reminded her of her students. She'd have to be careful whatever she decided to do to set a good example for her students without arousing the disapproval of their parents. But surely they wouldn't object if she and Clay were friends since they'd known each other as children and practically grew up together.

She could speak to him when she stopped by the store and let him know she was glad he'd come home. Whether they could truly be friends or not lay completely in God's hands at this point. Whatever He directed her to do, she'd do it.

Chapter 3

IRST DAY ON the job and things so far had gone about as expected. A number of old customers had ignored Clay and gone straight to Pa. Only four had actually complained about his presence, and he'd itched to comment, but Pa kept right on talking to the customers and told them how pleased he was to have his son home. Clay shrugged. He could ignore the busybodies just as well as they ignored him.

He only hoped his working with Pa didn't run off customers. If it did, and business was hurt, he'd leave town and go someplace where they didn't know his past.

He turned from placing merchandise on a shelf and bumped into Mrs. Pennyfeather.

"Excuse me, ma'am. I didn't see you."

She pulled herself to her full height and peered at him with beady brown eyes. The feather on her black hat fluttered as she shook her head. "Humph, you shouldn't even be here in the first place. Some nerve you have, returning here after all you've done." She patted her dark curls, lifted her beaklike nose in the air, and strode across the floor and out the door.

Pa shook his head. "Pay her no mind, son. You know how she thinks she's better than anyone else in town."

Clay only nodded and went about shelving more goods. The words stung and made him even more aware of the effect his actions had on others. If only he could get back those two years he'd wasted running with Laramie and his boys. Those two years had cost him five more. Even if they hadn't robbed anyone here in Prairie Grove, the gang's reputation followed them everywhere.

It'd been a mistake coming back home after that last bank robbery, but the gang separated and the only place Clay wanted to come was home. Because of that he'd been the only one caught and sentenced. He hadn't actually been inside the bank at the time of the robbery, so the judge had been lenient and given him only a five-year sentence. It could have been a lot worse. The bad part was that no one else in the gang had been caught. The law knew who was responsible, but Laramie and his cohorts had been able to escape capture all these years. Clay's anger against the other men still throbbed at times, but he'd learned to live with it while in prison. Seeking revenge would only land him in more trouble.

Clay shook himself to get rid of those dismal thoughts and finished stocking the shelves. When he was finished, he headed back to join his mother, who sorted out the sewing notions. She glanced up when he approached her.

"I heard Mrs. Pennyfeather. Don't let her bother you. She's so full of hot air she could float a balloon from here to Wichita and back."

He chuckled, and the smile on Ma's face warmed his heart. He'd do anything for her. As an only child he'd been spoiled and not disciplined near as much as he should have been. That's why Pa's turning him in had been such a shock, but he never doubted his mother's love, or Pa's for that matter. He'd done what any law-abiding citizen would have done, and it took courage when the person was his own son.

Ma nodded toward several bolts of fabric. "Put those up there on the shelf for me, if you would. These are a few new things for the winter months ahead. Women have already been in to buy more wool for colder weather."

Clay placed the pieces on the shelf, making sure he had them with matching colors like Ma wanted. "Ma, you look tired. Why not go up and rest before you have to prepare supper. Pa and I'll handle things down here."

Ma bit her lip. "I am a bit worn." She moved the buttons and spools of thread from her lap to the counter. "Maybe you could finish sorting these for me, and I'll go up for a little nap."

"Of course I will." He leaned down and kissed her forehead. "All the matching colors together, starting with the dark blues."

She laughed and shook her head. "You still remember after all these years." Before she left, she hugged his neck. "Don't worry about what anyone says. You're a Barlow, and we love you. Don't you forget that."

As if he could. Clay watched her slow ascent up the stairs. He needed to ask Pa if she'd been in to see the doctor. He didn't like the paleness in her face or the lack of sparkle in her eyes. If Ma had some kind of medical condition, he wanted to know about it.

When a lull occurred a little later, Clay stepped up to the

counter. "Is everything all right with Ma? She doesn't seem to have the energy she once did."

Pa furrowed his brow and ran his hands through his thinning hair. "Doc Lawford says she has a blood problem. Something to do with the iron in her blood. It's too low and she's weak. Supposed to rest a lot more than she does, but she won't quit helping with the store."

"Do you think my return will add to the burden? A lot of people don't want me here." If his presence caused distress for his mother, he'd be on the next train out of town. Maybe he could go down to Oklahoma Territory and start over.

"Don't worry about what others think. Your being here is the best thing for her. She's worried so much about you these past five years."

"I'm sorry for all the trouble I caused you both. I understand why you did what you had to do."

Pa patted him on the shoulder. "Thank you, son."

Pa said nothing more, but the warmth in his voice led Clay to believe a smidgeon of trust had been gained.

Pa walked over to the door and picked up a broom. He headed out to the boardwalk and began sweeping dust and debris from the area in front of the store.

The day had been busy with people coming in buying one thing or another. A few people now called in their orders over the new telephone Pa had installed. Pa had made many changes in the past five years, and Clay wanted nothing more than to regain a little of what he'd lost with his pa and help the store be even better. Clay figured his knack with numbers would come in handy in helping with the books and accounts.

He could stock the shelves and keep the store in order, which meant Ma could spend more time upstairs resting.

Still, he would have time on his hands. With so little to do in town, he'd have to find something to occupy his time when not working.

The music from the saloon drifted in from down the street. Maybe he could spend some time down at the Red Garter. No, that would only lead to trouble, and Ma would certainly disapprove. He'd have to find some other form of entertainment if he planned to recover Pa's trust.

Merry's steps dragged somewhat as she debated what to say to Clay. He'd be at the store with his pa, and if she dropped in as planned, she'd have to say something to him. She stopped at the boardwalk in front of Barlow's when she saw the owner sweeping. He spotted her and leaned on his broom. "Good afternoon, Miss Warner."

"Good afternoon, Mr. Barlow." She smiled. "I need to pick up fabric for a couple of new shirts for Henry. He's growing so fast that his arms are hanging out the ones I made him last summer."

"Go right on in. Clay's there, and he can help you. Mrs. Barlow is upstairs resting."

Merry frowned. "Oh, is she ill?"

"Just a little tired, I think." He stepped back so she could enter.

"I hope she feels better soon." Merry's heart began to pound. She hadn't anticipated encountering Clay alone.

Clay glanced up from the ledger he studied, and his eyebrows raised a notch. "Miss Warner."

"Hello, Clay. I . . . I came in to pick out some fabric to make new shirts for one of the boys." Heat filled her face, and her heart threatened to jump right out of her chest.

"Ma said your family had come back to take over running the home. I'm sorry about your grandfather. I really liked him." He laid down his pencil and stepped from behind the counter.

He towered over her by almost a foot, and he'd grown lean and even more handsome than she remembered. His dark brown eyes still drew her to him just as they had seven years ago. She swallowed hard and found her voice. "Thank you. Yes, we came back to help Grandma with the children. We have nine there now. Henry is thirteen and growing out of his clothes."

He pointed to the back and allowed her to pass and head to the fabric shelves. "Did your brother come back with you?"

"No, Zach is still in Barton Creek. He's working for one of the ranches as a wrangler. He should be up here for Christmas though. It's a new ranch, and his boss just married last year. We were there for the wedding, and when Lucy Starnes, the new wife, learned we were leaving Barton Creek to come back here to take care of the children's home, she gave us a big donation to help keep Holly Hill open." She stopped suddenly. Her mouth babbled on as if the people of Barton Creek and her brother were the most important subjects of the day.

"I'm sorry. You don't care about that." She stretched up for a bolt of fabric, but she couldn't quite reach it.

Clay reached over her and pulled it down. "Sounds to me

like you made good friends in that town. Is this the color you had in mind?"

Heat again rose in her cheeks. "Yes, the light brown is perfect. I'll need three lengths."

"All right, I'll cut it while you get whatever else you need."

He headed for the counter at the front and laid out the fabric there. She watched as he measured then picked up the scissors to cut. Not one word of what she'd rehearsed back at school came from her mouth. He must think her to be an awful ninny.

After she selected the buttons and thread, she made her way back to the front just as Mr. Barlow returned with another customer, Mrs. Hickman. The woman narrowed her eyes when she saw Clay behind the counter. She nodded at Merry before marching back to the canned goods.

Mr. Barlow shrugged and followed the woman. Merry peered up at Clay, and his face glowed bright red. In a low voice he said, "Some people don't appreciate my coming home."

"I can't believe she was so rude." She started to reach for his arm but snapped her hand back to her side. "Some people are glad you're back. I remember how much fun we had as children. We were good friends then. Maybe we can be again."

Clay's eyes darkened almost to black. "It may not be such a good idea. You wouldn't want to ruin your reputation by befriending an ex-con."

"You served your time, and now you can help your parents out when they need it." She swallowed hard, realizing she did have to consider how a friendship with Clay could affect the parents' view of her as a teacher. Still, she didn't want to shut Clay out of her life.

"I'm glad they need me, because I sure need them." He grabbed brown paper from the roll and wrapped her purchase then tied it with string.

Merry's mind filled with many things she wanted to say, but Clay's tone of voice told her he wasn't open to hearing them. What had she expected—to pick right up where they left off at age sixteen? He had changed. She had changed. And it would take time to get to know each other and build the friendship anew.

Clay handed her the parcel, and Merry put on the biggest smile she could muster. "Thank you, and I hope to see you more often in the days ahead."

She turned to walk away, but his muttered words still reached her ears. "Not if you know what's good for you."

Heat filled her face again. Those words stung worse than the wasp she'd encountered last summer. Had being in prison hardened him to the point he couldn't be friendly with those who cared about him? Of course he didn't know she still cared. Somehow in the days ahead she'd have to show Mr. Clayton Barlow that he was just as worth knowing now as he had been when they were in school together.

Chapter 4

Over a week had passed since Clay's return, and Merry had made no more headway in her attempts to be friendly with him. Every time she walked into the store, he avoided her, managing to find something else to do in the back. As she rode to town with the children Saturday morning, determination rose in her to try again. Perhaps today would be different, and he would at least speak to her.

Papa slowed the wagon and turned to the youngsters in the back. "Now, you older ones may spend your pennies however you like, but remember to mind your manners. You younger ones stick with Merry. She'll help you with whatever you want to buy."

Grins and nods greeted his words, and he climbed down to come around and let the back down so they could get out. Henry didn't wait for the others and jumped over the side to land on the dirt street in front of the general store.

Merry squelched a laugh as he dusted himself off and looked around. Henry's money would most likely still be in his pocket when it came time to go back to Holly Hill. He wouldn't spend a penny unless it was mighty important. Someday that boy would make a fine businessman.

Papa reached up and helped Merry from the wagon. "You keep close watch over these young'uns. They can get a bit rambunctious sometimes." He turned to Emmaline. "You and Susie look after the twins. We'll meet back here at noon and go back home to eat. Mama has a big pot of soup that'll be ready for us."

The girls nodded, and each grabbed the hand of a twin and started off down the street. Merry wrapped her arms around the shoulders of Stevie and Teddy. "Where shall we go first?"

Kenny piped up, his brown eyes shining. "Let's go see if Mr. Barlow has any new toys. I'd sure like to get another top."

That would be a better way for him to spend his money than on candy. Papa always gave the children a little money on Saturdays when they went into town. He said they'd earned it by doing their chores well and without complaint. The practice seemed to work well, as rarely did Papa ever have to ask any of the children to do something twice.

"That sounds like a good idea. Let's go." Perhaps she'd catch the attention of Clay, but then with so many customers on Saturday morning, he'd be busy helping others. She swallowed a sigh and followed the boys across to the store.

Inside, the boys headed straight for the section where Mr. Barlow had set up a toy display. Merry stopped and glanced around the store. Mama had given her a list to fill, but that could wait until just before meeting Papa. She walked among the aisles, glancing about in hopes of spotting Clay.

She turned the corner of a shelf lined with tins of fruit, meat, and beans and bumped right into his chest. One of his buttons clipped her nose, and she stepped back, rubbing it. Heat filled her face. "Oh, my, I wasn't expecting you to be right there."

"Obviously." He still held her upper arms with his hands as though to steady her. "Are you all right?"

She glanced down at his hands, and he immediately dropped them to his side. She lifted her chin to see his face. "You've been back a week now. How have things been?"

He turned away and busied himself with putting items on a shelf. "OK. I'm really too busy to talk right now. Is there something I can help you with?"

A crash sounded from the front. The boys. She'd completely forgotten about them. Merry swirled around and dashed to the front of the store where Stevie and Teddy stood in the midst of broken glass, their eyes wide open with fear.

"Oh, no, what happened?"

Mr. Barlow stepped up with a broom. "It was an accident. Stevie wanted some peppermints, but the jar was heavy and overturned on the floor when he tried to get a few."

She picked up the boy and set him over in a clean spot then turned and did the same with Teddy. "Why didn't you wait for Mr. Barlow to come help you pick out the candy?"

Tears slipped down Stevie's cheeks. "I'm sorry, Merry. I didn't know it'd be so heavy."

"No harm done, Miss Warner. I'll just sweep up this mess, and you can get on with your shopping."

"Please let me pay for the candy, Mr. Barlow. It's what Papa would want us to do." There went her plans to purchase pieces of lace to dress up the blue shirtwaist she'd planned to wear Sunday.

"It's not that much, and besides, like I said, it was an accident."

How kind of him, but the boys needed to learn to be more careful. "No, I insist. It's only right."

Mr. Barlow rubbed his chin a moment then hunkered down to eye level with Stevie and Teddy. "How about I take two pennies from each of you, and we'll call it even. Next time wait for me."

Both boys fished in their pockets for their precious pennies then handed them over to Mr. Barlow. He grasped them in his hand and stood. "There now, that ought to take care of it."

"Thank you, Mr. Barlow. The boys will be more careful from now on."

Kenny sauntered up with a smirk on his face. "I told them not to get the candy, and now I still have my money. Think I'll get this yellow and red top."

He set the toy up on the counter. "How much is it, Mr. Barlow?"

"Well, it's a brand-new line and costs a quarter, and that includes the string."

Kenny's face fell and his eyes clouded over. Mr. Barlow once again stooped down to talk with Kenny. "How about if I put this aside with your name on it? Then when you have a quarter saved up, you can buy it."

Now Kenny's eyes sparkled, and a grin spread across his face. "Really?" He turned to Merry. "Is that all right, Merry?"

"I'm sure it is." She grasped Mr. Barlow's hand when he stood. "Thank you so much. You've been a true friend for these boys today."

Robert pulled on her skirt. "Merry, I'll buy some licorice for Teddy and Stevie. I have the nickel I saved from last week."

Merry blinked a tear from her eye. "Oh, that would be a nice thing to do, but since you may see something else you want to buy, I'll take care of the candy." She turned to Clay. "Four of the licorice sticks, one for each boy, please."

Clay smiled and shook his head. He opened the candy jar with the black strips of licorice and extracted four then handed one to each boy.

Merry plopped a few coins on the counter before turning to the boys with the candy in hand. "I suppose one licorice stick won't ruin your dinner. Go ahead and enjoy them." She smiled as the four of them marched over to a bench and sat down to devour their treat.

Even with the money spent for the licorice, Merry had enough money for the lace. She handed Mr. Barlow Mama's list. "Could you fill this while I look at some lace in the back?"

"Sure thing, Miss Warner. Mrs. Barlow is back there with the fabric; she can help you." He laid the list on the counter and inclined his head toward the shelves down the aisle.

Merry headed back to the fabrics to find Mrs. Barlow. She spotted the woman by the thread. "Good morning, Mrs. Barlow. Your husband said you hadn't been feeling well. I do hope you're better."

"Thank you, Merry. I do feel much stronger after a good rest. Having Clay here is such a big help. He's doing so much of what I did to help out, and then some."

"I'm glad to hear his first week home has gone well."

A shadow passed across Mrs. Barlow's face.

Merry inched closer and whispered, "Has it gone well, Mrs. Barlow? With Clay being home again?"

Mrs. Barlow sighed. "I just wish some of the women in this town would keep their mouths shut and their thoughts to themselves."

"I understand. I saw Mrs. Hickman's and Mrs. Pennyfeather's reactions last week, and I must say they were quite rude." What Clay feared must be happening more often than she had seen. What a shame. They weren't even willing to give him the benefit of the doubt.

Mrs. Barlow nodded her head. "Several others have done the same. Some of them even threatened to take their business elsewhere." A giggle escaped her throat. "Now that's a laugh, seeing as how we're the only general store in town. Where else will they get sugar, flour, meal, and such?"

Merry joined in the humor of the moment. How true. Sometimes people must put their tongues to working before their minds could communicate common sense. "Don't you worry about us. Mama and Papa would shop here with you no matter what happened or even if another store did open up."

"Thank you, dear. Your parents are fine people, and we're proud to have them as customers. Now what I can I help you with?"

Merry proceeded to describe what she wanted, and Mrs. Barlow lifted down several samples.

Clay hadn't been at church with his folks last Sunday. How she wished to ask Mrs. Barlow why, but that would be nosy and was actually none of her business. Yet how could she ever show friendship to Clay if he avoided her and didn't even attend church?

Clay finished cleaning up the broken candy jar while his pa filled Merry's list, all the time aware of Merry in the back with his mother. Watching her with the children had given him more respect for the young teacher. Of course she'd always been the sensitive one. That's why the teasing had hurt her so much all those years ago. At least he had quit and they had become friends. The threat of Zach had helped a bit. Four years older, Zach had towered over Clay then. Zach's now being a cowboy on a ranch sounded as natural as breathing.

The lilt of Merry's voice talking with Ma drifted to the front of the store. Clay listened for it even as he assisted other customers with their purchases. He dropped a few coins to the floor and bent to pick them up. He had to get his mind off Miss Warner.

He handed the change to his customer, thankful that none of the men seemed to mind his taking care of them. Most of the ladies avoided him and waited until Pa could help with their goods. The few who spoke to him were ones like Reverend Tate's or Sheriff Devlin's wives. Those ladies didn't have a mean bone in their bodies.

"Clay, can you tell me if any of those candles your father ordered came in?"

He shook his head and blinked his eyes. "I'm sorry, Mrs. Lawford, I didn't realize you were standing there."

The doctor's wife laughed and reached over to pat his arm. "That's all right. I could tell you were lost in another place. Now about those candles."

Candles? Oh, yes, the ones they'd unpacked yesterday.

"They're right back there on your right. Would you like me to show you?"

"No, dear boy, I know my way around." She smiled and headed to the shelf with the candles. Another of the kinder ladies in town, and he appreciated her acceptance.

When he turned back to the counter, Mrs. Pennyfeather stood there with her mouth puckered up like a prune. "May I help you, Mrs. Pennyfeather?"

Her nose went up. "No, I'll wait for your father. It's a wonder you haven't stolen him blind and high-tailed it out of here by now."

Clay swallowed his anger. He couldn't let her remarks get to him, or he'd be right back in trouble. He raised his eyebrows and smiled. "No, ma'am, I wouldn't do that. I like it here."

Her eyes grew large and her back stiffened. Before she could comment further, his father strode to the counter. "Good day, Mrs. Pennyfeather. What can I do for you?" He winked at Clay then turned his attention to the woman in front of him and led her away.

Merry laid her purchase on the counter, frowning. "That was most unkind of Mrs. Pennyfeather."

He steeled himself against Merry's gentle words. "Here's the order you gave Pa. Will that be all for you today?"

"Yes, I suppose it will." The sparkle left her eye as she plunked down the money for the lace and then the bills for the groceries and supplies.

Why couldn't she be as rude as the others so he could brush her off and forget about her? He dropped the lace in a small paper bag and handed it to her. "Thank you, Miss Warner."

She said nothing but stared at him a few moments with hurt clearly written in her eyes. She picked up the other packages and bags then turned to her young charges, still sitting on the bench. "Come, it's almost time to meet Papa. We don't want to be late."

On the way out the door Kenny stopped and turned to look back at Clay. "That Mrs. Pennyfeather sure was mean." He peered up at Merry. "Why did she say that to Clay about stealing his pa blind? His pa ain't blind."

Merry grabbed the boy's shoulder and hustled him out the door. "No, Mr. Barlow isn't blind, and it wasn't very nice of her to say so."

They disappeared from sight, and Clay blew out his breath. What a week this had been. How would he ever regain the trust of women like Mrs. Pennyfeather, who were always ready to expect the worst of him?

Then an idea shot into his head. He'd look up Jimmy and visit him, that is, if his wife approved. Maybe if he could renew some old friendships, he could prove to the town that he had changed.

The aroma of Ma's stew wafted down the stairs. His stomach rumbled, reminding him how much he'd missed her cooking and how he looked forward to a delicious lunch. With Jimmy's friendship and Ma's cooking, he could survive anything. The concerns of the morning disappeared.

Chapter 5

MERRY STEPPED DOWN from the carriage then turned to help the younger boys, who ignored her and jumped down on their own accord, delighting in the thud made by their feet hitting the ground. Merry laughed as they scrambled up the porch steps to the front door of the house. Four little boys under the age of ten certainly made for an interesting time at church on Sunday mornings.

Henry clicked the reins and led the horse back to the carriage house. Papa pulled his horse to a stop so the girls and Mama could get out. With so many children they had two carriages to take to church each Sunday and sometimes into town on Saturday when they didn't take the wagon. Merry helped the girls as they stepped down. They made a pretty picture this morning with their bright bonnets and cloaks. Papa helped Grandma Collins from the carriage.

She hugged Merry. "I must say that blue is quite becoming to you, and the bit of lace you added is quite attractive. You've grown into a beautiful young lady."

"Thank you, Grandma. I hope I may live up to your

expectations." Grandma Collins had been a schoolteacher early before she married Grandpa and had a family of her own.

"I'm sure you will. Now, I must get inside and help your mother."

Merry nodded then fingered the lace trimming she'd added to her shirtwaist. Clay hadn't been at church again this morning. She'd heard rumors that he probably spent his Saturday night at the saloon and was too tired for church. She hoped such rumors were only that.

Some people were just too nosy for their own good, and she'd be just that if she asked Mrs. Barlow such a question. It really shouldn't be anybody's business what Clay did with his Saturday nights. Even though she abhorred the idea of his being in a saloon, an adult man could choose his own entertainment. But how could Clay regain the trust of the town if he spent time at the Red Garter? She blew out her breath and followed her grandmother into the house. Unless things changed a great deal in the days ahead, she'd best lay aside any plans to get Clay to pay attention to her. His not attending church and his complete indifference to her didn't bode well for any friendship with him.

Merry pushed thoughts of Clay aside to get dinner on the table, filling platters and bowls with slices of ham and steaming vegetables. Emmaline joined her in the kitchen and tied an apron around her waist. "Hmm, Grandma's rolls smell heavenly. Can't wait to have one with a little honey on it."

The rolls did fill the kitchen with a delightful aroma, making Merry's mouth water. She and Emmaline helped Mama get all the food on the table then rounded up the children to be seated. As they all sat and calmed down for the prayer, Merry's heart swelled with pride at the handsome picture made by the boys and girls she thought of as her brothers and sisters. Ranging in age from six to fourteen, they all held a special place in her heart.

Merry only half listened to the conversations going on around the table. Clay filled her thoughts. If the rumors were true, he'd run the risk of falling back into some of his old habits. His lack of attendance at church demonstrated that his faith had suffered a setback too.

Being gone from Prairie Grove all those years, she hadn't been able to see for herself what happened to him. She'd only heard stories and tidbits in letters to Mama from Grandma. Knowing what a bad influence Karl Laramie had been when she'd been in school only made the stories and tales more likely than not.

Her grandmother's voice broke into her thoughts. "I'm sorry, Grandma, what did you say?"

"I asked if you had any ideas for the Christmas play for the children. Christmas is just around the corner, you know."

"Oh, yes, I have. Of course the story is always the same, but I may add a little more to it this year. I promised Reverend Tate I'd use all the school-age children this year. We don't want any hurt feelings."

Kenny hopped in his chair. "As long as I don't have to be no angel, I'll be in it."

Susie added her opinion. "Silly. Girls are angels. The boys will be shepherds."

"Kenny, you won't have to be an angel, but I do expect you to use correct language when you speak."

A scowl twisted his mouth. "Aw, that's not fair. This ain't…isn't school. It's home."

Papa reached over and placed his hand on Kenny's head. "Maybe so, young man, but we want all our boys and girls to know how to speak correctly, and that means at home and church as well as at school."

Emmaline raised her eyebrows. "Do you have someone picked to play Mary and Joseph?"

"Not yet. I'm working on it, but we have to take care of the Thanksgiving program first." Three older girls in class, and all three would make a beautiful Mary for the play. They'd have to draw straws for that. It was the only way she knew to be fair. "I do have a narrator in mind. Jesse Grainger has a very nice speaking voice, and he can memorize very well."

Susie leaned in a conspiratorial fashion and grinned. "I imagine if Trenton Marshall is Joseph, Emmaline will want to be Mary."

Emmaline's cheeks turned a deep shade of crimson. "I would not. He's a…a…well, he teases too much."

Merry hid her own smile. She'd noticed the looks that passed between Emmaline and Trenton and the teasing he directed at Emmaline. Of course, to Merry that teasing signified the boy's caring about Emmaline. At fourteen he'd grown several inches since summer and was a very nice-looking boy. His family owned a farm not far from town, and everyone had great respect for them.

Conversation then turned to other things, and once again Merry's mind wandered to Clay. Prison had done nothing to take away from his handsome face or muscular build. Of course, Mama would say character counted for more than his good looks. And right now his character appeared to be in question. Perhaps it was a good thing she had not been able to renew their friendship. The last thing she needed was a broken heart.

Clay awakened to the aroma of pot roast filling his room. He lurched to sit up and rubbed his eyes. Bright daylight shone through the window, reminding him that he slept late. He shoved back the covers and headed to the basin of water on the chest across the room.

After splashing cold water on his face, he toweled dry then grabbed at his pants to get out his pocket watch. A groan escaped his throat. Already past noon, and he'd missed breakfast. No matter. He'd been too tired to even wake up for it.

He finished dressing then made his way out to the kitchen, where his mother pulled a pan of bread from the oven. Clay sniffed loudly. "Hmm, nothing like good homemade bread on Sunday." He circled Ma's shoulders with his arm and planted a kiss on her temple.

She grinned and batted him away. "Won't get you a taste any earlier. Go on and sit down. I'll have it on the table in a minute."

Pa sauntered in and stopped when he spotted Clay. "Well, I see you decided to join the land of the living."

Clay pulled out a chair and sat at the table. "Sorry, but I had a late night and was too tired to get up earlier."

"Well, you missed a fine sermon and a glorious Sunday morning." Pa pulled out a chair and seated himself across from

Clay. "Must have been a mighty entertaining evening for you to stay out so late."

The look on his mother's face clearly showed her disapproval, but she said nothing and placed the platter of roast and a bowl of mixed carrots, potatoes, and onions on the table. "It was more like early morning rather than late night, if I recall. I hope it was worth the loss of sleep."

The evening had been pleasant but not exactly entertaining and definitely not worth the loss of sleep even though he and James and few of the other guys had a good visit talking about old times. Hard to believe James was the only one of the group married. Grace Ann had been nice enough to keep them supplied with coffee while the men talked.

"It was OK, Ma. Maybe I'll tell you about it later." He chuckled at her raised eyebrows and Pa's frown.

Pa threw his napkin onto the table. "We heard rumors this morning that you'd spent your evening at the saloon."

No wonder they'd both frowned so much this morning. "No, sir, I was with Jimmy and few of the boys I knew back in school. We were at Jimmy's house all evening."

At the look of relief on Ma's face Clay reached over and placed his hand on her arm. "Ma, I would never do anything to embarrass you like that. I don't know where or how the rumors started, but they're untrue. Please believe me."

She patted his hand. "I'm so relieved to know that. I didn't think they were true, but I didn't want to be nosy and ask outright."

With that settled, Clay finished his meal with gusto. One thing for sure, if he kept eating like this, he'd gain back all the weight he'd lost in prison.

After they'd finished the meal, Clay offered to help with washing and drying the dishes. Pa retired to the parlor for his Sunday afternoon pipe followed by a nap. Ma would join him later, but now Clay had her to himself.

She poured hot water over the dishes and asked, "Why did you not get up and go to church with us this morning? It really doesn't look good for you to be out late on Saturday evening and then not appear in church on Sunday. I know you didn't go last week because you didn't want to cause a stir, but you can't avoid church forever."

He shook his head. "I'm sorry, but I just don't have much use for church these days. Too many stares and whispers. Besides, God didn't help me any in prison, so why would He do anything for me now that I'm home?"

Ma set the pan back on the stove and wiped her hands on her apron. She had something on her mind, and he may as well brace himself for a lecture. Sure enough, she grabbed his arm and guided him back to the table, where she plunked him down in a chair then sat down across from him.

"I hope you don't go judging the whole church because of a few bad apples. Not all our church people are like Mrs. Pennyfeather. As for God, well, He took good care of you while you were in prison. You didn't get sick like so many do. You served your time and came out of it healthy and able to work. We prayed for you every night, and God answered our prayers by having you come home to us."

"Maybe He did, but Karl is still running loose while I served time. How could that be fair? I know Pa did what he thought best, and I don't hold it against him now, but five years of my life are gone." He'd resolved that anger and put it aside because he'd seen what hot tempers and angry words could do to a man, and Clay wanted no part of that.

Ma reached across for his hands and clasped them in hers. "Calling the sheriff hurt your pa more than you could ever know. We both agonized over the situation, but we were afraid if we didn't stop you then, you might end up dead in some robbery somewhere. We love you, son, and nothing will ever kill that love."

"And that's what brought me home and keeps me here. I don't want to see you and Pa hurt any more, and if my presence causes others to criticize and shun you, I won't stay. I don't want that for you and Pa." He could always find a ranch willing to hire on an extra hand, even one who was an ex-convict.

She patted his hand. "Don't you worry yourself with that. Words can never hurt us. We have God on our side, and He's looking out for you too."

He took her hand and squeezed it. "Knowing you were here waiting for me helped me through some dark days. I love you, and I promise never to disappoint you again."

Not that he'd be able to keep that promise 100 percent, but he'd do his best. So far he'd done his best to please his parents, and he planned to keep doing so. Why, he'd even go to church if he had to.

Chapter 6

ONE OF THE activities Merry remembered best from former days in Prairie Grove included the annual fall festival the first Saturday of November. What fun it had been as a young girl to go into town and see all the booths and activities. Now Merry opened her window and breathed deeply of the brisk morning air. What a glorious day this would be, a day of sunshine and mild temperatures, perfect for the festival. On her way home from school yesterday she had seen the decorations downtown and the beginnings of booths where games and food would be offered for one and all.

She closed the window and hurried through her morning grooming in order to go downstairs and help her mother and grandmother with breakfast. She met Emmaline in the hallway.

"I see you're up early this morning too." Merry wrapped her arms around the girl's shoulders. "This year I'm going to keep tabs on all the boys and let you girls have fun on your own. I think the four of you can take care of each other."

Emmaline's face lit up with a smile. "Oh, thank you, Merry. The twins are no trouble at all, and Susie is a big help."

Merry squeezed Emmaline to her and winked. "You just might have some time to talk with Trenton."

"Oh, my, he won't even notice me, and if he does, it'll only be to torment me." Her cheeks burned bright red. She slipped from Merry's grasp and hastened on down the stairs.

It wouldn't be too many years before Trenton did more than tease Emmaline, and from the look in his eyes when he tormented her, that time would be sooner rather than later.

After breakfast Papa hitched the horses to the big wagon for the ride into town for the festival. Mama helped Merry get all the children into the wagon bed and settled. Merry then climbed up to join them.

The children laughed and talked about all the things they wanted to do that day. Keeping up with four little boys under the age of ten would be a handful. Henry would be off with his friends from school. Merry had hid her smile when Mama admonished him to be careful and not get into trouble. Henry, Trenton, and the other boys their age would find plenty of mischief for the day, and it would all be in good fun.

Stevie snuggled close to Merry. "Papa Warner gave us some money to spend on the games. Will you help me find one I can do so I can win a prize?"

She cupped her hand on the back of his head and with her other one brushed his carrot-colored bangs from his forehead. "Of course I will. You boys are going to have a great time today. I bet Mr. Hankins will even have a few horses saddled for rides again this year. I also heard a rumor that we may see some of those rubber balloons we saw in the catalog at Barlow's store."

He peered up at her and scrunched up his nose. "Are those the things you blow up with air and they burst with a loud pop?"

"Yes, they are, but you don't want to waste your pennies blowing them up just to pop them."

He thought a moment. "I suppose that would be kinda silly."

Kenny joined in the discussion. "Well, I'm saving up for that top in Mr. Barlow's store, so I'm not going to spend mine on games except maybe the fishing one."

"Now that sounds like a fine plan. I have a little saved, so I'll get each one of you a treat later in the morning."

The four little boys laughed and giggled as they discussed whether they would choose popcorn or candy. Merry studied the four. How sad that none of them had been adopted. Kenny and Robert came only a year ago when their parents died in a train wreck, but Stevie and Teddy had come as babies just before her family left for Barton Creek. Grandma and Grandpa Collins cared for them as if they were their own boys, but it would have been so much better if some loving family had wanted them.

Henry and Emmaline lived at the home when Merry and her parents lived in Prairie Grove, but the other girls had arrived while she had been in Barton Creek. The fact that none of the ones there now had been adopted saddened Merry. She'd do everything in her power to make sure they had a happy time until they were old enough to go to work for someone or get married.

Emmaline tapped her arm. "You're in a far-off place. Are

you thinking about a beau? That Clay Barlow sure is a handsome fellow. You ought to set your sights on him."

Heat filled Merry's cheeks. Although she hadn't been thinking about Clay, the mention of his name now brought back old memories and good times. "Since he's just out of prison, I don't believe he's interested in a relationship."

"But didn't I hear you say you were friends when you lived here?"

"Yes, we were, but then I moved away and he got into trouble." If she'd stayed in Prairie Grove, things might have been different. No, that made no sense. She had no influence over what Clay Barlow did. He'd chosen his own path.

"I still think he's handsome and so tall." Emmaline sighed and leaned against the wall of the wagon, a dreamy look filling her features.

Voices and music filled the air. Merry sat up and some of the children stood. Fall decorations with pumpkins, corn, squash, and bright yellow flowers adorned the sidewalks, and orange and brown bunting hung from the balconies of a few buildings. Merry shivered with excitement. She'd always loved this time of year as a child. Even though Barton Creek had similar celebrations, Merry had missed being here for this one. Prairie Grove was more home to her than Barton Creek could ever have been.

The boys jumped up and down and waved at people along the way. Papa pulled the wagon to a stop near the livery and jumped down from his perch to hitch the horses. Henry opened the tailgate on the wagon and scrambled down. He waved at Trenton, who ran over to greet Henry and help with the children.

Emmaline's face glowed with pleasure as Trenton reached up a hand to help her. Soon as her feet hit the ground, he smiled at her then let go of her hand to help the boys.

When the wagon was empty, Henry waved good-bye. "Trenton and I are going over to the games."

Mama held up her hand. "Don't forget to meet us back here at noon. You watch the courthouse clock and be sure you're on time. We'll eat without you if you're not here."

"Yes, ma'am. I'll be here. Don't want to miss Grandma Collins's fried chicken."

Merry laughed. She didn't plan to miss that chicken either or the rest of the picnic lunch Grandma and Mama had prepared. She grabbed the hands of the two youngest boys, Stevie and Teddy, then turned to the other two. "OK, Kenny and Robert, stay close to me."

She strolled down the streets with the boys in tow. Mama had offered to take them with her, but since she had to work in the Ladies' Missionary Guild's booth at the church, Merry had taken the responsibility of the four.

Stevie and Teddy pulled on her hands now and clamored to go over to the children's area. Merry looked down at Stevie, who pulled the hardest. "All right, but you mustn't try to run ahead so." She looked up just in time to bat her face against the back of a man standing in front of her. He jerked around with a frown creasing his brow.

Clay Barlow! Of all people, why did she have to run into him and almost knock him down?

Anger flared for a moment in Clay's chest, but it disappeared when he turned to see Merry and her young charges. He doffed his hat and nodded to her.

Her cheeks flamed red. "I'm so sorry, Mr. Barlow. I was talking to Stevie and didn't watch where I was going."

"No harm done. I probably shouldn't be standing in the middle of the street anyway. No telling what might run me down." He grinned at her to make sure she understood his teasing.

She ducked her head and pulled on the boys' arms. "Thank you. Now I must get these boys where we were headed."

"And where is that?" He glanced down at the boys, who stood with their eyes wide and mouths open.

Kenny's chest swelled out. "We're going over to the games and see if we can win some prizes. I bet I win a good one."

"I'm sure you will." Of course the children's games were rigged so that each one could win something. He couldn't say the same for the adult ones. Maybe the children's area would be more fun, especially with Miss Warner. If she could be polite and formal, he could be too. Besides, she could use some help with those four young boys.

"Hmm, do you mind if I accompany you, Miss Warner? I'd like to watch them win a few prizes."

The little boys grinned and begged her to say yes. Now her cheeks burned even brighter, and her voice came out in a squeak. "Yes, I suppose that will be all right." She introduced the four boys, who each reached out to shake hands as they had been taught.

Clay kneeled down to Stevie and Teddy. "Well now, let's go see what fun things we can find to do."

Taking their hands, he strode across the street and over to the park area where booths for the children were set up. A number of students from Miss Warner's classes spotted her and waved. Parents shook their heads and grabbed the hands of their young ones.

Hurt and disappointment gripped Clay's heart like a vise. Even on a day of fun like this some just didn't want to be friendly. He'd vowed to stay away from Merry to keep from tarnishing her reputation, and here he was in public with her. However, she didn't seem to mind as she headed toward the Go Fishing booth with Kenny and Robert.

Stevie and Teddy swung his arms, pointing. "That's what I want to do. Can we go see?"

Clay released their hands, and they scampered off to join the others. He sauntered up behind the boys to watch their faces when they landed a "fish." He and Pa had put together a box of items for the booth to use, and they'd been sure to include some fun items like finger puppets, whirly-gigs, a small bag of marbles, and paper windmills.

When Kenny opened his "fish bag" and found a ball and cup game, he jumped up and down and hollered his good fortune. He ran up to Clay and held up his prize. "This is the bestest prize I could have caught."

The boy's grin warmed Clay's heart. He ruffled the boy's hair. "I do believe it is."

Each of the others won prizes and expressed their delight to Merry, who hugged them and exclaimed how wonderful the prizes were.

Clay stood off to the side, watching. He wanted to offer them all a treat of a drink from the concession stand but hesitated to pay more attention to Merry than might be considered proper. Besides, she might mistake his interest in the children as desire to be with her. That wouldn't do, especially since, even after several weeks of his being home, many of the town folks still cast disapproving glances his way. Then Stevie and Teddy pulled Merry toward him.

Color filled her cheeks. "I'm sorry, Mr. Barlow, but they wanted to show you their prizes."

He knelt down to their level. "I see that you were very good fishermen today."

Teddy waved his windmill through the air and the paper whirred in the breeze. "See. Isn't it great?"

"It surely is." He glanced up at Merry, and his heart pounded in his chest. If only he had made wiser choices years ago, he could be courting her today. He swallowed hard. Those thoughts had to be buried and forgotten. She deserved someone much better than him.

Kenny joined the others. "Let's go see what else we can find, Merry. This is fun."

She smiled then shrugged. "All right, but Mr. Barlow has other things to do. Thank him for bringing you here."

The four little boys' voices rang in chorus. "Thank you, Mr. Barlow."

"It was my pleasure. I hope you have a good time the rest of the day." Merry grabbed the hands of the two youngest and turned to leave. She glanced back to say, "Maybe we can see each other later today."

Clay only nodded, but his heart still beat like a drum in

his chest. God sure had a cruel sense of humor. The one person from his past he most wanted to befriend was now out of reach to him.

A hand clasped his shoulder. "She's a beautiful woman. Remember when we teased her and pulled her long curls?"

Clay turned around to find James, grinning as he looked after Merry. "Yes, and I also remember how Merry finally stood up to us and threatened to send Zach after us."

"Yeah. He was a big galoot, and I was afraid of him, but I sure wasn't going to let her know it. Besides, he didn't keep me from teasing Grace Ann."

"And look where that got you." Clay chuckled then punched James's arm. "Seems to agree with you though." He glanced around. "Where is your wife anyway?"

James nodded toward the church. "She's over there helping the ladies with the bake sale. I hear music, so the cake walk must have started. Come on, let's go join the fun. Besides, I have something I want to talk over with you."

Clay followed James but kept his eyes on the lookout for Merry and the boys. He spotted them again by the tables where the ladies sold baked goods. He imagined the boys would be clamoring for cookies.

Sure enough, she handed one of the ladies a few coins and then picked up four cookies wrapped in waxed paper and placed them in her handbag. She probably planned to save them until after the boys had eaten their lunch.

What a wonderful mother she would be. No, his thoughts couldn't go that direction. He must leave her alone, in thought as well as action.

James pulled him over to a corner away from the crowd.

"There's something I want to tell you about, but you have to promise you won't say anything to anyone else yet."

Clay furrowed his brow and studied his friend's face. Something sure troubled James. "I promise if it isn't illegal."

"It isn't, at least not yet."

"Whoa, this sounds like trouble." Clay backed away and tilted his head.

"Wait, hear me out. It's a long story." James explained how he had hired a seventeen-year-old girl to help out during his wife's pregnancy. "You may have seen her around town. Her name's Lily Vaughn."

"Oh, yes, she comes into the store with her mother. Dark hair and kind of timid. Doesn't her father work in the land office?"

"Yes, and the family are faithful members of our church. But here's the thing. Grace Ann has spotted bruises on Lily's arms and legs."

"So what does that have to do with me?" The idea of a young girl being beaten soured his stomach, reminding him of the abuse he'd witnessed in prison.

"I thought maybe if I told you, the two of us could think of some way to find out more about her. I'm afraid her parents are abusing her, but with them being churchgoers and all, it'll be hard to prove."

"You should be talking to the sheriff or Mr. Warner. They know all about the law."

"I know, but I didn't want to bother them with this unless we have more proof. Grace Ann is trying to befriend her in hopes Lily may reveal what's going on, and I'm keeping a lookout. But we could use another set of eyes."

Clay shoved his hat back on his head then rubbed his chin. "I don't know. That might not be good with my reputation."

"Please, Clay. I know the real you, and you're too decent a man to let a girl continue to be abused if there's something you could do about it."

He didn't know about his decency, but James was right. Abuse of any kind, especially to a young woman, was worse than any beatings he'd seen in prison. "OK, but we have to have absolute proof."

James nodded. "I know. But with Grace Ann, you, and me all watching out for her, one of us is bound to see something. Thanks, Clay." He held out his hand, and Clay gladly shook it. At least one person other than his parents was willing to think the best of him. He only hoped he could live up to their good opinion.

Chapter 7

LAY SPENT THE rest of the afternoon with James until Grace Ann finished with her volunteer duties at the cake walk. After James left to meet with his wife, Clay wandered about the streets hoping to glimpse Merry once again, but he finally gave up and headed to the area where several ranchers had set up outdoor cookers and offered hot barbecued beef.

He paid for a packet of beef and went back home to eat. The situation with the girl James mentioned wouldn't leave him alone, and as he climbed the steps to the rooms above the store, he debated with himself about helping Lily.

Not enough trust had been built with the people of Prairie Grove to warrant his involvement, but he couldn't sit by and do absolutely nothing to help the girl if she needed it. James had said she was seventeen. That was old enough to leave home, but if what James said was true, that might not be possible. Even so, he'd look for signs of abuse and help his friend do something about it, if need be.

He set his wrapped meal on the table, retrieved a plate and

fork, then poured a cup of coffee. Footsteps tapped across the floor behind him, and he turned to see his mother.

"Clay, I didn't know you'd be home so early. Pa and I are going to the hotel to eat a little later. He decided to give me a special treat this evening."

"Not much else to do since the festival is closing down for the evening." He unwrapped his meat and potato and sat down at the table. "I brought supper home with me. Couldn't resist the smell of that beef."

Ma sat down across from him. "Yes, it did smell delicious. I'm glad you have something for supper. I didn't think about cooking you anything."

Clay laughed and patted her hand. "That's all right. You need a night off, and this is plenty for me."

Ma clasped and unclasped her hands. "Did you have a good time today?"

"Yes, I really did. Spent some time with Miss Warner and four of the boys from Holly Hill. That's a lively bunch she has to corral, but they were having a great time. Those bags Pa and I filled for the fishing game were a big hit with them." He glanced around the kitchen. "Where is Pa anyway?"

"He's helping with the clean-up crew, but he'll be along shortly."

Clay laid his fork across his plate. "Ma, do you know the Vaughn family?"

She looked a bit startled at his question, but she answered readily. "Yes, they're new to town, just moved here in September. Mrs. Vaughn doesn't get out much except to come to the store and church. Their daughter is a quiet, shy girl. I don't think I've heard her say more than a dozen words any time she's come in with her ma."

"What about Mr. Vaughn?" Clay sipped his coffee and watched for Ma's reaction.

Her brows knit together, and she pursed her mouth. Finally her mouth relaxed, and she said, "Mr. Vaughn works in the land development office with Mr. Johnson, who's about ready to retire. I've seen him at church, but I don't really know him. Seems like a nice enough fellow, but something about him doesn't sit well with me, and I can't put my finger on it. Why do you ask?"

Might be he's hiding the beating he gives his daughter. Clay picked up his plate and headed for the sink. "No reason. I wondered about them, since they're new to town."

Pa burst through the door. "Sorry I'm late, Cora, but I'll get cleaned up straightway and we can go down to the hotel and eat." He kissed the top of Ma's head and disappeared into the other room.

Clay rinsed off his plate and set it aside to dry. The evening loomed ahead long and boring. Too bad they didn't have a dance at the town hall after the festival, but after a long day, most folks wanted to get on home for the evening.

Pa returned, and in a few minutes he and Ma left to enjoy their dinner together. Must be really special for Pa to take Ma to the hotel for dinner. Most people in town ate at the diner, leaving the hotel to guests.

After washing up himself, Clay moseyed back down to the street. In half an hour he found himself at the base of the hill leading up to the house at the top of Holly Hill. Even at this distance the light from oil lamps colored each window in a soft glow.

What a beautiful place for orphaned children to live. Mr. and Mrs. Collins had been loving parents to so many children. Mr. and Mrs. Warner were good to carry on the tradition of taking in children who lost parents in a tragic way. Merry too. She would make some man a fine wife someday, but most likely that man wouldn't and couldn't be him.

The blast of a whistle pierced the air. Clay jumped. That sound came only when a storm threatened or a fire burned somewhere. He glanced back toward town and spotted the orange glow of flames in the evening sky. The clang of the fire wagon broke through the night, and Clay ran back into town.

A few blocks away a house blazed with orange flames lighting the dark sky. By the time he reached the yard, fire had swallowed up the entire house, with the volunteers pouring water on it in vain.

A woman lay on the grass with a small boy beside her. One of the volunteers knelt beside her, and another woman ran up to help. Clay went over to do his part in helping with the long hose from the wagon.

The man in front of him turned. "Go help the pumpers. We need more water."

Clay ran back and grabbed hold of the pumper bar. The man there stepped back. "Thanks for coming. My arms are plumb wore out." Clay went right to work pumping the water.

All around them people shouted and called out for the doctor and more water. A crowd collected around the edge of the yard to watch the inferno. When the fire finally died out, only the brick chimney still stood amidst the pile of rubble that had once been a house.

Despite the chill air, perspiration dotted Clay's face from the exertion on the pumper and the heat of the fire. With the last embers put out, Clay stopped pumping to wipe his forehead with his handkerchief. Then he noticed the group of people standing where he'd seen the woman earlier. Heads shook back and forth, and he heard a few sobs.

Clay pushed his way through the crowd to see four sheet-covered mounds. Mrs. Tate, the pastor's wife, held the little boy he'd seen earlier. He hurried to her side. "What happened, Mrs. Tate?"

"The Henderson family is gone, except for little Jonathan here. I'm going to take him to my place right now, but we need to figure out what will be best for him." She cradled the sobbing child against her chest and swayed back and forth with him.

Clay blinked tears from his own eyes. "What about the Warner bunch at Holly Hill? Mrs. Warner will know exactly what to do for him."

Mrs. Tate nodded her approval. "That's a fine idea. Louise is wonderful with those children, and he won't be alone with the other little boys around." She thrust the boy to his arms. "Here, you take him while I go to find Reverend Tate. Doctor Lawford has already checked him and said he's fine."

Clay clutched Jonathan to his chest and glanced around for help. He had no idea what to do with a boy this size. The boy, no more than four, shivered in Clay's arms. His brown eyes, as sad and frightened as any Clay had ever seen, stared from beneath dark locks of hair around his face. Someone had wrapped a blanket around the child, who wore only a nightshirt under it. He didn't need to be out in this cold. Clay turned and marched toward the church and the parson's house in back.

Before he reached the church, Ma found him at the same time Reverend and Mrs. Tate did. While Mrs. Tate explained to Ma the circumstances, Reverend Tate spoke to Clay. "My wife told me your suggestion, and I think it's an excellent one. Mrs. Collins has never been one to refuse a child, and I'm sure her daughter is no different. She and I will go with you to deliver him."

Clay stepped back, his eyes opened wide. "You want me to take him?"

"Yes, it was your idea. Besides, you're young and strong and can carry him better than the missus or I can."

Ma patted his arm. "I'm going with you too, so perhaps we should get the wagon. Might be much easier on every one. Stanley will have ours hitched in no time."

She strode off toward the livery where Pa boarded the horses. The reverend and his wife took off right behind her. Clay shrugged and shifted the boy's weight in his arms. Sobs came from the folds of the blanket.

"Shh, little fellow, it'll be all right. We're going to find you a nice warm bed."

"I want my mama."

"I know you do, but she's not here right now." How in the world would he ever explain that to a child? He wouldn't have to. That was the reverend's job, and the quicker they got the boy to Holly Hill, the quicker Reverend Tate could help Jonathan understand what had happened.

A day that had begun as a special Saturday had ended in

such tragedy. Clay shook his head. How could a kind, loving God take away a child's parents in such a horrible way?

Merry climbed into bed filled with worry about where the fire might be. Papa had gone to help as soon as he heard the fire alarm, but Mama and Grandma stayed behind to make sure the children stayed in bed. With tomorrow being a church day, they needed their sleep.

The door opened with a bang downstairs, and Merry jumped from her bed and donned her robe. She padded out to the stairway where the muffled voices of her parents wafted upwards. When she entered the parlor, her parents and Grandma wore grim expressions.

Mama turned to Merry and blinked her eyes. "All except Jonathan in the Henderson family perished in a fire, their home destroyed."

"Oh, Mama, that's terrible." Such a tragedy for a wonderful family and a precious little four-year-old boy. The two older Henderson children had been her students, and her heart ached for the little boy. "Where is Jonathan now? Is he all right?"

Papa nodded and squeezed Mama's shoulder. "Yes, he's fine. Reverend Tate stopped me as I was headed home to tell me they're bringing Jonathan to us."

Mama pulled away from Papa and grabbed Grandma's arm. "Then we must make sure to have things ready for him. Merry, find something for him to wear. His clothes probably smell like smoke, so he'll need something clean. Grandma and I will fix up a bed with the younger boys."

Merry followed them upstairs and into the room they used for storage. Boxes filled with donated items for the home sat in the room. She found the one marked for sizes four to six and opened it to find a clean night shirt, a pair of pants, a shirt, shoes and socks, and undergarments. Now he'd have something not only for tonight but the morning as well.

With the clothes in hand, she hurried to the room where the younger boys bedded down. Mama and Grandma worked quietly to set up a cot for Jonathan without waking the other boys. Wouldn't they be surprised to find a new little brother in the morning?

She laid the clothes on a chair and went back down to the parlor. A knock on the door sounded as she reached the bottom step. Papa met her in the entryway, and they opened the door together to find Clay on the stoop holding a blanket-wrapped bundle. His mother and the reverend and his wife stood with him.

Papa opened the door wide to let them enter. Clay glanced at Merry. His eyes widened and her heart jumped right to her throat. Of all things for Clay to see her in her nightclothes with her hair hanging down her back!

She excused herself and ran upstairs to change. After slipping into her clothes, she twisted her hair up and secured it with a comb. Now she looked a sight more presentable.

Grandma met her in the hallway. "I'm going to put the little one to bed. Go on down and help your mother with coffee for our guests."

"Yes, ma'am." She breathed a prayer for Clay to still be with Reverend and Mrs. Tate. At the bottom of the stairway, she glanced left into the parlor where Papa, Clay, and Reverend

Tate conversed, and excitement stirred once again in her chest. She turned to the kitchen where the fresh aroma of coffee filled the air. No need to interrupt the menfolk in their talk. Grandma and the other women sat around the kitchen table.

Mama poured coffee into cups on the table then set a plate of fresh banana bread alongside. "I have sugar and a little milk if you prefer that," she told Mrs. Tate.

The men entered, and they all sat around the large oval table. Reverend Tate picked up a cup of hot coffee and added sugar. "This is nice of you, Mrs. Warner, and we do appreciate your taking in young Jonathan."

Mama sat down next to Papa. "It's no trouble at all. With as many as we have around here, one more won't be any problem."

Merry glanced upward. "At least none of them were awakened by the noise." As she returned her gaze to the table, it caught with Clay's, and her heart beat faster. Before his eyes flicked away, she sensed something there. Yearning? But for what?

"Were you…" Her voice squeaked. Heat filled her face, and she swallowed before trying again. "Were you there at the fire?"

His lips formed a grim line, and he spoke to a spot somewhere beyond her left ear. "Yes. I helped with the pumper wagon. Your papa and Reverend Tate helped too."

"It must have been terrible." She could only imagine the horror he must have experienced in watching the house burn and four people die. Nothing else to say came to her mind. Thankfully at that moment Reverend Tate rose from his seat.

"It's getting late, or should I say early. It's best we get back to town and see what else I need to do. The Henderson family belonged to our congregation, but I have no idea about any relatives except that Mr. Henderson had a brother in Wichita. I'll send a wire there to inquire about family."

Merry followed them to the door with Mama and Papa. Before she could stop to think about what she was doing, Merry laid a hand on Clay's arm. "Thank you for bringing Jonathan here," she said. "We'll take good care of him."

He looked down at her. "I know you will. You understand better than anyone what he's going through." For the first time that night he looked straight into her eyes, as if searching for that understanding for himself.

"Thank you," she said automatically, not knowing what else to say.

Clay nodded, a veil going over his eyes. He went out to the wagon while her parents said good-bye to the Tates and to Mrs. Barlow.

What a day this had been. It had shown her that Clay's compassion for others had not completely disappeared after his years of running with a gang and serving time in prison. Yet she mourned the loss of the fun-loving, uncomplicated young man she had known in her teens. Now a shadow followed him wherever he went.

Merry wrapped a shawl around her shoulders and followed her parents outside to say good night to their guests. She stood by the wagon as Reverend Tate assisted Mrs. Tate and Mrs. Barlow into the wagon. Then she stepped back with her parents to watch the wagon drive off into the darkness, carrying Clay and all her hopes and fears for his happiness.

Chapter 8

ON SUNDAY MORNING Merry went in to awaken the younger boys. If she could get to them before they saw Jonathan, she could explain what happened and let them help Jonathan get through the day.

When she entered the room, Jonathan already lay awake. So quiet, yet his little body shook. Merry hastened to his side and knelt beside the bed then gathered the child in her arms. "You're safe here, Jonathan."

"I want my mama." He clung to Merry, and sobs wracked his small frame. Merry sat on the bed and rocked him back and forth. How could she tell him everything would be all right when nothing would ever be the same for the boy?

"Merry, who's that?" Teddy sat up in bed and rubbed his eyes.

"It's Jonathan Henderson. His house burned down during the night."

Stevie, Kenny, and Robert now sat up and stared at Jonathan and Merry. Stevie frowned and shook his head. "What about Charlie, his brother? He's in our class at school."

Merry gulped and swallowed hard. How could she have forgotten how the children here would feel? Now little Charlie was gone, as was Amy, their sister. Tears flooded Merry's eyes. "Charlie died with his parents and sister. Jonathan is the only one left."

The boys looked at each other and blinked their eyes. Death was not new to them as each had experienced the death of his own parents. Stevie and Robert both ran over to Merry and Jonathan and wrapped their arms around them. The death of their parents was recent enough for them to cry with Jonathan.

Stevie patted Jonathan's shoulder. "I still miss my mama, but Mama Warner and Merry are good, and they love us. You'll like it here."

Jonathan hiccupped and sniffed. His red-rimmed eyes blinked at Stevie. "I wanna go home."

Merry hugged him tighter. "I know you do, but your home is gone. You have to stay with us."

Mama opened the door and took in the scene. She hurried to the bed and picked up Jonathan. "I think it's time for you to get ready for church. Grandma and I will take care of Jonathan." Her smile beamed love for all of them.

She left the room with the sobbing boy in her arms. Mama and Grandma would know exactly what to do for Jonathan. That was their job.

Merry planted her hands on her hips. "Let's get dressed for church."

Teddy pulled on her arm. "Merry, what about Charlie?"

Merry knelt and gathered the boys around her. "Charlie is

in heaven with his parents and sister, just like your parents are. He's spending Sunday with Jesus."

Stevie stuck out his bottom lip and blinked back tears. "I'm gonna miss him. Me and him was friends, and we was going to have a game of marbles at recess tomorrow."

She let his lapse of correct grammar pass. This was not a time for correction. "We'll all miss Charlie."

"But why does God let bad things happen like the fire?"

She grasped Stevie's hands in hers. "I don't really know. Sometimes accidents just happen. Sometimes God decides He needs someone up in heaven and sends His angels to get them. It's hard to understand even for me, but someday we'll get to see them again. And you know what? I bet your parents are looking down on you from heaven and thinking what good boys you are."

Kenny buttoned his shirt. "I didn't even know my parents. Only mama I know is Mama Warner." He ducked behind his bed and bent down to pull on his pants.

Merry stood with her heart aching for these four boys and the losses they'd experienced already in their young lives. She blinked back her own tears. "I'll leave now so the rest of you can dress. If you need me, I'll be right across the hall."

Out in the hall she blew out her breath. This would be a difficult day for everyone. So much loss under one roof, but at least they all had this place to call home.

She finished her dressing and headed back downstairs, stopping first to rap on the boys' door to remind them to hurry.

In the dining room the girls helped set the table for breakfast. Emmaline glanced up at Merry. "I saw the little boy Reverend and Mrs. Tate brought in last night. He's so little, and he was crying. It's so sad. Grandma Collins is sitting with him in the parlor. I'll miss seeing Amy at school. She was such a pretty little girl, and so quiet."

The other three stopped their work and peered at Merry. They expected her to say something, but what? *Lord, give me Your words now.*

"Last night was a terrible tragedy, and little Jonathan will likely have nightmares about it. It will be up to all of us to help him get through these next days and weeks. You know what it's like and how Jonathan is feeling right now, although I imagine he's a little more frightened because of his age. Let's just love him and let him know he's welcome here."

"What about other family? Does he have someone who will want to take him?"

Merry wrapped her arm around Emmaline's shoulder. "I don't know, but Reverend Tate is going to find out and let us know." If he had family somewhere who could take him, it would help him get through this difficult time.

Mama pushed through the door from the kitchen with a platter of eggs and bacon in her hands. "Ah, there you are, Merry. Are the boys all ready? Grandma is staying at home with Jonathan this morning."

"Yes, the boys should be here any minute. I expected Grandma would want to keep Jonathan here instead of going to church. His sad little face breaks my heart."

"Yes, it's hard for a child of any age to lose his parents, especially in something like a fire." She set the platters on the table and headed back to the kitchen for more.

Merry hurried to follow her just as the clamor on the stairs announced the arrival of the younger boys. Henry walked through the back door with Papa. They'd been up and out taking care of chores even on Sunday morning. Papa said cows didn't know Sunday from Thursday.

Henry removed his gloves. "Whillikers, I'm so hungry I could eat all that breakfast this morning." After hanging his coat and hat on a peg by the door, he reached for a biscuit.

Merry swung around with the tray out of his reach. "No, you don't. Go on in and sit down with the rest. You'll get yours soon enough."

His eyes twinkled with mischief. "You know I could grab that whole platter out of your hands." Then he shrugged. "But I won't."

In a few minutes the whole family gathered and sat waiting for Papa to say grace. Merry glanced at Jonathan sitting beside her. Mama had placed several books on a chair for Jonathan so he would be higher to the table. His dark eyes were still damp with tears, and Merry wanted to reach over and hug him. Instead she took his little hand in hers and smiled at him. Grandma held his other hand in hers.

Not much conversation flowed around the table this morning. Merry suspected each child remembered losing family; even the ones who had come as babies understood the sense of loss for little Jonathan.

After breakfast Merry helped clean up the kitchen then checked on her charges to make sure they were ready to leave. Everyone but Grandma Collins and Jonathan boarded the two carriages for the ride to the church. Merry sent a silent prayer heavenward that Reverend Tate would be able to find some family for the little boy. No matter what one's age, everyone needed a family to love, and to be loved…and a place to belong.

Clay rolled over in his bed. The aroma of bacon frying this morning didn't entice as it normally would. His head ached from the lack of sleep the night before. By the time he and Ma returned home with Reverend Tate and he'd taken care of the horses, it had been three in the morning before he climbed into bed. How could Ma rise at her usual time on Sunday after so little sleep?

He groaned once and then turned to bury his head in his pillow and hoped sleep would return quickly. Two more hours and he would get up.

Then images from the night crowded into his mind. The flames of the fire leaped higher than ever, and the four shrouded bodies on the front lawn lay larger than life.

Clay bolted upright and blinked. All the sights, sounds, and horror of the fire flooded his mind with pictures he wanted to forget. Then little Jonathan's face appeared. A child lost his parents and his sister and brother. How could God be so cruel?

Unable to sleep with the images crowding his head, Clay rose and dressed. Another long Sunday loomed ahead. Perhaps he'd go to Holly Hill later this afternoon and see how Jonathan had fared during the night.

When he entered the kitchen, Ma turned from the stove. "Good morning. I figured you'd sleep in this morning after our late night."

He leaned down and kissed her cheek. "You're the one who should be in bed. You need your rest."

She waved the spoon in the air. "Oh, posh, I'm fine. I've

been getting stronger every day since you've been home. Sit down and have some eggs."

"That sounds good. I smell bacon and biscuits too."

Ma laughed. "Oh, yes, your pa likes a good hearty breakfast on Sunday mornings before church."

Pa walked into the room. "That I do, and this one smells wonderful, just like all the rest." He sat down at the table and picked up his napkin to spread on his lap. "Thank you for taking care of getting Jonathan to Holly Hill last night. I helped George Mason carry the bodies to his funeral parlor. Such a sad situation."

Ma poured Clay and Pa cups of coffee. "It is indeed. At least Jonathan is in good hands at Holly Hill. Mrs. Collins and Louise Warner both have ways with children like no one else I've ever seen. I do believe Merry is developing the same instincts."

Clay could vouch for that just from the few times he'd observed her with her students and with the younger boys at the home, but he didn't dare comment.

Ma placed platters of eggs, bacon, and biscuits on the table and then sat down. She reached across for Clay and Pa's hands. "We have much to be thankful for this day and much to seek in prayer for Jonathan."

"That we do, my dear." Pa squeezed Ma's hand and bowed his head.

As his father spoke the words of prayer, all the things that happened in the few weeks since his return rolled through his mind. The only bright spots had been seeing Merry again and Ma's improvement. The whispers and unkind remarks behind his back and Jonathan's plight all served to further his distance from God. No matter how much his mother might coax, he had no plans to attend church this morning.

Pa finished the blessing and filled his plate with eggs and bacon. "I'm hoping Reverend Tate will be able to locate family for Jonathan. I never heard his parents speak of any other relatives, but then most of our conversations revolved around business. He talked a lot about the future and how the new automobiles would change his wagon repair and building shop, and what he was planning to do to expand."

From what he'd seen of Lester Henderson's business, he would have done quite well in automobile repair. What a waste of a young father on the verge of true success. A sour taste filled Clay's mouth. Another reason he had no desire to trust God with his future. He pushed back from the table.

"I'm not feeling well. Going back to bed. I'll see you after church." He turned a deaf ear to his mother's pleas and left the room. His bed sounded like the best place to be just now.

Cora blinked back tears. Her son had come home, but part of him got lost somewhere along the road. Five years in prison had changed him, and not necessarily for the better. "I do wish Clay would come back to church with us."

Stanley reached over and patted her hand then held it. "So do I, but he's had a hard time with the criticism and complaints since his return. It'll take time for him to adjust. The old Clay is in there somewhere, and we just have to wait and pray for his return."

Her husband spoke true, but the criticisms were hurtful to

her as well. "Did you see the way Clay looked at Merry Warner at the festival yesterday?"

"Hmm, no." He moved his hand and picked up a biscuit. "Can't say that I notice such things."

"I remember the way they liked each other back in their school days before the Warner family moved away. If she'd been here, she may have been able to keep Clay from getting into so much trouble."

"Maybe so, but ifs are not going to change the past now. I do know that the Warner girl has taken to stopping into the store in the afternoons after school much more often than she did before Clay came home."

Cora leaned back in her chair and signed. "How nice it would be if the two of them could get back together. She's just the one to bring our son back to church."

Stanley shook his head. "Oh, Cora, don't look to a girl to change his ways. The change has to happen inside of him, not just to impress some young woman. And besides, I wouldn't want him courting someone until his own affairs are in order."

Cora sighed. She had to admit Stanley was right. Until Clay got his heart right with God, he wouldn't be a fit husband for any young woman. Still, nothing would do her heart and health more good than to see Clay settled down with a wife and family. Just the way he'd handled Jonathan last night gave a good indication of the kind of father he'd be. She could only pray that God would continue to work in his heart and life and make him fit to be a good Christian husband as well.

Chapter 9

ERRY GATHERED UP her belongings from her desk and prepared to go home, glad that another week of school was over. The children had all left for the day, and even the ones from Holly Hill had raced homeward for some of Grandma Collins's hot chocolate and sugar cookies without waiting for her to walk with them.

So far no word had come from any family for Jonathan Henderson. Merry's heart ached for the little boy who clung to her like a sticky burr. He had completely captured her heart, and she spent as much time as possible with him when she came home from school, although Mama and Grandma both advised her against becoming too attached to him.

The children in school would come to terms with the deaths of their classmates in time, but all week since the funeral she'd had to contend with weepy girls. Merry had let them voice their grief and talk about the Henderson children.

Today she'd assigned parts for the Thanksgiving program, and talking about the play helped take their minds off their sadness. The older children had taken their parts without argument, but the younger ones had their own ideas. All the boys wanted to be Indians and all the girls Pilgrims. Even though she had explained she needed some of both for each part, it had taken drawing parts out of a hat to get them evenly distributed. None of the girls had drawn to be an Indian, but the boys had. That had brought a lot of excitement and celebration.

She walked toward town, mentally calculating how much black material she'd need to make Pilgrim costumes for the children from Holly Hill. Mrs. Barlow had promised to order plenty of black, white, and brown fabric so all the parents could make the necessary costumes. The fabric should be in today.

She stopped to admire the poster advertising the box supper they always had the Saturday after Thanksgiving. One thing about Holly Hill, any excuse the church or town could come up with for a celebration meant one would be held. Merry already planned what to prepare for her basket and how to decorate it. She remembered the good time she'd had as a sixteen-year-old the last year they'd lived here. All single girls fifteen and older had auctioned their boxes to help raise funds for improving the play yard at the school, repairing the swings, and providing new equipment for the boys to play ball games. While the couples shared box suppers, the adults and younger children enjoyed a potluck supper. The one this year would go to raise funds for a new addition to the church.

If Clay happened to buy her box as he had back then, he'd have no excuse not to spend time with her. Despite her apprehension as to what the school board might think, she truly wanted Clay's friendship. If she gained that, then maybe she could find out what was behind the sadness she sensed whenever he was near.

She sighed and opened the door of the store. Best not to get her hopes up. A lot had changed since that long ago day when Clay had kissed her. Friendship might no longer be possible.

Merry glanced around for any sight of Clay but did not see him. Mrs. Barlow appeared at the bottom of the stairway to their living quarters. She spotted Merry and hurried over to her.

"Some new cloth came in on the train today. Clay went over and picked up our order. He's in the back now putting it on our inventory." She turned her head toward the storeroom. "Clay, bring out some of that fabric we ordered."

So that's where Clay hid out. He'd been doing that every time she came into the store, not even coming out to inquire after Jonathan.

Mr. Barlow finished with his customer. He waved to his wife and Merry. "I'm heading over to the bank to make a deposit." He grabbed up a bag and left.

Mrs. Barlow led Merry back to the piece goods. "The whole town's excited about the Thanksgiving play. It'll be the first one we've had in a long time. Reverend Tate says you'll be directing the one at church for Christmas as well." Mrs. Barlow's face beamed her approval of all Merry had done.

"That's right, but we're not doing anything toward it until we get through this one. The children are really excited about both." Indeed they were. Today she'd had trouble getting them back to their studies after assigning their parts for the play.

Maybe the play rehearsal should be the last activity of the day instead of right after their noon break.

"Here's the fabric, Ma. I just got it on the inventory."

Merry jumped at the sound of Clay's voice. She stepped back and patted her chest. "Oh, my, you startled me." She reached for the fabric, and her hand brushed Clay's. Heat rose in her face, and the strangest sensation shot up her arm. She gulped and grasped the bolt far away from his hands. Every time she came near to him, her cheeks flushed and embarrassment overtook her. He'd probably begun to think red was the natural color of her face.

"Thank you. I haven't seen much of you since the fire. Your pa must be keeping you busy." Her voice squeaked and caused more heat in her face.

"Yes, he gives me plenty to do. If you'll excuse me, I'll get back to it." He backed away then headed to the store room.

Mrs. Barlow smiled after him. "Don't mind Clay; he doesn't mean to be rude. He's just working extra hard to prove himself to the town." She took the bolt from Merry and began rolling out a length. "Do you need more than you did the other day when we ordered it?"

"At least two yards more. And I need more thread and two yards of white." Merry was relieved to hear Mrs. Barlow's explanation for Clay's behavior. She had begun to wonder if Clay would ever soften toward her. But obviously he had a lot of work to do to regain his good name in town.

"Then go on back and get what you need while I cut these pieces." Mrs. Barlow nodded to the area where the sewing notions were displayed.

Merry made her selections of thread and looked up when

the bell over the door rang. Three women entered the store and approached Mrs. Barlow. Merry stood still, just out of sight, but near enough to see them and hear their comments.

Mrs. Pennyfeather stood by the counter with her nose in the air as usual. That woman had to criticize and complain about everything. The feather on her hat shook as she squared her shoulders. "Cora, did you know that Karl Laramie and his gang were said to be in the area?"

Merry peeked through the display and noted the ashen color of Mrs. Barlow's face as she answered the woman. "No, I hadn't heard about it. Are you sure?"

"The sheriff's going out with some men now to investigate. Wouldn't surprise me any if they'd come back to get Clay. After all, he ran with them before."

Mrs. Barlow gripped the edge of the counter as the woman continued to belittle Clay. Merry wanted to step out and give Mrs. Pennyfeather a good scolding for doing that to Mrs. Barlow. She looked like she might faint at any minute. Mr. Pennyfeather headed the school board and just might fire her, but Merry couldn't let the woman go on with her comments.

She stepped from behind the display. "Mrs. Barlow, can you help me a minute? I'm sure those ladies are familiar enough with the merchandise that they can find what they need."

Mrs. Pennyfeather's mouth dropped open, and the faces of the other ladies turned red. They stopped their talking and stood with those dumbfounded looks on their faces.

When Mrs. Barlow reached Merry, her hands trembled and all color had drained from her face. Merry grasped Mrs. Barlow's hands and spoke so that the ladies couldn't hear. "I didn't really need your help, but I couldn't stand what those women were saying. I hope the sheriff does find Karl and his gang and puts them in jail."

A tear slipped down Mrs. Barlow's cheek. "Thank you, Merry. I don't understand why some of the ladies can't seem to forgive Clay. He's paid for his crime and wouldn't get involved with Karl again. He promised me he would never get in trouble again."

"I believe him." Merry glanced toward the front of the store. "The ladies are leaving, so let's go finish with the fabric."

They made their way back to the counter. Mrs. Barlow folded up the cut cloth. "I'm so glad you were here, Merry. I don't know how much more I could take from them. I've calmed down now and feel better."

"It's the least I could do after what you and Clay did to help little Jonathan. I just hope Reverend Tate finds relatives for him soon."

"He's heard nothing yet from the wires he sent to Mr. and Mrs. Henderson's homes in Missouri and Pennsylvania, but then it's been only six days since the fire."

"I do hope they find someone. Jonathan is a very lonely little boy and misses his family something terrible." She picked up the package Mrs. Barlow had wrapped. "Thank you again for ordering the extra cloth."

She headed for the door, but out of the corner of her eye she spotted Clay just inside the storeroom door. How much of Mrs. Pennyfeather's comments had he heard? It just wasn't fair. She'd like to help Clay, but since he wouldn't have anything to do with her, that help would be hard to offer.

Clay pounded his fist against the wall in the storeroom. Would the criticism and blame never end? Mrs. Pennyfeather and her friends caused a deep hurt in Ma every time they came into the store and gave their opinions. Merry had rescued Ma from further humiliation, and for that he had to be grateful.

He wished he could have seen the look on the ladies' faces when Merry interrupted them with her request for Ma's help. And his heart warmed at her simple statement of belief in him. Just thinking of Merry always cheered him up, but until all the people of Prairie Grove accepted him, he'd have to steer clear of her. He didn't want to bring hurtful gossip on her head.

Heaviness settled in his heart. If Karl lurked anywhere near town, that meant trouble brewed also. In addition, he had no faith that the sheriff would make any arrests. Never had he seen one so cunning and elusive as Karl Laramie and his gang. Clay had been the stupid one for getting caught, but in reality, it was the best thing that could have happened to him. He'd lost five years of his freedom, but he'd learned his lesson about the law.

Clay raised his eyes toward the ceiling. *Is that what You wanted, God? Did You do that to me to teach me not to follow the wrong people? If so, it worked.* Still, God could have given him a clue before he got himself thrown into jail.

The back door opened, and Pa stepped through into the storeroom. He shrugged off his coat and hung it on a hook near the door. "Looks like you've been busy while I was at the bank."

"It's all inventoried and ready for the shelves. I'll take care of that now." Clay picked up an armload of merchandise. "I just heard Karl Laramie might be in the area. Is it true?"

"Yes, it is. The sheriff took a small posse to check it out. I don't know why Karl would risk coming back here." Then Pa's eyes narrowed. "You wouldn't be thinking about rejoining that gang, would you?"

Clay gulped and shuddered. His father still didn't trust him. "Never!"

Pa smiled and gripped Clay's shoulder. "I didn't think you would, but be careful. He might try to reach you." He tied an apron around his waist. "I saw Mrs. Pennyfeather and a few of the other ladies leaving. She had a set to her shoulders that told me her feathers had been ruffled. What happened?"

"The same old thing. She had a few hurtful words about me to say to Ma, but Merry Warner stepped in and put a stop to it."

"Hmm, figured as much since I also saw Merry leave a little after." Pa placed both hands on Clay's shoulder. "Son, don't let narrow-minded women like Mrs. Pennyfeather take away the joy of being home. What she says will not change the way your ma and I love you. We're proud to have you here helping us. Don't you forget that, especially... well, you know what I mean."

Clay swallowed the lump in his throat at the realization again of how much he owed to his parents. Their faithful love and support had kept him going those five awful years. "I know, Pa, and I appreciate being here." He hefted his load. "Now I need to get this out on the shelves so we can make more money."

He grinned and headed into the main store area. Several

other customers were now shopping. Clay nodded to his mother and headed back to place the merchandise on the shelves. Pa came in to relieve Ma, who declared she'd be upstairs finishing up supper for them.

Clay's mouth watered at the thought of the fried chicken she'd fix up. He'd seen the chicken parts in a bowl of cool water in their icebox earlier and could already taste the crispy coating Ma would use to fry them. He'd detected the scent of cinnamon in the air earlier in the afternoon, so that meant an apple pie might also be part of dinner.

He placed a few items on a shelf and let his mind wander back to Merry. How he and the other boys had teased her about the spelling of her name, causing her a lot of misery. They'd even called her "Merry Christmas" a number of times.

He chuckled at the memory. Instead of being angry, she had held her head high and said that since it was Jesus's birthday, she didn't mind the name at all, especially since her own birthday came just two days later.

The boys stopped teasing and calling her the nickname because she'd taken all the fun out of it. He'd never forgotten it, and that was the day he decided he loved her and would someday marry her.

Reality hit him like a sledgehammer. He may want to love her, but she could never be his. She deserved someone much better than an ex-convict bank robber. But if he planned to stay in this town, he'd have to be around her. That meant he would have to learn to be near without revealing his attraction to her. Maybe he should start by going to church. Seeing her there would be safer. A lot of people milling around would keep any conversation with her strictly on a friendly level.

He tossed a can of tomatoes between his hands and grinned. Going to church would most certainly bring delight to his ma as well as give him a chance to see Merry. And if through church God chose to explain Himself and His strange ways...then all the better.

His heart lighter, Clay began to whistle as he stocked the shelves.

Chapter 10

CLAY WAITED UNTIL his parents had left before he dressed to attend church. He planned to slip into the back and sit on a rear bench. That way he could observe Merry without her knowing.

He chose not to wear a suit since most of the men from the ranches outside town didn't. Suits were for funerals and weddings. However, he did shave and take extra care with grooming his hair.

Clay grabbed his hat and bounded down the outside stairs to the street and headed for the church. The lyrics and music of an old hymn being sung by the congregation floated in the clear cool air and brought back memories of happier days. He hummed along with the music at first before the words came rushing back. "What a friend we have in Jesus."

Friend indeed. He was supposed to bear all sins and grief, but the past five years proved that wrong. Maybe going to church wasn't such a good idea after all. Clay stopped a moment, but he didn't turn back. Instead he squared his shoulders to steel himself against what he would hear from Reverend Tate and continued toward the church.

The singing had concluded as he slipped through the door and to a seat on the back row. The woman next to him raised her eyebrows as though surprised to see him then smiled and patted his arm. He groaned inwardly. One of his mother's friends had to be in the last pew. No turning back now. He'd just have to make the best of it.

A few rows in front of him he spotted Lily Vaughn and her parents. They looked like any ordinary family attending church on Sunday, but the things James said ate at Clay's thoughts. He needed to get to know the girl better to see for himself. Perhaps he'd speak to them after the services. His gaze then scanned the sanctuary until he spotted Merry's blue hat with the velvet bow. He remembered blue to be her favorite color. She sat ramrod straight with her face to the front. Although Clay heard Reverend Tate's voice, the words he spoke went through Clay without stopping to take hold.

Merry turned her head and bent to smile at the child next to her. A finger brushed her lips, and she shook her head. Like any small child, he or she must be fidgeting. Clay remembered his mother doing the exact thing to him, but when he didn't stop, she pinched his ear. A nick of pain pierced his ear lobe at the memory. Merry wouldn't be so drastic as that, but it'd be interesting to see how she handled such a situation.

The opportunity never came, and Reverend Tate spoke the closing prayer. People all around him stood, but Clay scurried back outside to wait for the pastor. Many of the members might be friendly and speak to him, but Clay didn't want to risk Ma hearing more criticism, even if he was attending church.

The door opened and the congregation began their exit. A few glanced his way, but most stood in small groups talking.

When the Vaughn family stepped outside, Clay removed his hat and approached them. "Good morning, Mr. and Mrs. Vaughn. My name is Clay Barlow, the mercantile owner's son. You arrived here while I was gone." He turned his smile to Lily. "And good morning to you, Miss Vaughn. I've seen you in the store with your mother."

The girl's eyes narrowed, and she cast a furtive glance toward her parents. From his experiences in prison Clay spotted the cold fear in her eyes right away. James was right. Something was amiss.

Mr. Vaughn nodded his head to acknowledge Clay's greeting. "Yes, we'd heard you were back home. Now if you'll excuse us, we'll be on our way." He grasped the upper arms of both Lily and Mrs. Vaughn and led them away.

Before Clay had opportunity to further consider the man's behavior, Reverend Tate appeared at the door with Merry. The pastor spotted Clay and waved. He and Merry both hurried to where Clay stood by a tree.

"Good to see you this morning, Clay." He grasped Clay's hand and shook it with a firm grip. "We have some news about the Henderson family that Miss Warner just shared with me."

Merry's cheeks burned bright red, but her gaze held firm with Clay's. "It's most interesting. One of the older children in my class was a friend of Amy Henderson and says that Amy once told her that she had an aunt and uncle in Wichita. Their last name is Barnaby."

Reverend Tate grinned and nodded his head. "I've been trying to contact any Henderson family that may live close, but I didn't have a name except Henderson. This will give us something more definite."

Clay's heart pounded with the nearness of Merry, but he controlled his breathing. This was good information. A wire to Wichita just might find relatives.

Something grabbed him about the knees. He looked down and smiled at the little boy with his arms wrapped around Clay's legs. "Hello there, Jonathan. How are you this morning?"

He grinned and held his arms out for Clay to pick him up.

Once Clay had the boy in the air and secured in his arms, Jonathan hugged Clay's neck. "Where you been?"

Clay's heart sank. He hadn't been out to the home since the night of the fire a week ago. "I'm sorry. I've been busy at the store."

"You come now." Jonathan squirmed around to face Merry. "Can he, Miss Merry? I wants him eat dinner with me."

Mrs. Warner stepped up behind her daughter. "Of course he can, that is, if his own mama doesn't need him."

Jonathan's small hands gripped either side of Clay's face so he looked squarely at the boy. "Does your mama need you?"

Clay let go a deep laugh that filled him from the toes up. "Now I suppose my ma can get along without me for a little while." He ruffled the boy's hair then set him on the ground and sent him to play with the other boys. "I don't want to intrude, Mrs. Warner. Ma does have dinner for us at the store."

She waved her hand in the air. "Pshaw. You're not intruding. We'd love to have you. Isn't that right, Merry?"

Merry's cheeks flamed again, and her gaze locked with his. "Yes, we would."

That was all the encouragement he needed even though it went against his better judgment. He had made sure to avoid being alone with her the past few weeks, but with the crowd at Holly Hill, he'd be safe in talking and just being near her.

"That's settled then." Mrs. Warner clapped her hands and called to the children, who came running to board their carriages. As he watched the troupe leave, he had to give Mr. and Mrs. Warner credit, as well as Mrs. Collins. They created more of a home atmosphere for the children than a lot of folks Clay knew.

He turned around to find his parents standing nearby. Ma's face gleamed with joy. She ran to him and threw her arms around his neck. "I'm so happy to see you here this morning. Why didn't you tell us? You could have come with us."

Clay disentangled her arms and shook his head. "I didn't want to cause a fuss. And I wanted to see how Jonathan was doing."

None of the joy left Ma's eyes. "Oh, I saw how he ran up to you and hugged your legs. He remembers how good you were to him the night of the fire."

He glanced from his mother to his father then back to her. "Mrs. Warner invited me to share lunch with them today. Is that all right with you?"

A light shone in Ma's eyes now that added to the one already there. "That's wonderful. You can have dinner with us any old time." She patted his shoulder. "Go and have a good time."

He planted a kiss on her cheek then hurried off to get his horse for the ride up to Holly Hill House.

Merry's hands still trembled as she clasped them together in her seat in the carriage. Emmaline leaned over and grinned. "It'll be nice for Mr. Barlow to join us for dinner, won't it?"

"Yes, I suppose it will." Her knees had almost given way when he'd accepted the invitation. Jonathan had climbed into her lap when they left the church. Now he wrapped his arms around her neck. She hugged him close. Such a precocious little boy, and she loved him dearly. "How are you feeling, Jonathan?"

He leaned back and tilted his head. "I feel good. Mr. Clay's coming. He took care of me after the fire. I 'member him."

"I'm sure you do remember. He's a very nice man."

Jonathan nodded and laid his head against Merry's shoulder. He'd been so quiet about the night of the fire. This was the first time he'd actually mentioned it. The first part of the week he'd cried almost every night for his mama and papa and had nightmares. For the past few nights the nightmares had subsided, but he still had trouble sleeping. The mention of the fire today in connection with Clay might be a sign that healing had begun. A long road still lay ahead, but hopefully with the love that surrounded him, the road would be a little smoother.

Papa turned the carriage into the driveway leading up to the house. Every time Merry saw it, her heart filled with love and pride. The stately, two-story clapboard house with stone accents had a porch all the way across the front with a roof jutting out from just below the second-floor windows to cover it and give ample shade in the summer. Grandpa Collins had built it a number of years ago after he sold some of the land surrounding the old house. As prosperous ranchers, Grandpa and Grandma decided that taking care of orphaned and abandoned children was what God called them to do, so they'd sold most of the land and rebuilt the house with more bedrooms and space for the children. Donations from friends throughout the cattle industry kept the place in tip-top shape with some funds left over for special treats for the children.

Two large oak trees graced the front lawn, and a rope swing hung from one of the limbs. Green holly bushes filled with bright red berries filled the flower beds across the front and gave the home its name. How beautiful it always looked during the Christmas season. Merry was happy to call it home.

At the front doorway Papa climbed down from the carriage to assist the ladies in stepping down. The other carriage stopped behind them, and Henry turned around. "OK, everybody out. I'm hungry, and I want to get these horses into the barn so as I can eat."

The boys jumped down and raced up the walk. Merry reached up to the carriage seat to get Jonathan.

"I can do it, Miss Merry." Jonathan shoved her hand aside and scooted to the edge then dropped to the ground. "See? I can do it myself."

"Yes, you surely can." She gave him a little shove from behind. "Now catch up with Teddy."

He scampered away, and Papa drove the horses around to the back. Merry began gathering hats, gloves, and scarves left behind in the other carriage. Emmaline and Susie helped.

Both girls mumbled about the boys being so careless, but they made sure they had everything.

"Aren't you girls done yet? I'm in a hurry."

Merry stepped back from the carriage. "All finished, so go."

Henry snapped the reins then drove around to the back of the house. Merry picked up her skirts to head up the walk but stopped at the sound of a horse behind her.

"Wait up, Miss Warner, and I'll walk with you." Clay sat atop his black horse and grinned down at her.

She waited while he dismounted and hitched his horse to the post at the gate. He joined her, and they strolled up the walk to the house. "It was good to see you in church this morning," Merry said.

Clay lightly pressed her elbow as they climbed the steps to the porch. Heat rose in her arm as though a hot coal touched it. Her knees trembled, and she gave thanks that his hand held her steady.

"I wanted to see how Jonathan was doing. I was happy to hear you have discovered a possible lead to his family."

Merry's voice caught in her throat. She swallowed hard and nodded as he opened the front door for her. Before she could remove her cloak, the younger boys, including Jonathan, surrounded her and Clay.

Stevie's blue-green eyes danced with excitement as he grabbed Clay's hand. "You can sit by me at dinner, Mr. Clay."

Jonathan pushed his way to Clay's other side. "No, he'll sit by me." His little mouth puckered in a pout and his eyes pleaded with Clay.

"I think Mr. Clay has two sides, so both of you can sit by him." There went any chances of sitting next to him herself, but perhaps his being between the boys would be better for her in light of how her heart pounded and her tongue thickened like custard cooking on the stove.

The boys tugged at Clay's hands and led him to the dining table, where Grandma Collins had set an extra place. He settled the boys into their chairs then took his place between them. Merry sat beside Jonathan and grasped his hand while Papa said the blessing.

As conversation worked its way around the table, Clay helped Jonathan with his food and cut up his roast beef for him. The little boy gazed up at Clay, and Merry watched how gently Clay handled the child. He'd make a good husband and father. Her heart jumped, and she almost choked on a piece of potato. She grabbed for her glass of water and drank deeply to push the potato on its way.

At one time she'd harbored such thoughts for Clay, and lately some of those old feelings had begun to resurface. But he had spent five years in prison, and several years before that he was running around in a gang. A shudder went through her at the image of Clay in jail with horrible men who had committed all manner of crimes. No wonder he often seemed sad and avoided her. Still, his being at church today was a good sign and one that could bode well for his future.

After dinner Mama shooed her out of the kitchen and told her to entertain their guest before Papa bored him to death. When Merry entered the parlor, the men stood, and Papa greeted her with a hug.

"Here's my girl now. I was just telling Clay how good you'd been with helping Jonathan getting settled here at Holly Hill."

"He's such a precious little boy. I hope we can find his family soon," Merry said.

Mama's voice called out to Papa from the kitchen. He grinned, shrugged his shoulders, and left the room. Merry's hands dampened with perspiration, and she wiped them down her skirt. Clay stood so close she could detect the scent of bay rum, probably from his morning shave.

Clay looked down at her. Was that a hint of gladness she detected in his eye?

"It was kind of your mother to invite me to dinner. The children are amazing. Are they always that good at the dinner table?"

Merry laughed at the observation. "No, they're not. You were special company, so the boys used their best manners." She walked away a few paces then turned to face him. "Clay, why do you avoid me whenever I come into the store? Don't you want to be friends?"

His face paled, and she noted how his throat moved up and down before he answered. "I want to be friends, but the town's schoolmarm has no business being friends with an ex-convict."

"You were in prison once, but now you're not." She stepped back closer to him and reached out her hands. "I still care about you. Please can't we at least be friends?"

He turned away from her. "Merry, it isn't in your best interests. Your reputation is important in this town. It's best for us not to be more than two adults who speak to each other on occasion."

Another crack split her heart. She blinked back the moisture in her eyes. How could she argue about her reputation?

Especially after the way Mrs. Pennyfeather and her friends behaved.

He turned back to face her. "Karl Laramie is rumored to be back in the area, and people most likely expect me to join up with them again." Bitterness tinged his last words.

"Would you, Clay? Would you join up with them again?" Her heart thundered so loud that surely he must hear it.

"No, I wouldn't, but..." His voice trailed off and he stepped back. "Tell your parents I appreciate the hospitality, but I must get back to town." He grabbed his hat and headed for the door, but just then four little boys appeared and way-laid him.

Jonathan clung to Clay's legs. "Please don't go. Stay and play with us."

Merry grasped Jonathan and picked him up in her arms. "Honey, he has to go back to town. His own ma and pa need him there." Her words said for him to go, but her heart pleaded for him to stay.

He shoved his hat onto his head. "I'll be back to see you, Jonathan. I promise." With one last glance at Merry he opened the door and headed out to his horse.

Merry set Jonathan back on the floor and sent him off to play with Teddy and Steve. She stood at the window and watched Clay ride down the hill to town until he disappeared. Ma had been right. Clay wasn't the same boy she'd loved seven years ago. Something in his eyes spoke of hard things he'd seen and done.

Until he proved himself to the good citizens of Prairie Grove, she'd have to be content with whatever friendship she could get from Clay. However, it did make her want to ask

God if He'd forgotten how old she was getting. Twenty-four her next birthday and unmarried didn't bode well for her future.

Merry let the curtain fall back into place. She had a classroom full of students she loved, a houseful of children she adored, parents and a grandmother who loved her, and a God who would supply all her needs. Why then did she suddenly feel so empty and alone?

Chapter 11

FOR TWO DAYS Clay stewed because of the hurt he'd seen in Merry's eyes. He had to do something to turn her attention away from him. Her smile caused his insides to twist with the pain of knowing he would never have the standing to court her.

The bell over the doorway jingled, and Mrs. Vaughn and Lily entered. A dark blue bonnet covered Lily's dark curls and matched her eyes. "Good day, Mrs. Vaughn, how can I help you this morning?" As soon as he spoke, Lily lowered her head.

Mrs. Vaughn handed him a list. "These are the provisions I need for this week. Lily also needs to look at some piece goods."

Clay took the list, but Pa stepped up behind him. "I'll take care of Mrs. Vaughn. You go back and help Lily with the cloth. You can reach up and get down what she needs better than I can."

Mrs. Vaughn's mouth pinched as though she was in pain. "I suppose you can do that, Lily." She narrowed her eyes. "I'll be right here."

Lily simply nodded and followed Clay to the section with the bolts of fabric and other sewing notions. Clay stopped and stepped back to allow Lily to select what she wanted. "It was good to see you at church Sunday. Mrs. Shanks tells me that you're helping her at home." Actually James had told him, but that didn't matter right now.

"Hmm, yes, I am." She ducked her head and glanced backward toward where her mother and Pa stood by the canned fruits.

"That's very good of you. Your mother must be proud of you helping out in such a way."

"She's not my mother, and all she wants is the money I make."

Lily spoke so low that if Clay hadn't been standing right next to her, he wouldn't have heard a word. "What's that you said?"

"Nothing." She pointed to a bolt of brown cloth on the shelf. "I want some of that brown and perhaps some of the cream colored too. Four lengths of the brown and three of the cream will be plenty."

Clay reached for the fabrics and then laid the bolts on the counter for cutting. He wanted to find out more about the girl, but what could he say after the statement she'd made? Had she intended for him to hear? The question gnawed at Clay as he measured and cut the lengths for her.

"Are you going to be working for Mrs. Shanks today?"

She twisted her hands and kept her head down. "Yes."

He folded the cut fabric. "I'll be delivering groceries to her later today, so I may see you then."

Lily's eyes opened wide in fear, and she grabbed the fabric

from him. Without a word she scurried back to the front and plopped the fabric on the counter to be included with the other purchases.

Something definitely didn't add up with Lily. If Mrs. Vaughn wasn't her mother, then what was she, and why did she lead people in town to be believe Lily to be her daughter? He returned the bolts to the shelf. Now his curiosity niggled him. He wouldn't rest until he could get the answers to his questions.

The bell over the door tinkled again as Mrs. Vaughn and Lily left. Sheriff Devlin stepped back to allow them to exit then came on into the store. He waved at Clay. "Good morning, Clay. You have time to talk a few minutes?"

Clay slid the second bolt of cloth onto the shelf. "I can spare a few minutes." His heart pounded. What could the sheriff possibly want to know? His gut clenched. This must have something to do with Karl.

Sheriff Devlin moved to a corner to be out of earshot of the two customers now entering the store. "Has Karl Laramie tried to contact you yet?"

So it was about Karl. "No, sir, he hasn't. I'll let you know if he does, but I don't really think he will."

"You ran with him once. How does he avoid capture?" The sheriff narrowed his eyes and peered at Clay.

"He keeps moving. Doesn't stay in one place long enough for anyone to find him. I wouldn't have been caught if I hadn't come back to see Pa. I haven't seen or heard from him in the past five years, and I don't think I will now."

"I believe you, but if he does try to make contact, you have to let me know immediately."

"I'll do my best, Sheriff." He stepped back. "Now if you'll excuse me, I'll get back to work."

Devlin stared at Clay a few more seconds then seemed satisfied and left. Clay's heart still pounded in his chest, and he found it hard to swallow. The last thing in the world he needed at the moment was for Karl Laramie to come nosing around looking for him. After what he'd seen and experienced in prison, he wanted no part of that life ever again.

He picked up a box and headed for the shelves to unload cans for the shelf. His palms grew damp with perspiration. If Mrs. Pennyfeather or any of her friends caught wind of the sheriff's visit, they'd have rumors flying around faster than a bullet seeking its target.

Nothing he did turned out the way it should. Except for maybe working the fire and helping Jonathan. The little boy had won his heart, and Clay wanted nothing better for him than to find some relatives to care for him, preferably before Christmas.

The bell jangled again, and this time Mrs. Warner and Mrs. Collins came in with Jonathan in tow. Clay headed toward them, and the curly-haired little boy ran straight to Clay.

He wrapped his arms around Clay's knees and tilted his head up. "Hi, Mr. Clay, we came to get stuff for Miss Merry."

Clay reached down and hefted the boy to his arms. "You have? Miss Merry must be getting ready for the Thanksgiving program at the school."

Jonathan nodded. "I gets to be a Pilgim boy. That's 'cause Miss Merry needs Pilgims."

"Now that will be fun." Clay tousled the boy's dark hair.

Jonathan giggled as Mrs. Warner reached for him. "I think you've bothered Mr. Clay enough for now. He has work to do."

Clay chuckled and tried to release the boy, but he held tight around Clay's neck. "Don't want down."

"It's all right, Mrs. Warner. I'd finished stocking shelves when you came in." He patted the boy's back as he turned toward the toy section of the store, where he had just completed a display for Christmas.

"Look what we have back here, Jonathan. All kinds of new things for Christmas. What do you want Santa Claus to bring you this year?"

Jonathan leaned his head back and peered at Clay. "A ma and pa."

Clay swallowed the lump in his throat. "Perhaps he'll be able to get one for you." Finding Jonathan's family before Christmas had suddenly become even more important. He only hoped no one would promise such a thing for the boy before they had any news from Wichita.

"He will. My granny told me Santa brings what we want."

"Your granny? When did you see her?" If they could find the granny, they might then find other family members.

"Last time Santa Claus came. She's in heaven with Jesus now. Ma and Pa are too."

His little face had such a solemn expression that Clay hugged the boy tight. "I hope you get a ma and pa for Christmas."

Before Clay released him, Jonathan whispered, "You can be my pa. It'll be our secret."

Clay swallowed hard again. "But you need a ma too."

"Miss Merry can be my ma. She takes care of me." He giggled in Clay's ear. "That's a secret too."

The hushed words burned Clay's ear. His hold tightened. Oh, how he'd like for that to happen, but it couldn't this Christmas, and most likely never.

Finally he set Jonathan on the floor and gave him a set of wooden blocks to play with. "We'll have to wait and see what Santa can do about that. You sit here and play with the blocks while I go help Mrs. Warner and Grandma Collins."

Mrs. Warner grasped his arm at the counter. "I heard what he wants for Christmas. We're doing everything we can to find his family before then, but Reverend Tate still hasn't had any word from Wichita."

He patted her hand. "I know, but he'll keep looking and maybe have some good luck in the next week or two. We still have plenty of time."

Pa handed her a package. "Is there anything else you need, Mrs. Warner?"

"No, this is it. We mainly wanted to get Jonathan out and about. It gets lonely at the house with all the other children at school. Merry's practicing with the children this afternoon, so we'll have lunch here in town as a treat and then take him over to the school."

Mrs. Collins passed them with Jonathan in tow. The little boy grinned up at Clay. "'Member our secret."

"I will." Clay waved then grabbed up the broom and began sweeping. How could he forget a secret like that?

Merry called her charges back to the classroom after their noon recess. Mild temperatures had allowed them to play outdoors, and they came in smelling of crisp air and, in some cases, dirt. They washed their hands at the pump sink in the cloakroom before taking their places at their desks.

"This afternoon we'll have a run-through of the play for next week. If you don't know all of your lines as yet, you still have this weekend to learn them, so today you may look at your script if you need to do so."

All eighteen eager faces smiled up at her. Grandma Collins stepped through the door with Jonathan in tow. "I brought your littlest Pilgrim to do his part."

Jonathan peeked out from where he hid behind Grandma's skirt. His eyes darted about the room from student to student. Merry held out her hand and smiled at him. He took one tentative step forward then ran to jump into her arms and bury his face in her shoulder.

"I'm so glad to see you, Jonathan. We were just about to begin our practice. Are you ready?"

He nodded his head, and she set him on the floor but still held his hand. "All right, everyone, take your places."

"I'll leave him with you and be back for him later. I still have a few errands to run." Grandma kissed the boy's forehead. "Now you be good for Miss Merry, and do your part well."

Jonathan nodded then waited while the others lined up on opposite sides of the rooms with Pilgrims on one and Indians on the other.

Merry checked her tablet. "All right now. Pretend you have

baskets of food, and you Pilgrim girls stand around the table there and pretend it's the one we'll use. Now, let's start at the beginning." She led Jonathan up to Emmaline, who grabbed his hand and held it.

The Pilgrim girls began moving about the table as though setting it. Phoebe Marshall pushed her long blonde curls to the back and gazed about. "I do hope the Indians dress properly today. With the weather so cold, they should be wearing coats."

Emmaline pretended to set a bowl of food on the table. "I'm sure they will. Chief Powtow said he'd bring food from their bounty to share with us."

Bert Norris puffed out his chest. "The chief and his tribe will come in peace today as we celebrate our plentiful harvest this year. Without their help with the maize, we would have starved to death last year."

Merry beamed with pride as the play progressed. Then, out of the corner of her eye, Merry detected a spot of color. She turned to the window just in time to see Clay jump out of sight. What in the world was he doing outside her window?

She nodded toward the children to keep going and moved to the window. She poked her head through the opening to see Clay pressed against the wall with a most startled expression.

"Clay Barlow, what are you doing? Spying to make sure we do it right? If you're so interested, don't stand out here; come on inside. I think the children would appreciate an audience."

His eyes opened wide, and he shook his head. "I...I don't want to be a distraction. I'm making deliveries, but your mother said you'd be rehearsing the play this afternoon, and I thought I'd take a look to see how they were doing."

By now the children had stopped their dialogue and stared toward the window. When Jonathan realized Clay stood there, he made a dash for the window.

"Mr. Clay, Mr. Clay, come see me in the play."

Merry laughed. "Now you can't refuse an invitation like that."

"I guess not." He backed away but turned and headed for the front door. In a few moments he stepped into the room.

Merry's hands became damp and clammy. She balled them into fists and nodded for Clay to come have a seat. Strange that he would come to the school to see how the play was going, but any opportunity to be near him presented another chance to offer him friendship.

"All right, boys and girls, let's show Mr. Barlow what we're doing." She stifled a giggle as he squeezed his large frame behind a student's desk. She should have directed him to Bert's since it had a larger chair and more room.

The children resumed their places and began where they had left off. Jonathan's eyes never left Clay. The child did that with her back at home. He wanted to be near her all the time. The only thing she could figure was that she was closer to his mother's age and appearance than either Mama or Grandma. And Clay was more like his father, Mr. Henderson.

She shook her head to rid it of those thoughts and concentrated once again on the children. Only once did a child forget lines, but he recovered quickly and went right on. When they reached the end, they all turned toward Merry with expectant looks on their faces.

Merry stood and clapped her hands. "Excellent practice. Just don't forget everything between now and the performance when we have real props and our costumes. We'll go over it again a few times before then to make sure you're good and ready."

Whooping and hollering and laughter followed this announcement. Merry didn't shush them because they'd been on their best behavior for the afternoon and deserved a time of jubilation.

Clay unwound himself and eased out of the desk. "That was very good. You have a nice way of handling them all. Do you ever have trouble?"

"Trouble? Of course I do." She laughed and lifted her shoulders. "They wouldn't be normal if they didn't cause a little ruckus. Tricks, pranks, and mischief are all a part of growing up. We just have to learn how to channel behavior in the right direction."

"Reminds me of when we were students here." Clay stooped to pick up Jonathan, who had run up to him.

Merry shook her head. "Oh, do I ever remember you and James and how you teased me and the other girls. I think Mrs. Grody enjoyed using the switch on you boys. She rapped my knuckles a time or two. I hope I never have to resort to such punishment."

"I'm sure you won't." He shifted Jonathan's weight and set him back on the floor. "I have to continue with my deliveries, so I'll let you get back to your students."

Clay headed for the door. Jonathan called after him, "'Member our secret."

Clay's face flamed red, and his throat moved up and down. "Hmm, I will." Then he raced from the building like something chased him.

Merry raised her eyebrows. Now what kind of secret could a four-year-old have with a grown man? A secret was a secret, and it wasn't likely she'd find out anytime soon unless one or the other of the two decided to tell. She shrugged off the notion and headed for her desk to finish off the day.

Chapter 12

CLAY POINTED THE wagon toward the Shanks's home. He shouldn't have stopped at the school, but hearing the laughter and knowing that Jonathan was in the play, he couldn't resist. What that little stop accomplished didn't sit well with the plans he must make to learn more about Lily.

He wanted to kick himself. His arrival and then staying like that only served to be an encouragement for Merry, and he couldn't afford for her to get her hopes up about friendship. He must be more careful in the future.

Grace Ann Shanks stood at the kitchen door when the wagon rolled into the yard. "I saw you coming down the road. I'm glad you're here. I have a hankering to make a cobbler for supper, and I'm about out of sugar."

"Got it right here." Clay grinned and hopped down from the wagon. He lifted the box of groceries and provisions and headed for the house.

He entered the kitchen with the aroma of cinnamon and sugar hanging in the air. Smelled like a home ought to smell with all kinds of good things cooking in the oven. James was one lucky man.

Clay set his load on the counter top just as Lily came into the room.

She glanced at Clay but kept her eyes on Grace Ann. "I'll put these away for you, Mrs. Shanks."

"Thank you, Lily, and then I want you to sit down here and have tea and cookies with us." Grace Ann reached for the pot on the stove. "Clay, you're going to stay for a few cookies and a cup of coffee, and I won't take no for an answer." She nodded toward the table. "Have a seat, and I'll get the cookies."

"Then I won't say no." Clay grinned and pulled out a chair. If the cookies tasted as good as the aroma in the room, he'd be in for a treat. Maybe Lily would open up some with Grace Ann there.

A few minutes later a plate of cinnamon sugar cookies and a cup of steaming coffee sat before him. Grace Ann joined him with a cup of tea for Lily and her. As the girl seated herself reluctantly, she glanced at him, and the fear in the girl's eyes sent chills through his bones. He'd seen a lot of fear in prison, but this was different.

He stirred sugar into his coffee, a habit he'd picked up in prison to make the stuff they served halfway drinkable. No sense dilly-dallying around with chitchat. He might as well ask directly. "Lily, I'm not sure you intended for me to hear your comment at the store, but I did, and I'm curious as to why you said Mr. and Mrs. Vaughn aren't your parents."

Lily dipped her head and moved her hands to her lap. Grace Ann reached over and grasped Lily's shoulder. "It's all right, Lily. Tell him what you told me."

When Lily glanced up, tears filled her eyes, and she blinked. "My real parents are dead. Ma died several years ago. Pa did his best with the four of us children. As the oldest I took care of the baby."

Her story was so similar to many families on the prairie. Holly Hill existed for those very reasons. If hardships and disease didn't take the children of the family, many times it took one or more parents. Living on the prairie took its toll on both men and women.

Lily continued. "If it hadn't been for that terrible storm coming through in the spring of ninety-seven, we might have been OK. The storm took our house and the lives of Pa and my middle brother and sister. My youngest sister was with me in town and survived. We had nothing to go back to, just the land."

"Where is your sister now?" Clay couldn't imagine the horror of losing his family in a storm.

"She's living with a family down in Texas. I heard about a cousin who had come up to Oklahoma and decided to set out to find him, but I ran low on money. Mr. and Mrs. Vaughn found me in Oklahoma City trying to find food and a place to stay. At the hotel Mrs. Vaughn said she and her husband would take me to my cousin's place. They seemed so nice, and I believed them."

"What happened then?" So far her story had touched his heart with sadness for her, but it didn't explain the fear she exhibited.

"The next thing I knew, we were on a train bound for Kansas. They told me they'd take me with them, and I could be their daughter. They took the little money I had and gave me no choice but to go with them."

"Is that when you came here?"

Now her hands twisted and turned on the table. "Yes, in September, and they told everyone I was their daughter." Her eyes bored into his soul as she gazed at him across the table.

Grace Ann smiled and gripped Lily's hands. "Go on, sweetie. Tell him the rest of it."

A half sob escaped Lily's throat. "Please don't tell let Mr. and Mrs. Vaughn know I told you anything."

At Clay's nod she continued. "It wasn't bad at first. They were very nice on the train, and Mrs. Vaughn told me how much they'd always wanted a daughter. When we first arrived, she bought me a new dress to wear to church. She said we'd go to church because that's what respectable people do." She paused to sip her tea as though to gain courage to continue.

"After the first week I learned I had to work to earn my keep. I helped Mrs. Vaughn with her sewing and doing laundry for people in town, and that wasn't so bad, but I never got any money for it. I still hoped I might save enough to go back to Oklahoma to look for my cousin. When I complained about not earning any money, Mr. Vaughn hit me."

Anger rose in Clay like a billowing wave. No man had the right to hit a woman for any reason. "Why didn't you tell anyone?"

"I didn't know anyone. And they threatened me with more beatings if I did, so I decided to just lie low, do what they said, and wait for the right time."

"But Mr. Vaughn still beats you?"

"Yes, he gets drunk sometimes, and then beats me if

something isn't done right. The only reason they let me work for Mrs. Shanks is they got greedy for the extra money I could make."

Clay sat in silence, disgust and anger fighting in his stomach. "We have to tell the sheriff."

Once again fear all but screamed from Lily's eyes. "No, please don't tell the sheriff. Mr. Vaughn will beat me good then. He says there's no law saying he can't beat a disobedient daughter."

"But you're not really his daughter." Except how could she prove she wasn't? It would be their word against Lily's. That area of the law wasn't familiar to Clay, but Mr. Warner would know. After his help with Jonathan, maybe Mr. Warner would be more inclined to listen and give advice. "I don't know about that, but we need to get you out of Prairie Grove."

Grace Ann bit her lip. "That's what I've been telling her, but she's too afraid of Mr. and Mrs. Vaughn." She leaned toward Clay. "I know you and James can do something about this." She grasped his arm. "Please, Clay. We have to help her."

Clay stood and shoved his hat onto his head. "I'll see what I can do, and I'll talk more with James."

Grace Ann hugged him. "Thank you, Clay. You're a good man."

Clay nodded to Lily then strode out to the wagon to head back to town. Speaking to Mr. Warner wouldn't break the promise he'd made not to tell the sheriff since Mr. Warner no longer served as a lawman. If Mr. Warner didn't know what to do, then he and James would have to find another way to help Lily.

Merry spotted Clay returning to the store in the wagon. He would go around to the back and come in that way. She wanted to see him and ask him about the box supper social coming up soon, but Mama and Grandma looked ready to leave.

"Mama, I forgot something I need. You go on home with Grandma and Jonathan. I'll make my purchase and then walk home."

"We can wait for you, my dear. We have time. Supper is almost ready, so we don't have to hurry back. Papa's there, and he can take care of the children."

No use arguing with Mama over a carriage ride. May as well let her wait. "All right, I won't be long. I promise." She hurried back into the store and then tried to think of something she could purchase to make her excuse legitimate.

Clay came through the door from the storeroom. A cloudy look that could be anger or deep thought covered his face. Merry hesitated then stepped up to him. "Excuse me, Clay. I just wanted to thank you again for providing a bit of an audience for the children this afternoon. It really helped them get a feel for what they should do."

His head jerked just a bit, and he stepped back. "Merry, I didn't know you were here."

"Of course you didn't. I stopped by with Mama and Grandma. They're out in the carriage now." Thread, that's what she could use as her excuse. "I had to make a little purchase before we leave."

"Then don't let me keep you from your errand." He reached for his apron and tied it around his waist.

Merry bit her lip. Now or never. "Um, Clay, do you plan to be at the box supper the church is having the Saturday after Thanksgiving?"

He stared at her, his brows knitting into a frown. "I'm not sure. I clean forgot that was coming up."

Heat rose in Merry's face. "Oh, I see. I thought maybe you could bid on my box, not that I'm supposed to…" She stopped short and whirled around. "Never mind." How humiliating to be hinting at the possibility of his bidding on her box. She hurried to the back of the store and picked up two spools of thread. If she didn't come out with at least some little package, Mama would start in with the questions.

Merry completed her purchase, avoiding contact with Clay. He must think her to be one brazen woman. He hadn't shown any real interest in her as an individual, only her students and Jonathan, and she'd practically thrown herself at him again.

She climbed into the carriage beside Mama and pulled Jonathan to her lap. At least here was one little boy who loved her, but even he wouldn't stay around if they found his family. If only she could turn the clock back five years and be the one to stop Clay from getting into so much trouble.

Chapter 13

*T*UESDAY AFTER DINNER Louise Warner helped her
mother dress the children in their costumes for the
play. Good thing Merry had decided to stay in town and make
sure all was ready for the performance at seven. If she hadn't,
there would have been a bigger rush to get back to the school
and set up everything.

The door knocker sounded loudly enough for her to hear it
on the second floor. Someone must be in a hurry. Frank's voice
floated up the stairwell as he answered and addressed whoever
was there. A moment later he called her name. "Louise, will
you please come down? Clay is here."

Clay was here? What could that mean? "Emmaline, please
help these boys finish getting everyone dressed. I'll be back in
a minute."

Jonathan jumped down from his perch on a chair. The
white collar of his Pilgrim child's costume framed his wide-
eyed face. "Mr. Clay's here? I gotta go see him."

Louise set him firmly back in the chair. "We don't have time
for you to see him now. After the play when the refreshments

are served, you'll have plenty of time to talk to him. Now sit here and be quiet while the others get their costumes on."

She hurried down the stairs to the parlor to find Clay and Frank by the fireplace in deep conversation. "Excuse me, I'm sorry I didn't come straightway, but we're getting the children ready for the play."

Clay rolled the brim of his hat in his hands. "I thought you might be, but I didn't want to wait any longer."

"Is there a problem?" Louise asked.

Clay stared at Louise for a moment then nodded toward the parlor door. "May we speak privately?"

"Of course." She closed the door behind her. This must be serious if Clay wanted privacy. Could he be here about Merry? She crossed to the settee by the fireplace and sat next to Frank.

Clay began, "I promised a young lady I wouldn't speak to the sheriff, but I need some legal advice about how to proceed in helping her."

Louise frowned and grabbed for Frank's hand. "Who is the young lady, and is she in trouble?"

Frank patted her hand. "Now, Louise, let the boy have his say."

His words soothed her, but the expression on his face reflected the seriousness of the matter, especially if it involved legal advice. She prayed Clay wasn't in trouble again.

"You know the Vaughn family from church?"

Louise nodded. "Yes, I've met them. They have a very pretty daughter. Lily's her name, I believe."

Clay rolled the brim of his hat in hands again. "I've been wrestling with this thing on my mind this past week. I discovered that they aren't her parents."

Louise gasped and Frank's grip on her hand tightened. "What…what do you mean, and how do you know? Is she adopted?"

"No, she isn't adopted. James and Grace Ann have been concerned about her, and they asked me for help. I spent some time talking with Lily and Grace Ann and learned that Mr. and Mrs. Vaughn picked her up in Oklahoma City and brought her here. They told her they'd take care of her, but they haven't."

"Clay, what on earth do you mean? They may be new to town, but so far they've been fine, upstanding members of our church and our community." Louise couldn't believe such a tale about Irene Vaughn. Lily was rather shy and didn't speak much to people, but she looked to be well cared for.

As Clay continued to tell them what he had learned, Louise's heart sank to the pit of her stomach. To think that such a thing could be going on right here in town, and no one knew anything about it.

"So you see, Mr. Warner, I want to know if we can legally take her away from Mr. and Mrs. Vaughn and help her find her cousin in Oklahoma."

Frank rubbed his chin and shook his head. "That's a fine line there, Clay. Could Lily be making up the story to spite the Vaughns? They could have adopted her, and she doesn't like living with them."

"James and I thought of that, but just yesterday she came to work for Grace Ann and showed her new bruises where Mr. Vaughn beat her because she talked to a few girls at church."

Louise squeezed her eyes shut. She'd seen Mr. Vaughn grab Lily and drag her away from two girls after church, but she hadn't thought anything about it. Frank had to do that with the boys on occasion when they were lolly-gagging behind. But to beat her for it. Unthinkable.

"Those are serious charges. If they aren't her real parents or her adoptive parents, the sheriff can take her away from them."

"I don't know what she's afraid of, but she doesn't want the sheriff to get involved. James and I came up with a plan, but we haven't worked out all the details as yet. When we do, I'll let you know."

Frank placed his hands on Clay's shoulders. "Be careful you don't get mixed up in something that will get you in trouble. I think you need to let the sheriff know what you're doing when you decide."

"I'll think on it, but I won't unless Lily is willing. I was hoping I could count on your help."

Louise jumped up. "Of course we'll help. Soon as you have something decided, let us know." She couldn't stand by and let any kind of abuse continue if they could do anything about it. The girl could come here and be protected until her real family could be found. What those two were doing bordered on slavery, and that was reprehensible.

Frank scowled at her but didn't correct her or say no. He peered at Clay through narrowed eyes. "You heard that Karl and his gang robbed the bank over at Bennington. That means they're still around these parts. Have they tried to contact you?"

"No, sir, they haven't, and I told the sheriff I would let him know if they did."

"Good. Now, we have a play to attend, and from the noise in the hallway, those boys are ready to go."

When they stepped into the entry hall, five little boys dressed as Indians and Pilgrims greeted him. Jonathan grabbed Clay around the legs, and Clay hoisted him into the air. "You make a mighty fine little Pilgrim boy."

Jonathan giggled and hugged Clay's neck. Louise blinked back tears. What a fine young man Clay was proving to be. He'd worked hard since his return to help his ma and pa. A shudder ran through her at the thought of what he must have endured while in prison.

He set Jonathan back on the floor. "I have to go now, but I'll see you at school in a little while."

Jonathan nodded and followed the others out to the wagon for the ride into town. Clay shook Frank's hand. "Thank you for your advice."

Frank nodded. "Let me know what you and James decide."

Clay returned his hat to his head, smiled briefly, and took his leave.

Louise squeezed her husband's hand. It would take an elaborate scheme to help Lily. If the least little thing went wrong, they might all suffer the consequences. "Have we made a mistake in agreeing to help?"

"I don't think so, my dear. God wants us to help those less fortunate than we are and those in dire circumstances. Lily qualifies as both, and God will carry us through. We have both Him and the law on our side."

God would help, but she intended to do a lot more praying between now and whenever they carried out their plans.

Merry set the last of the props in place and placed her hands on her hips. She surveyed the stage area and grinned with pleasure. It really did look like a harvest table with bountiful fruit and grains. The children had been a little nervous as they left after school. Tonight was the real thing and not another practice. She had reassured them that they'd do fine.

She sat down at one of the desks and picked up the basket she'd brought this morning so she'd have a little something to eat before everyone began arriving. An apple, a piece of Grandma's homemade bread, cheese, and two sugar cookies would help her through the evening.

After devouring her light supper, Merry made her way to the table where the refreshments would be set up. Over the table she spread Grandma's tablecloth embroidered in fall hues of orange, gold, and brown. The parents had insisted on serving punch and cookies after the play tonight, and Merry hadn't argued with them about it. Having parents involved suited her just fine.

"Oh, Miss Warner, we're here early to set up our refreshments."

Merry turned to find Mrs. Marshall and Mrs. Norris with several other ladies bearing trays of cookies and jars of punch. "Right over here, ladies. The tables are ready for your food."

The women chatted among themselves as they arranged the plates, napkins, and cups. If the amount of cookies piled on those platters was any indication, they thought the whole town would turn out for the play.

"Thank you so much for bringing everything. I'm sure our guests will appreciate it."

The husbands of the women entered and began bringing in extra chairs. "Where shall we put these, Miss Warner?" Bert's father held several chairs in his hands, his size filling the doorway.

Merry waved her hands toward the area she'd cleared of desks. "Right over here, Mr. Norris. We may need to move the other desks too."

The town blacksmith had no trouble setting up and moving desks. He removed his coat, and his muscles bulged under his shirt's sleeves.

Another figure appeared in the doorway, and her heart skittered in a million directions at once. Clay carried two more chairs and set them with the others. He glanced at her but said nothing. They couldn't talk now with all the parents filling the building, but they would talk later. Merry would make sure of that.

The boys and girls arrived and hurried to gather behind the makeshift curtain she'd hung across the front. A strong length of clothesline and two quilts worked just fine to hide the back stage area. Merry left the adults to their tasks and hurried to join the children.

"Merry...I mean Miss Warner, my collar came loose." Imogene held up her collar for Merry to see.

Merry grasped the collar and smiled. "I'll fix it in no time, sweetie; just hold still." Even though the children had been told to call her Miss Warner at school, remembering was sometimes difficult for them. She refastened the collar and stepped back to admire her young charges. Bert made a perfect Pilgrim father although he'd first wanted to be an Indian chief.

The big clock on the schoolroom wall inched toward seven, and Merry readied all her students. "Let's have a quick prayer before we begin." They all bowed their heads, and Merry offered up a prayer.

"Father, we thank You for this opportunity to share with our parents, family, and friends the story of the first Thanksgiving. Help us remember all our lines and cues. Help us to have a good time and fellowship afterward. In Your name we pray. Amen."

Merry stepped from behind the curtain and introduced the play. As the children took their places, smiles and beams of pride spread across the faces of those in the audience. The play began, and the children portrayed the early settlers and Indians with great pride of their own. Only twice did a student stumble over a line, and to Merry that was as near perfect as she could wish for.

Bert shook hands with the Indian chief, Trenton Marshall. "May this day be the beginning of a time of friendship between our people. May God watch over us and protect us as we go through the winter ahead."

Trenton nodded. "So be it."

At the end of the handshake Bert and Trenton turned to the audience. The other children lined up on either side of them and then bowed. Merry's heart swelled with love for the children as the parents clapped and stood. A few of the men whistled, and some shouted their approval. Her very first Thanksgiving pageant had gone well.

When the applause died down, Merry stepped to the

platform. "Thank you for coming, and thank you to all of those who helped with costumes and props. We couldn't do this without you." Her hand waved toward the refreshments. "Our ladies have baked cookies and provided punch for us, so enjoy."

People began mingling and heading toward the cookies. She faced her young charges. "Well done. I'm very proud of you, as are your parents. This is our last time together until after the holiday, so I want to wish all of you a very happy day of giving thanks and eating good food." She grinned and tilted her head toward the refreshments. "Now go join your parents and have some cookies."

They didn't wait to follow her orders. How nice it would be if they responded that quickly to all her commands in the classroom.

Mrs. Pennyfeather tapped Merry's shoulder. "I must say, my dear, that was quite a nice production. You managed to keep the children well behaved throughout. I've had my doubts, but you seem to have done a fine job with them this semester. Let's hope it stays that way." With a twitch of her nose she turned her back and waved at someone else.

Trust Mrs. Pennyfeather to follow her compliment with a warning. Merry shivered, the words lingering in her mind.

From the corner of her eye she caught a rapid movement. Jonathan had found Clay and now clung to his neck. Merry grinned then strolled over to relieve Clay of the little boy.

She reached up for Jonathan. "You can't take up all of Mr. Barlow's time. Come with me, and we'll have some cookies."

Jonathan shook his head. "Don't want to leave." Then he peeked at her with one eye. "Will you bring me a cookie?"

"It's all right, Merry. I was telling him what a good job he did as a little Pilgrim boy tonight." Clay stroked Jonathan's back and smiled down at Merry.

"If you're sure it's not a bother, I'll get you both a few cookies."

A minute or so later she returned and handed Clay the cookies. He shifted Jonathan around and held one under the child's nose. "I bet this is your favorite kind."

Jonathan nodded and grasped the cookie in his hand then began to nibble on it. Clay bit into his and chewed. All the while his eyes never left Merry's face.

Heat rose in her cheeks, but she didn't look away. "Thank you for helping with the chairs. I really appreciate it."

"I enjoyed it. Anytime you need someone to help out in the classroom, let me know."

Clay shifted Jonathan again, his little head nodding and his eyes drooping. Mama strode up to Clay and held out her arms.

"Let me take this little one off your hands. He's had a big day." She grasped Jonathan and cradled his head against her shoulder. "We'd better take the children home now, even though they're so keyed up, we'll probably never get them to bed."

Merry laughed. "At least tomorrow there is no school, so it won't hurt if they're up a little later."

"Can you find a ride home, dear?" Mama asked.

"I'll bring Merry home, Mrs. Warner," Clay offered.

Merry's heart jumped. Mama beamed with pleasure and nodded then left with Jonathan.

The townspeople began preparations to leave. A number

of them came up with their congratulatory remarks and offers to help with projects any time. Merry thanked them and told the men to wait until the next day to come back and get the chairs.

Clay headed for the podium to take down the quilts and clothesline. He coiled the line and set it beside Merry's desk. Mrs. Marshall had already boxed the props and set them aside, so Clay moved the table back to where it had been before. As he folded the blankets, Merry glanced around and realized he was the only one left.

Merry approached as he stacked the blankets on the desk. "Thank you again, Clay. If you don't mind, I'll finish cleaning up tomorrow. It's been a long day, and I'm bushed."

"I can imagine you are, what with all the work you put into it."

"It's a good thing the parents are so willing to help." She placed her copy of the script in her desk drawer. "I couldn't do it all without them."

He grinned and stepped closer, only inches from her. The aroma of soap and a hint of peppermint filled her nostrils as she breathed in to steady her nerves.

"I can see this town is proud of their school."

Her heart thrummed a faster beat at his compliment, her feet rooted to the spot. His nearness sent shivers of delight straight to her soul.

He stood there, staring into her eyes, and she could no more turn away than she could fly out the window. Perspiration drenched her palms, and she pressed them into her skirt.

"Merry, you're so..." Then his face bent toward her, and she lifted hers to feel the brush of his lips against her cheek.

Lightning bolts of pleasure raced through her veins before his arms went around her and he pulled her against his chest.

Feeling the crush of his mouth on hers weakened her knees to the point she clung to him for support. She returned the kiss with all her love flowing from her to him.

Suddenly he dropped her arms and stepped back. "I'm sorry. That should never have happened. Forgive me." With that he grabbed his hat and coat and bolted for the door.

Merry stood still, her fingers touching her lips, swollen from the kiss. Pain stabbed at her heart, and doubt crept in. It had been so long since he'd been around a woman that he probably was only reacting to being alone with her. The kiss meant more to her than it possibly could to Clay.

She blinked and glanced around the room. He'd forgotten he was supposed to take her home and had run off now just as he had after his first kiss all those years ago.

His face appeared in the doorway, his cheeks a flaming red. "I forgot. I need to take you home."

She grinned and blew out the last remaining lamp stand. Now she'd have a few more minutes with him. "I'm not sure I would have forgiven you for forgetting this time."

The air had grown chilly, but the memory of the kiss warmed her insides once again as she walked beside Clay. His jaw was set in a hard line, and he didn't smile. Had the kiss been that bad? For her it wasn't, but then maybe he expected more.

Merry cleared her throat. "Thank you for walking me home." She'd walked that way more times than she could count, but it helped to have a companion, even a silent one.

His eyes stared straight ahead. "You're welcome."

She breathed deeply. If he could be so aloof, then so could she. They walked in silence until they were halfway up the hill to her home. Clay stopped and touched her arm. She glanced down at his fingers then back to his face.

He dropped his hand. "I'm so sorry for what happened at the school. Please forgive my forwardness, and I promise it won't happen again."

A sob clogged Merry's throat so she couldn't swallow or speak. So the kiss meant nothing. She gathered up her skirts and ran the rest of the way up to Holly Hill, leaving Clay Barlow far behind.

Chapter 14

WITH THANKSGIVING NOW behind her, Merry looked forward to Christmas and the Christmas program. First, however, she intended to enjoy the box supper social whether Clay attended or not. Her lips still burned with the kiss he planted there after the Thanksgiving play, but he hadn't spoken to her since. Of course, she hadn't seen him since that time either.

His words on the walk home still pierced her heart, but she would not let them ruin the good time she planned to have tonight. Many cowhands from the surrounding ranches would be in town for the event, and she just might get to eat with one of them. She'd put Clay behind her and enjoy the evening.

When the wagon stopped at the entrance, she jumped down with the other children and headed inside the town hall, where the social would be held. She added her brightly decorated box to the others stacked on the stage of the main room.

Today, the town's annual salute to the beginning of the holiday season would be held indoors due to the colder temperatures brought in by winds from the north. The ladies had outdone themselves in decorating. Bright orange pumpkins, yellow gourds, and squashes made up colorful arrangements around the room. The beauty of the decorations was outdone only by the array of meats, vegetables, and desserts that filled the room with sweet and spicy aromas.

Her box contained dinner for two with fresh cured ham, homemade rolls, and her specialty, pumpkin pie. Mama and Grandma took charge of the children today to give Merry time to enjoy the festivities without added responsibility. If Clay came, maybe he would remember how she liked blue and bid on her box, but then again maybe not. Heat rose in her cheeks at the memory of how forward she'd been in suggesting that he bid.

A group of women, all younger friends from her own school days, gathered in the corner. Merry hurried to join them. "You all sound like you're having fun already. I can't wait to see who bids for our boxes."

Laura Wilson hooked her arm through Merry's. "We were just talking about that. Some of the cowboys from the ranches have come into town, and they'll bid for sure. I've seen a few very handsome ones standing around the room."

Carol Sims giggled. "Did you know that Dora Stuart put a box up with ours?"

"I can't believe she's still unmarried." Merry remembered the woman from her earlier days. "But of course, with her cranky ways, it must be hard to attract a man." Dora had to be in her forties, and she had the worst disposition of any woman in town. She ran the new lending library with a firm hand and made sure borrowers took care of the books.

Laura leaned her head toward Merry. "Yes, and wouldn't it

be funny if old man Barnes from the livery got her box? Her with those fussy ways, and him with…well, you know."

Merry did know. George Barnes may not be any older than Miss Stuart, but he was nowhere as neat and prissy as the librarian. Seeing those two together would be a sight to behold.

Carol tilted her head and grinned. "You wouldn't be hoping for Clay Barlow to win your box now, would you? He's certainly the most handsome single man in town."

Heat rose in Merry's face. "Whatever would give you that idea?"

Carol and Laura both laughed and winked at each other. Laura shook her head. "Now, we all know how sweet you were on him back in our school days…before he got into trouble and all."

"That was then and this is now." Her feelings hadn't changed at all, but she had to be careful not to let them show.

Laura all but swooned. "I think his being in prison and coming home is so…so…romantic. Mama says he did his time, and he still has that reputation, but I'd give anything if he'd pick my box."

So would Merry, but it was best to keep that quiet.

A tall man entered the hall, and her breath caught at the sight of Clay. "There he is."

Both Laura and Carol spun around to see. Laura gripped Merry's arm. "Oh, I think I'm going to faint."

"Oh, for mercy's sake. Get ahold of yourself. You're twenty-one years old and not some giddy schoolgirl." Her own knees threatened to betray her right in front of her friends.

Laura's lip poked out in a pout. "You don't have to remind

me of my age. It's bad enough for Mama to keep doing it." She sighed. "Besides, I feel just like a schoolgirl, and he's better looking now than he was at eighteen. Just let me enjoy looking at him."

Merry enjoyed looking at him too, and she followed his movements with interest until he turned and saw her with the girls. His long strides carried him straight to their spot.

"Good afternoon, ladies." He grinned, and the crinkles around his eyes only served to emphasize the depth of his dark chocolate brown eyes.

Both Laura and Carol tittered and batted their eyelashes. Merry kept her gaze steady and prayed her voice wouldn't squeak or crack. "Good afternoon, Clay. Are you here to bid on one of our boxes?" She swallowed a groan. What a stupid question.

"Of course, and if any of you will give me a hint, I might just bid highest on it." He spoke to all three, but his eyes held firmly on Merry's face.

Once again heat rose in her cheeks, and her knees quivered again. "Now that wouldn't be exactly fair, would it?" Maybe it wouldn't hurt to drop the hint that hers was decorated in blue.

Carol all but grabbed Clay's arm. "It wouldn't really be cheating, but it's best not to tell."

"I suppose I'll just have to guess and take my chances."

"Oh, but you might get Miss Stuart's box, and that wouldn't do at all." Carol again batted her eyelashes in that way she had to make her look all innocence and light.

"Hmm, that would be something." He touched his forehead where a curl or two of dark hair hung. "If you'll excuse me, I'll visit with you later and might even claim a dance or two."

With that he walked away. Laura and Carol bent their heads together and whispered between themselves, but Merry's attention stayed on Clay's back until he disappeared out the door. Her heart beat like a drum, and her nerves danced a jig in anticipation of what might come later in the evening. A dance with Clay might prove that his kiss Tuesday night meant something.

Clay left the hall to return to the store to help Pa close up for the day. Seeing Merry and her friends a few minutes ago reminded him of his stupid mistake in kissing Merry. Despite all his resolve in tamping down his feelings for her, he'd gone and done the one thing that would encourage rather than discourage her.

Still, his mind wandered back to her. If he guessed correctly, Merry's basket would be decorated with something blue. That had been her favorite color years ago, and it probably still was. He shouldn't bid on it, because his attraction to Merry was just too strong. Perhaps he could bid on Laura's box and not have to worry about being near Merry. He simply didn't trust himself to be with Merry alone for any length of time.

Trenton Marshall grasped his arm. "Say, Mr. Barlow, I was told to give you this note." He thrust it into Clay's hand then ran off like a posse followed him. Clay furrowed his brow. Who could be writing to him? He unfolded the note and read:

Clay, Mr. Vaughn won't let me come to the social tonight. He and Mrs. Vaughn will be there. Please come to see me tonight while they're out. I need your help, and I need it bad. Lily.

He crumpled the note and jammed it into his pocket. Sometime during the evening's festivities he'd have to slip out and go to Lily. If things weren't bad, she never would have sent him a note and risk the wrath of Mr. Vaughn. If Lily had been beaten again, Clay didn't know what he'd do, but he would have to do something. Lily couldn't stand the abuse much longer without completely breaking down.

He leaned against the wall of the store and closed his eyes. Lily and Merry both tugged at his heart. He loved Merry, but Lily spoke to him as one who needed him. He wanted to make a difference, and saving a girl like Lily could be a start. It would certainly make a difference for Lily.

The only people he could trust with Lily's problem were Mr. Warner and maybe Reverend Tate. Both men were the kind who'd want to help a girl in distress and pay no attention to what others might say. Mr. and Mrs. Warner already wanted to help. Maybe he should speak with Reverend Tate too.

He shoved off the wall, but he heard a noise from the back alley. He turned to peer in that direction.

"Psst, Clay, over here."

Clay followed the sound, and a hand reached out and grabbed his arm. It pulled him back behind the building. "Looks like our little jailbird has been living a life of ease."

Karl! Clay jerked his arm away. "What are you doing here?"

"Came to get you, my friend." Karl's white teeth gleamed through the wide grin he wore.

"I'm not your friend, and I'm not going anywhere with you." Clay's eyes darted about the area, on the lookout for the sheriff or anyone else who might see them.

"Is that so? From what I hear, the town ain't treatin' you right, so you may as well ride with us."

Clay's heart hammered in his chest. The last thing he needed was to be seen with Karl. "The town's fine, and I'm doing just fine without you. Aren't you afraid of getting caught coming into town like this? The sheriff heard you might be in these parts and has been looking for you."

"That don't worry me any. With so many coming in for all the goings-on, they won't notice me unless you go back and tell. I don't think you want to do that, do you, friend?"

Clay clenched his teeth. "I said I'm not your friend, and nothing can keep me from going for the sheriff right now."

Something cold poked his side, and he realized Karl had pulled his gun and now pushed it into Clay's gut.

"I could shoot you right here and be gone before anyone could get here and find you dead in the alley." He leaned close enough for Clay to smell liquor. "But because of our ol' friendship, I ain't gonna do that. You go on back and have your fun, but if you say anything to anyone about me bein' here, you might be picking up the bodies of people you care about, and I ain't talking about just your parents either. With that pretty little gal Merry back in town, I'm guessing you'd like to pick up with her where you left off."

Cold perspiration ran down Clay's back, and bile rose in his throat. He was threatening Merry. "Karl, if you harm one hair on anyone's head, I'll hunt you down and kill you myself."

Karl hooted. "I'd like to see that. Think about it, Clay, and keep your mouth shut."

Karl turned and disappeared before Clay had time to react. He slumped against the wall of the store. Karl had some nerve coming into town and even greater nerve grabbing Clay, but if he didn't do exactly what the outlaw wanted, no telling what would happen. He would keep quiet about Karl's presence for now, but no way on earth would Clay go back and join up with that gang of thieves and killers.

His anticipation of this evening and the box supper now soured on his stomach, but he had to go back and act like nothing had happened. He had to make sure Merry was OK. Despite his misgivings, he planned to stick closer to Merry in the days ahead. Karl would get nowhere near her if he could help it.

Chapter 15

AFTER HIS DECISION to stick close by and protect Merry, Clay returned to town hall and scanned the tables. He picked her box out of the group right away. It was the only one wrapped with a blue cloth with a bit of holly attached to the handle. It had to be hers, and he would wait until the auctioneer held it up before bidding on any of them. If he was wrong in his choice, he'd still have a chance to have a dance with her later.

Bids on both Laura's and Carol's boxes were won by two cowboys from the Masterson ranch. That place had a reputation for nothing but the best in cattle and strict rules for their hands. The girls would be safe with those boys tonight.

The note in his pocket crinkled when he moved. Lily needed protection too. Two girls were now threatened with harm—one very much aware of the danger she was in with the man who called himself her father, and the other one so innocent and unaware of the danger that was hers. Both depended on Clay for safety, although Merry didn't realize it yet.

The auctioneer held up the blue-covered box, and Clay's

hand shot up with the first bid. He glanced over at Merry, whose face shone bright red. Her gaze met him for a few seconds before she looked down and twisted her hands. He'd been right. Joy surged through him until a stranger upped Clay's bid.

The bidding hopped back and forth between Clay and the man. Something about him didn't sit right with Clay. When the bidding got up to three dollars, the crowd gasped in surprise. Most had gone for under that, but Clay didn't care what the other man bid; he'd bid higher and hope Pa would give him the money. He didn't want that man sharing dinner with Merry.

Finally the other man grinned and saluted to Clay. The truth hit Clay in the gut with a cannonball. That man had been with Karl in his last bank robbery. Where was the sheriff when he needed him? Clay stood there, indecision whirling. He could either go and find the sheriff, or he could pay for the box and spend time with Merry. Merry won out.

He had the bid for just under four dollars, and four was all he had on him. He paid for the box and handed it to Merry. "I believe this is yours, isn't it?"

She bit the corner of her lip and nodded. "I was afraid you wouldn't get it. That man kept going up higher with his bid."

Her uncertain manner told him he'd hurt her by his behavior on Tuesday. Well, he wouldn't do it again tonight if he could help it. "Yes, but I was determined to get it for myself."

"How...how did you know it was mine?"

Clay grinned and patted the blue cloth. "This is your favorite color, and none of the others had any blue on them." He tweaked the holly. "And this is a dead giveaway."

Her cheeks turned pink as she gazed straight at him with eyes more green than he'd ever seen them. "I remember a lot of things about you, Merry." Even after seven years so many of Merry's traits came flooding back to his mind. He grasped her elbow. "Shall we find a corner and enjoy your meal?"

She nodded, and he led them to a corner where tables had been set up for dinner. He handed her the basket, and she spread the cloth on the table then began taking food from the basket. His mouth watered at the sight of the ham, homemade bread, and, best of all, slices of Merry's pumpkin pie.

After he stumbled through blessing the meal, he bit down on a thick slice of homemade bread slathered with butter. "I always knew you'd be a good cook."

Merry cut off a piece of ham and popped it into her mouth. "And why is that? I never did much of it all those years ago."

"But what you did was always good. Those sugar cookies you baked for the class were the best I've ever eaten." And he hadn't had any like them since then. So many things about Merry he'd liked when they were sixteen, and now at twenty-three, they were an even greater attraction.

For the next five minutes his tongue stuck to the roof of his mouth, and words lodged in his throat. He could only eat and stare at Merry, who kept her head down and her hands busy. Finally Carol and Laura, along with their escorts, joined the table to share their desserts. Clay sat back and listened to the chatter among them as he ate his pie. If the dance didn't start soon, he wouldn't have more than one with Merry before he had to hurry off to see what help Lily needed.

He spotted Mr. and Mrs. Vaughn across the room with a group of people from the church. Clay itched to mosey over and inquire as to why Lily wasn't present, but from what he'd learned, that would only arouse their suspicion. No telling what excuse they were giving the others for her absence.

Finally the musicians lined up on the platform, and the men moved the tables out of the way. As her dinner partner, Clay claimed the first dance with Merry. Holding her in his arms now brought back the vivid memory of the night he kissed her behind the church after one of the socials there the Christmas she was sixteen and only a few months before they moved to Oklahoma. What a fool he'd been. Five years wasted in that dung heap of a prison.

"Clay, what's the matter? One minute you were smiling and now you're scowling. Is my dancing that bad?"

"No, no, Merry. Your dancing is fine. My mind wandered for a few moments and remembered how I missed such fun while I was in prison." At least that was partly true as far as his thoughts went.

"Well, then, I'd like to see that smile come back. It's much more attractive than a scowl. I can't imagine anything more horrid than being in prison." Her green eyes gleamed as she cocked her head to one side and lifted an eyebrow.

"Then don't try. It was bad, and that's all you need to know." How good it was to hold her and be as carefree and happy as he was at this moment. "You're as good a dancer as you are cook."

"I would hope that I'm better." She grinned up at him in such a way that he wanted to hug her close, but he kept his distance.

He'd done it again. He had to stop letting her get her hopes up only to dash them down again when it couldn't be like old times. Too many things had happened in the past seven years. Neither of them was the naïve sixteen-year-old from that time. He had a reputation, and Merry had responsibilities. One could ruin the other, and he didn't want that to ever happen.

He swept his gaze around the room, but still no sign of the sheriff. He must still be at the jail. If there was time later, Clay could pay him a visit. If not tonight then maybe tomorrow.

The music ended, and another young man came to claim Merry for the next dance. Clay relinquished her hands and headed for the punch bowl. After the next dance he'd have to leave, or he wouldn't be able to find Lily and see what new problem had arisen.

When another cowboy claimed her after the third dance, Clay said, "I have an errand to run, but I'll be back soon as I can."

She nodded then danced off with the cowboy. Clay checked his pocket watch. Mr. and Mrs. Vaughn should be here at least another hour. That gave him time to go by their place and check on Lily.

At the door he saw James and Grace Ann. He strode up to James and leaned over to whisper, "Lily sent a note. She's in trouble and needs to see me. Maybe you and Grace should go too."

James nodded and leaned down to speak to Grace Ann. Her eyes opened wide. "Yes, of course we must."

With one last glance at Merry, Clay hurried out with James and Grace Ann and headed for the Vaughn place. He'd get back in time to escort Merry home.

When they reached the house, Clay knocked on the door. The three of them waited, but no one came. They heard someone calling from the back of the house and went around there. Lily stood at a back window that was raised about six inches.

At the sight of her, Grace Ann cried out and reached in to grab Lily's hand. Clay's mouth gaped open. A huge bruise covered Lily's cheek, and her arms bore welt marks. Her face shone pale in the light from the room, and recent crying had caused her eyes to be swollen.

"Oh, I'm so glad you came. I don't know what to do." She bit her lip, and more tears streamed down her cheeks.

Grace Ann held Lily's hands tightly in hers. "What happened?"

"Mr. Vaughn was furious when I burned the meat he and Mrs. Vaughn planned to take to the box social. That was when he beat me. Then they locked me in my room. I was lucky that a boy came by looking for his lost dog, and I sent the note through him."

Clay stepped back, and his breath escaped with a swoosh of sound. James beat his palm with his fist, and Grace Ann cried and held on to Lily. "Clay, James, we have to get her out of this house someway."

All thoughts of Merry and taking her home left his mind.

Merry waited and waited, but Clay never returned. Her feet grew tired from dancing with some of the clumsy young men who stepped on her toes more than once. She plopped down in a chair and fanned her face.

Laura joined her. "Whew. I'm worn out. It's been fun, but I'm about ready for a rest."

"That's why I'm sitting this one out too." Although if Clay were here and wanted to dance, she'd find the energy for it.

Laura glanced around the room. "Where is Clay? I haven't seen him for a while." She giggled. "I'm so glad he won your basket. I thought sure that strange man would outbid Clay, but he finally stopped and let Clay have it."

"I thought the same and was so surprised by the amount Clay paid for it. I don't know where he is now. He said he had an errand to run and left a little before nine." Merry looked toward the door once more in hopes he'd walk through, but only a few people leaving with young children came into view. "It's almost ten now and time to leave." Papa had already left, expecting Clay to escort her home.

Laura yawned and covered her mouth. "Sorry about that. I guess I'm more tired than I realized. I for one will be glad to get home and get these shoes off."

"I will too. Tomorrow morning will come too quickly, and Papa says if we can be out and about on Saturday night, then we can be in the Lord's house on Sunday morning." Since Clay hadn't returned, she had no good reason to remain here. If she left now, she could be back at Holly Hill with a twenty-five-minute brisk walk.

"I think I'll call it a night, Laura. It's time to head on home."

"But you can't walk all that way alone. It's late, and you need someone to go with you."

"I'll be fine. I've been up that hill more times than I can count." Still, it would be rather dark. If only Clay had stayed around, he could walk her home. She didn't want to bother anyone else with making the trip.

"No, you stay right here. I'm going to get my brother. He'll take you in the carriage with him and Betsy. You're just a little ways beyond them." Laura jumped up to find her brother.

Merry had no intention of waiting around for Edward and Betsy Wilson and disrupt their evening. She retrieved her shawl and hurried out into the night. At the top step of the town hall, she paused. A figure darted out from the alleyway and headed her way. It looked like Clay. She stepped back into the shadows as he raced by and headed off into the night.

Her heart sank to her toes. He'd left her at the dance just like he'd done all those years ago. He'd been so nice and friendly most of the evening, but he must have gotten cold feet. Merry pulled her shawl tighter and straightened her shoulders. What Clay did was none of her business, but the hurt filled her just the same. She pushed back tears and started the trek back to Holly Hill.

Why did she even bother with him? Because she still liked him, but a lot of good that did. Most likely she was destined to be a schoolmarm the rest of her life and be cranky and mean like Miss Stuart.

The shadows deepened, and she picked up her skirts to walk faster. Suddenly footsteps sounded behind her and a hand grabbed her arm. "Just a minute, missy. I need to talk to you."

She whirled to see the man's face, but it was shadowed by a wide-brimmed hat, and she could see nothing in the darkness. "What do you want?"

"Listen to me, and listen good." He poked her shoulder. "You tell that nice friend of yours, Clay Barlow, that he'd better think about what he was told this evening. He'll be in a heap of trouble if he don't, and people he cares about will be hurt. No one will be safe."

"What are you talking about?" She wrenched her arm free and stepped away.

"Go on home now, but don't forget what I said. You better tell him to do just like he was told, and nobody'll get hurt. You understand?"

Merry nodded again and took another step away. Just as suddenly as he'd been at her side, the man disappeared. If she wasn't so angry at the man's words, she'd probably faint, but anger outweighed the fear.

Who was that man, and why was he warning Clay about something? Maybe Clay planned to join Karl and his gang of outlaws again. But if he planned to do that, why the warning? Confusion filled her soul. None of this made any sense at all.

She quickened her steps toward Holly Hill. She didn't really know Clay now like she had seven years ago, and it was quite possible he would go back to his old ways. Whatever that man meant by his warning couldn't mean anything good for anybody.

She shook her head. The Clay she'd seen with Jonathan was not the same one who'd robbed banks and gone to prison. He couldn't be. As angry as she was for his forgetting to come back and see her home, her anger grew at the possibility Clay would rejoin Karl.

Mama would know what to do. She ran the last part of the way and burst through the door. She stopped dead in her tracks and squelched the cry that rose in her throat.

Clay sat in the parlor with Mama, Papa, and Grandma.

Chapter 16

FTER THE INITIAL shock, anger returned. Merry drew her hands into fists and placed them on her hips. "What are you doing here, Clay Barlow? I waited all evening back at the dance for you."

Clay jumped from his seat and strode to her side. "I'm sorry I didn't make it back, but something came up, and I had to see your parents."

Mama stood with surprise written on her face. "How did you get home? Papa was coming back for you so you wouldn't have to walk in the dark."

"No one was there, so I did walk. I'm fine now, but that still doesn't explain what he's doing here." She took off her coat. "I'm tired and don't feel like listening to any lame excuses."

She headed for the stairway, but Mama's hand grasped her arm. "Please wait, Merry. You need to hear what Clay has to say. He needs our help with Lily Vaughn."

Merry hesitated, her gaze going from Mama to Papa and then to Clay. What did Lily Vaughn have to do with anything? Then a light dawned. That's who he'd gone to see. The worried expression in his eyes touched her soul, but her anger at having to walk home alone, being accosted, and his being with Lily was too much for one evening. "After what happened to me, I don't care what happens to him or what help he needs."

Mama squeezed her arm. "What do mean? Did something happen on the way home?"

Clay stood to the side with his hat in his hands, his eyes clouding over. She couldn't tell her parents what happened to her with him standing there. "Nothing. It was just dark and scary." I'm going to bed now."

She turned and raced up the stairs. Thankful she had a room of her own, Merry flopped across the bed on her stomach and let the tears come. All the events of the evening rolled through her mind like a runaway train, and she could do nothing to stop them.

Things had been going so well, and Clay had seemed to really enjoy being with her, but then he'd left to run an errand and never returned. Apparently her well-being meant nothing to him.

Mama knocked on the door. "Merry, please come back down. Clay needs our help."

What help could that man possibly need from them? Then she remembered what the man said when he held her so tight. If Clay didn't go back to Karl's gang, someone could get hurt. She jumped from the bed and swiped her hands across her cheeks.

She hesitated once again with doubts about Clay and his behavior this evening stabbing at her heart. Mama and Papa could handle whatever problem arose. She didn't want to face

Clay again and hear some tale about what he was doing and why he left her at the town hall without an escort.

"No, Mama. I don't want to see him right now. I'll talk with you and Papa after he's gone."

Her mother's footsteps sounded in the hallway, and Merry once again fell to her bed in tears. Clay should have stayed at the dance with her rather than running off. Then that awful man wouldn't have threatened her. Trust in Clay dissolved like sugar in Papa's coffee.

It would take a heap of explaining to make any sense at all of this evening, and right now no explanations would be enough.

Louise returned to the parlor, her heart heavy. Her daughter had been hurt by Clay's leaving her at the social, but if she'd just listen, she'd understand. "I'm sorry. She won't come down." She placed her hand on Clay's arm. "She's upset, so nothing will help right now. I'll talk with her later, and maybe she'll be ready to listen by then."

"I'm so sorry, Mrs. Warner. I had no idea she would be so hurt. If only she'd let me explain why I wasn't there to take her home."

The anguish in Clay's eyes broke her heart. Two young people very dear to her hurt so badly. They would be so good for each other, but circumstances and misunderstandings got in the way. "I'm sorry too, Clay. Now sit down and let's finish our discussion. We need to help this girl."

Clay sat with his hands between his knees. "I was about to tell you what I thought might work and see what you thought."

Frank nodded and crossed one leg over the other knee. He puffed on his pipe and stared at Clay. "What about the sheriff? Did you say anything to him?"

"Not yet. Lily's afraid of the law for some reason. James and Grace Ann were going to tell Reverend Tate, so I high-tailed it up here to let you know what's going on."

"If things are as you say, then Mrs. Warner and Mother Collins and I will do all we can."

"They are that bad and worse. If we don't get Lily out of there, Mr. Vaughn just might beat her to death."

"Have you spoken with your parents about Lily?"

"Not yet. I wanted to get your help first, and then I'll ask them about what I need from them. If they don't want to help, then I'll have to come up with another plan, but I really can't see Ma saying no to a girl in trouble like Lily."

Louise nodded. "I can't see that either. Your mother is as kindhearted as they come. What is it you want us to do?" Whatever it may be, she prayed Frank and her mother would be agreeable.

"I want to get Lily out of the Vaughn household and some-where safe. I think I have a way to do that, but I need a place to bring her and hide her until we can get her away from Prairie Grove."

Frank leaned forward. "I see. You want to bring her here, I presume."

Louise's heart beat faster. How could they hide the girl? With all the children around, the word would surely leak out. It might even bring danger to the children. This was much more serious than she had ever thought it could be. Still, she couldn't turn away a girl in distress.

"Yes, sir. I thought maybe in a house this big and with so many children, they wouldn't think of looking for her here."

"Well and good, but we can't keep it a secret with so many little eyes and ears around. They could say something that would bring Mr. Vaughn and the sheriff to our doorstep claiming we kidnapped his daughter."

"I…I…guess I hadn't really thought about that." Clay's head drooped, and he stared at the floor. "What else is there to do?"

Louise's mother crossed her arms over her chest. "Well, seeing as how this is my house, I do have a say as to what we can and can't do with it."

"Of course, Mother, we won't do anything without your permission, but I don't think we even need to ask since it's too dangerous for the children," Louise said.

"I think we can solve the dilemma. You know the room in the attic where Zach spent so much of his time? It still has a bed and furnishings in it. We can fix it up for Lily and put her up there, and I don't think any of the younger ones will even know. If Emmaline and Henry find out, they're old enough to understand and help us keep her hidden until we can find a safer place."

Louise's heart swelled with gratitude for her mother. Always the problem solver, she had come up with a near perfect solution to help Lily. "Oh, Mother, that's a wonderful idea. Zach loved it up there. Does it still have that little pot-bellied stove to keep it warm?"

"Of course, I haven't moved a thing since you all moved out. It won't take any time to have the place fixed up and ready. Since I keep it locked, none of our younger children even know the room exists. It's too far away to be a convenient bedroom for them, and I didn't want them playing up there."

"Then that's the perfect place for her." Louise sat back with relief. Her mind raced with all that would need to be done in the days ahead.

Frank wrinkled his brow and pursed his lips. After a moment he said, "We can do it, but how will you get her here without anyone knowing she's gone? And when will you do it?"

"I haven't worked out all the details on that. The main thing for me was to know I'd have a place to bring her for safety. I plan to discuss the other steps with my parents. I figured it'd be easier to convince them if I had your approval and help first."

Mrs. Collins heaved herself from her chair and stood. "Smart young man. Now, would any of you like more coffee?"

Clay jumped up. "I think I'd better get on back to town and start working things out with Ma and Pa. I'll let you know as soon as the plan is in place."

Frank clamped his hand on Clay's shoulder and walked with him to the door. "I'm glad we figured out a way we can help. After all, that's our business…taking in stray children and giving them a place of security. Lily's not much more than a child herself."

Clay shook Frank's hand. "Thank you for listening and being willing to open your home to Lily. I hope Merry will understand too and forgive my neglect."

Louise stepped forward. "She will. Mother and I will make sure she does. Merry can be touchy, especially if she feels she's been mistreated, but we'll talk with her and help her see that you didn't mean to forget her."

That daughter of hers had better listen. Merry shouldn't let their budding friendship be marred by misunderstandings.

Louise pursed her lips. Somehow those two must be brought together. They cared for each other, even if neither one of them would acknowledge it.

Merry stood at her window and watched Clay mount his horse and leave. Her throat tightened, and she bit her lip. How could he have left her that way? He must have no feelings at all for her.

She still needed to talk with Mama about what happened on the way home. That she couldn't keep secret. The man hadn't said who in particular would be in danger, but he had implied that it might be her family.

Perhaps Mama would be with Papa, and they both could help her. She tiptoed down the stairs, but halfway down she heard voices and Clay's name. She stopped and leaned over to listen.

"Mother, I'm so glad you thought of Zach's old room for Lily. She'll be safe here until we can find a more secure place for her."

Pa's voice sounded from the parlor. "Such a pretty girl. I can see why Clay would want to help."

Merry sat on the steps with a thump. Clay and Lily Vaughn? Was Lily why he had forgotten her? And Clay planned to bring Lily here, but why? And why were her parents involved?

Merry's heart broke into fragments at the double betrayal. Without a sound she gathered up her skirts and dashed back up the stairs to her room. Once again she flung her body across her bed and broke into sobs.

All the time Clay had been dancing with her, he'd been thinking of Lily. Obviously he wasn't the man she thought him to be. With his womanizing ways he was closer to Mrs. Pennyfeather's assessment than she could believe. Perhaps that old busybody was right after all.

Clay's heart sat like lead in his chest as he made his way back to town. Somehow he had to make Merry understand what he was trying to do and why he had gone to see Lily tonight. If her mother couldn't get through to her, then all hope would be blown away like the dust of a drought. She'd see what he'd done as another betrayal of their friendship.

A few words blistered the air before he lifted his eyes toward the dark sky. "God, You've done it again. I love Merry and thought I could be around her and not have it hurt, but it does. Now You've taken away any chance I might have had to be friends. She'll never trust me after this. I should have told her first before I went to help Lily."

He rode into town and to the stables to leave his horse. Perhaps it was better this way. Now he wouldn't have to endure the pain of being around Merry and knowing he couldn't tell her of his love. She'd avoid him like a dread disease from now on.

After bedding down his horse for the night, he left the livery and headed across the street to home. Tomorrow he'd talk with his parents about a plan to help Lily. Knowing Ma, she'd have some ideas that would help. He couldn't fault the

Lord on that account. God had given him good Christian parents who cared about people. He hoped he'd never do anything again to lose their trust.

He reached the entrance of the outside stairway where a sheet of paper tacked to the handrail drew his attention. He grabbed it and unfolded it to read the message, fear lacing his heart. *Remember what I said. Keep quiet, and no one will get hurt. K*

Karl! That man didn't deserve his protection after all he'd done. He turned toward the sheriff's office. Devlin needed to know the men were near town.

Then Clay stopped. What if something happened to his parents or to Merry? Karl was mean enough to carry through on his threats. *God, I need some direction here. If anything happens to Ma or Pa or Merry, I could never forgive myself.*

His heart heavy with doubt, fear, and indecision, Clay clumped up the stairs to his home.

Chapter 17

CLAY SAT AT the breakfast table Sunday morning with his heart in his throat waiting for his parents' response to his request for help for Lily. Neither one of them spoke for a few minutes, and Clay sensed their doubt and fears.

"Please, Ma. You have to help her. Her situation is desperate." If Christians were supposed to show compassion, this was the time to prove it.

Ma pursed her lips in thought. "I simply can't believe what you're saying about Mr. and Mrs. Vaughn. They're members of our church, and Mr. Vaughn works at the land office. Are you sure Lily's telling you the truth?"

"I saw the evidence, and even if he were her father, we can't let him go on beating her like that."

Pa stroked his chin. "I've seen a little of Vaughn's temper, so I see how he might take it out on the girl. If she's his daughter, we have no legal right to do anything, but if she's not, then we should help get her out of there."

"You say Mr. and Mrs. Warner are willing to help?" His mother's brow furrowed with her concern.

"Yes, and Mrs. Collins is fixing up Zach's old room in the attic for her."

Ma glanced at Pa. "We'll need to talk about this and pray over it. Come to church with us, and we will let you know our answer after the services."

Although he'd prefer the answer now, this was all he could hope for at the moment. He'd go to church with them, and perhaps he'd see Merry and have a chance to explain to her if her mother hadn't already done so. He could also speak with James and Grace Ann about their visit with Reverend Tate.

"All right. I'll go to church with you. I'll be waiting for your answer afterward." He pushed back from the table. "If you'll excuse me, I need to get ready."

In his room Clay went over his plan once again. This coming Saturday was the first-ever Christmas tree lighting in the town square. It would be the perfect time as everyone would be in town to see the electric lighted tree.

Lily's room was in the back on the ground floor. If he broke her window, he could get her out, and they could use the alleyway behind the store to get there. They couldn't wait long after getting away to head up to Holly Hill. He had to tell Lily so she'd be ready. With her bruised face, she wasn't likely to attend the tree lighting with Mr. and Mrs. Vaughn.

With the plan settled in his mind, his next step would be to talk with Frank Warner. But the first thing he had to do was to win Merry over.

He tucked a clean shirt into his pants then reached for his jacket. If Merry knew the whole story and why he had been to see Lily, her kind and caring heart would take over, and she'd be in the middle of making sure all went well.

Ma and Pa waited in the kitchen until he came down. Pa held Ma tight to his side. "We're taking the carriage. You can ride with us if you wish. Save you the time it'd take to saddle your horse."

A ride in the carriage wouldn't be so bad. "Thank you, Pa. I'll ride with you." He followed them downstairs and helped Ma aboard while Pa took the reins.

They rode the blocks to the church in silence. His ma stared off into the distance, her jaw firm and her hands clasped in her lap.

Mr. and Mrs. Warner greeted them in the churchyard. Clay helped his ma from the carriage, and she stepped up to Mrs. Warner. "Louise, we have to talk. I need to know more about this wild scheme our son has."

"Of course. Let's walk over by those trees." Mrs. Warner led Ma to a spot near the tall oak trees now shedding their leaves.

Clay turned back to find Pa and Mr. Warner deep in conversation themselves. Clay's gaze wandered over the crowd heading into the church. He didn't see Merry, although Emmaline and Mrs. Collins herded the children inside. Maybe she'd already gone in.

Inside the sanctuary he scanned the room, and his glance landed on the Warner pew, but no Merry sat there. All the spaces on the two Warner rows were filled, but Merry didn't appear, even after Mr. and Mrs. Warner joined the others.

Mr. and Mrs. Vaughn came in alone. Bile rose in Clay's throat at the sight of them marching down the aisle and into their pew like they were the best Christians there. Clay's fists clenched and unclenched. What a sham.

Clay sat beside his parents, his heart heavy with the suspicion that Merry had even skipped church to avoid the chance of running into him. The preacher's words slipped right by him until he heard him say, "Just as the Lord is our good Shepherd and hunts for that one little lost lamb until it's found, God wants us to seek out those among us who are lost and without Him and to bring them into the fold. Jesus will welcome them with open arms."

Was Reverend Tate speaking of Lily or of Clay himself? It didn't matter. Rescuing Lily wouldn't necessarily save her soul, but it would save her life. He narrowed his eyes and peered at the preacher. *Lord, if You help me get Lily away and into a safe place, I'll know You do care about each one of us no matter who we are. I once believed that, but after the past seven years, I'm not sure of anything anymore. Help me find the truth.*

After the service he avoided Mr. and Mrs. Vaughn and sought out James and Grace Ann. "What did you find out from Reverend Tate?"

James jammed his hat onto his head. "He wouldn't believe such tales about one of his most faithful members. Even after we said we'd seen the evidence, he didn't want to believe us. He said we'd have to have more proof than a few bruises. When we told him we didn't even believe Lily to be their real daughter, he told us of course she wasn't. She'd been adopted."

Grace Ann's eyes misted over. "He won't help us until we have proof that she isn't adopted. I'm sorry, Clay, but we still have to do something for her."

"I agree, and I'm working on a plan. I'll let you know as soon as I get a little more firm in what to do."

They accepted that and walked away toward their buggy. Clay pressed his lips together. Reverend Tate's attitude shouldn't have surprised him, but he'd prove how wrong the man was about Mr. and Mrs. Vaughn no matter what it might cost.

Merry dried her eyes with the corner of her apron. Mama had finally given up trying to get Merry to church this morning and believed the story of her not feeling well. The least she could do was to have dinner ready for the family when they arrived home.

Last night she'd pretended to be asleep when Mama came to her door. Nothing Mama could say could change the fact that Clay had abandoned her for Lily and left her open to assault by that stranger. Then the audacity of his coming here and seeking her parents' help for Lily went beyond her comprehension. All the dreams she'd conceived the past weeks were no more than that…dreams that couldn't possibly come true now.

She set the table with dishes and tableware. When she came to Jonathan's chair, she stopped and ran her hand over the smooth cherry wood finish. Poor Jonathan. First he'd lost his parents, and now his idol turned up with feet of clay. She winced at the comparison, but it was true.

She clenched her teeth and finished setting the table. After checking the roast to make sure it wouldn't cook dry and burn, she ran back upstairs and heaved her body onto the bed.

Nothing had gone right after Clay left the social last night. If only he'd stayed and finished the evening with her, none of this would be happening now. Her heart would still be in one piece and she wouldn't hold so much anger in her heart.

Merry pulled a pillow to her chest and grasped it tight. The sounds of the family arriving home from church traveled upstairs. Mama would be up in a minute wanting Merry to come down for Sunday dinner. She'd go down and eat, but then excuse herself and come back to her room before Mama and Papa started in on her about Clay.

A few moments later she met Mama on the stairs. "I was just coming down to help finish putting dinner on the table."

Mama peered at her with a probing stare that sent shivers up Merry's back. "Are you sure you're feeling better? You didn't sound so well this morning."

The tone of her voice told Merry that Mama didn't really believe the "not feeling well" story. Merry brushed past her mother and continued down the steps. "I'm better now, but I do believe I will skip dessert and go back to my room and rest some more."

The others stood around the table waiting for Merry. She slipped into her place as Papa nodded for them all to be seated.

Jonathan reached up and hugged Merry. "I missed you at church. Were you sick, Miss Merry?" He tilted his head and grinned. "Mr. Clay was there."

She glanced to her mother. How could they have exposed Jonathan again to that man?

Papa frowned and spoke, his deep voice filling the room. "We shall now ask the Lord's blessing and thank Him for our bounty."

Merry bowed her head and clasped the hands of those on either side of her, but anger still bubbled just below the surface. She jerked her head at papa's "Amen." She hadn't even heard the prayer.

Conversation flowed about her as the children talked about church and who they saw and what the preacher had to say and who all had been there. Merry listened with only a smidgeon of interest, her main desire being to finish the meal and disappear again to her bedroom.

As soon as she deemed it appropriate, Merry pushed back from the table and asked to be excused. Papa and Mama frowned, but neither spoke. Grandma shook her head but remained silent. Merry turned and fled up the stairs back to her room.

Louise joined her mother in the kitchen. The two worked alone as the girls were dismissed for the afternoon. "We have to do something about Merry. I would have insisted that she go to church with us, but doing so would have only made the whole morning miserable for all the others."

Merry could be stubborn when it came to getting an idea in her head and having someone change it. In this case, whatever idea she had was completely wrong. She believed the worst about Clay and why he wanted to help Lily. Of course Merry had a right to that because of the way he had left her at the social. The fact that her daughter walked home alone so late at night didn't sit well, but if Merry had waited for her father, she wouldn't have had to do that.

"What do you plan to do about getting her to listen to

reason?" Her mother handed Louise another stack of dirty plates.

Louise shook her head. "What? Oh." She plunged her hands back into the soapy dish water. "I don't know. Frank and I will have to talk with her before this goes much further. Perhaps after the children are down for naps or their quiet times, we can explain then."

Once Merry heard about what Clay wanted to do, she'd jump on the chance to help Lily. Merry wouldn't go against her nature of caring and wanting to help others in trouble. It was one of the things that made her such a good teacher.

"I'll be there to support you if you think it will help."

"Thank you. That may make a difference. If she sees we're all united in our efforts, she may be more willing to listen to what is planned." She placed the last dish on the counter to drain and picked up the dishpan.

After Louise emptied the pan by the back door, she wiped it out with a towel and returned to the kitchen. "If you'll take care of getting the children occupied, I'll see to Merry."

"Of course, and I'll pray all goes well." Her mother headed to the parlor where the children played.

Louise proceeded upstairs to Merry's room and knocked on the door.

A muffled voice responded, "I'm resting. I'd rather not talk right now."

Frank walked up behind Louise. "It's time for a firm hand, dear." He knocked on the door. "Merry Lee Warner, you are to come out right now, and I don't want to hear any arguments. I'll stand here and knock all afternoon or come in and get you if I have to. It's up to you."

Louise's breath caught in her throat. Rarely, if ever, did Frank use that tone of voice with any of the children. *Please, Lord, have Merry come out of her room.*

The door cracked open, and Merry's head appeared. Her swollen, red eyes attested to her sadness, but the set of her chin declared her anger louder than any words. This beautiful child of hers was one stubborn lass.

"That's better. Your mother, grandmother, and I wish to speak with you in the parlor. I suggest you wash your face and join us immediately." He turned toward the stairway then stopped to add, "I don't want to have to come back up here for you."

Louise reached out and squeezed Merry's hand. "It'll be all right. Just come downstairs and listen to what we have to tell you. Nothing is as it seems."

Merry sat in silence while her parents told her of Clay's plans. Disbelief, anger, relief, and concern cascaded through her mind like the colored pieces of glass in the kaleidoscope Grandma kept in the parlor. The only thing to truly register in her mind and bring complete relief was the fact that Clay wanted to help someone. She now concentrated on what Papa said about Lily being in danger. "But, Papa, we see Lily with her parents at church all the time. How could this be true?"

"James and Grace Ann Shanks have seen her bruises too. In fact, it was James who sought out Clay's help to begin with."

Merry scrunched her eyebrows together. She'd seen Lily with her mother in the store, but she never spoke to anyone except her mother and Mr. and Mrs. Barlow. "So Clay wants to kidnap her from her parents and hide her here?"

Papa sat back in his chair. "It isn't kidnapping if they are not her parents in the first place. We want to help her find her cousin in Oklahoma."

"I'm sorry I was so hard on Clay. But aren't you afraid that Lily will bring danger with her?" Now was the time to tell her parents about last night and the man who attacked her, but that would only bring more worry on their heads. If it happened again, she'd say something, but Lily's dire situation pressed more on her than what some man said. Besides, with Papa being a retired lawman, he could handle any trouble. She had to remember that.

Merry continued. "And what about the other children? How can we keep them from telling about Lily's being here?"

"We've thought of that." Grandma strode across the room and sat next to Merry. "I'm going to fix up Zach's old room in the attic for her. Clay will bring her here after the children are in bed. She'll stay up there out of sight, so the others won't even know she's here."

That might work, but it still didn't keep the concern from spilling over. "We have to take care of her. What excuse are we going to use to go up to the attic? I still think it's too dangerous."

Grandma patted her hand. "We'll do it when the children aren't around and during the late evening when they're in bed. Your pa will oil the attic door hinges and check the stairs to make sure nothing squeaks. It's really quite cozy up there."

Merry had visited her brother enough when he lived up

there to know the truth of Grandma's words. Lily would be very comfortable.

Finally her anger subsided to concern. No matter how careful they were, the chance of Lily being found still filled her heart with dread. But it wouldn't make any difference for her to protest once again. "It appears that all the plans have been made. When can we expect this event to take place?"

Papa leaned forward. "We're not sure. Clay was to speak with his parents today and get their approval. After that he'd get all the details worked out and let us know when and how he'll engineer her rescue."

"I see. So all we are supposed to do now is to sit and wait to hear." Clay was being inconsiderate and taking such advantage of her parents' kind hearts. He should know better than to bring such trouble into a house full of children. She didn't like the plan at all, but she had no voice in the decision.

Besides that, what if Clay was concerned about Lily's safety because he was attracted to her? Lily was a very pretty girl with blue eyes a color Merry had never seen before. Lily was young and fresh-looking too. She was more the type a man with his past might seek out than an old maid like Merry.

Clay may be concerned about Lily's safety, but it seemed that he'd given no thought to the safety of the children at Holly Hill. Life here would undergo a drastic change. The responsibility of keeping the children from finding out about Lily would most certainly fall on Merry's shoulders, and that was a responsibility she didn't care to have, especially if she learned that Clay cared more about Lily than her.

Chapter 18

ERRY AWAKENED AND lay in her bed, her parents'
words running through her mind faster than the
river at flood stage. The fact that he wanted to help the girl
escape the Vaughns brought fear. Although admirable, such
an attempt also carried danger...very real danger to all of
them. The memory of the man who waylaid her on the way
home returned. She should have told her parents right away.
Did that have anything to do with Lily? She squeezed her eyes
shut. Is that what the man meant by Clay remembering what
he'd been told? Everything became a jumbled mess. Whatever Clay intended to do, they would all be in danger, and that
scared her more than anything her parents told her.

Mama knocked on the door. "Time to get up or you'll be
late."

Merry sat straight up in bed then threw back the covers.
A new week of school and getting ready for Christmas gave
her no time to think about Lily, the strange man, or Clay. The
children had lessons to learn and didn't need her distractions.

Papa had the wagon and team ready after breakfast. With

the cold weather that had blown in last night, he didn't want them walking to school. The skies did look heavy and gray this morning. A ride into town would be most welcome.

She bundled in the bed of the wagon with the others and let their chatter and hopes that it would snow for Christmas go without comment. Her own thoughts flew in all directions. Maybe she should tell Clay about the man who had attacked her so as not to have her parents worrying about her. He would know what the threat meant. And she probably should apologize to him for her own rudeness Saturday night.

The idea of facing him today sent a shudder through her bones. She cast a glance at the store when they passed by, but it stood dark. Maybe he'd be there after school, and she could stop by to apologize then.

When they arrived at school, many of the students were already gathered, waiting for her arrival. Papa stopped the wagon and hopped down. "I'll go in and make sure you have a good fire going to warm up the place."

"Thank you." Merry jumped to the ground then made sure all the children did too. When she rang the bell a few minutes later, they needed no second ring to send them indoors where the warmth of the woodstove began to permeate the room. The cloakroom filled with coats, boots, gloves, and warm hats attested to the cold wind that had blown in from the north.

She called roll then started them on their lessons for the day. As she walked among the rows checking their work, she made notes of things that still needed to be done in preparation for the Christmas pageant. Satisfied that everything would be in place, she turned her attention to the multiplication tables the midgrade students were learning.

The five students came to the front and sat in a semicircle around Merry. The times six table presented few obstacles to the girls, so Merry kept an eye on her three older boys. Bert and Henry leaned close together and whispered then gestured to Trenton.

Merry swallowed her grin. Those three were apt to tease and make fun of the girls, but it was always in fun. The girls might protest, but their giggles confirmed they liked the attention. She cleared her throat. "Henry, may I help with something?"

He jumped back to his seat. "No, ma'am."

"Well, fine then. Let's keep your noses in your own books." She smiled with her mouth, but her eyes sent the warning that Henry would know well from escapades at home.

The boys settled down, and Merry continued with the girls, but her mind drifted elsewhere. The weekend when they had the tree lighting might be the best time for Clay to help Lily escape. Of course it was his plan, so whatever he decided would be what they would do.

Trying to imagine what life must be like for Lily went beyond Merry's comprehension. She'd been blessed with loving parents who had guided their children to fear the Lord and treat everyone with kindness.

She sighed. Grandma said that God had a purpose for every life, but sometimes He surrounded those purposes with unfortunate circumstances and even tragedies like the Henderson fire. Although she believed that for His children God could bring good from everything bad that happened, doubt did creep in on occasion. Trusting God to work out His plans was one of the most difficult things she had to do.

Clay's heart filled with gratitude for his parents' decision yesterday after church. They wanted to help him in any way possible with Lily. So he spent yesterday afternoon forming a plan, and now he was ready to talk about it. Yet all through breakfast they'd talked about anything and everything but Lily.

Ma removed the plates from the table and carried them to the sink. Pa sipped his coffee and eyed Clay over the edge.

Clay glanced at his mother then back to Pa. "I came up with an idea for how to help Lily leave the Vaughn's house."

Both parents stopped what they were doing and stared at him, waiting for him to speak.

"This tree lighting that the mayor has planned a week from Saturday will be the perfect time. James and Grace Ann will keep Mr. and Mrs. Vaughn occupied at the tree lighting while I take care of getting Lily out of the house."

Pa gazed at Ma a moment before answering. "Yes, but what then? How will you get her to Holly Hill?"

"I'll bring her here first. I think it's best to ride up there on horseback. I can keep to the old trail through the woods where we're less likely to be seen."

"If you can get her away before Mr. and Mrs. Vaughn get home, you'll have a better chance of hiding her. With the streets crowded, you should have no trouble going the back way. Have you told Lily any of this yet?"

"No, but I'll let Grace Ann know, and she can tell her."

"And what if she doesn't want to go along with it?" Ma reached out to grasp Clay's arm. "This is dangerous for her, especially if she gets caught."

Clay gripped Ma's hand. "I know, but she's desperate to get away from there." The sooner he could get Lily out of that place and into the Warner's home, the better it would be for her. His plan had to work.

Ma wrung her hands. "I still don't understand why Jimmy can't be the one to rescue her. Why do you need to be the one to do it? I hate the thought of you getting into trouble again."

"James and I discussed that, Ma. We figured suspicion would fall on James and Grace Ann first, since Lily works for them. We need to make sure they're at the tree lighting with the Vaughns. No one is going to suspect me of getting involved with this—I've barely talked to Lily."

Pa stood. "It's time to open the store. We'll talk more later after you hear from Lily."

Clay pushed back his own chair. He had to finish dressing and then get down to help Pa with the opening. With the weather so cold, they'd probably see only a few customers today. This was the kind of day to stay home by the fireside if at all possible.

Fifteen minutes later he joined his father in the store. Pa always came down before breakfast on cold days and got the little pot-bellied stove going so it'd be warm for the first customers.

Clay went about setting up the display of supplies the women might want for their holiday meal. If any came in today, that's most likely what they'd want. Fresh pumpkins sat by the door waiting to be made into pies and sweet breads. A display of sweet potatoes, various squashes, apples, and vegetables invited purchase with their colorful array.

When the first customer opened the door, the wonderful

aroma of yeast and cinnamon from the bakery across the street wafted in. At this time of year the sweet smells from that shop hinted at the great food that would follow during the Christmas season ahead.

At one point after a number of customers had come and gone, Clay stopped and shook his head. "I can't believe we've had as many people in this morning as we've had. I figured it'd be too cold for people to get out for anything."

Ma laughed and rearranged the squash. "Son, neither cold weather, rain, nor snow will stop a woman from starting her preparations for the holiday season. Four weeks may seem like a long time, but with menus to be planned and supplies to be set aside for all the baking and cooking that will go on, wise women get started early."

The bell jingled over the door, and she scurried off to help a friend with her purchases. Clay strolled over to gaze out the window. From this vantage point, if he leaned just right, he could see the school down the way. He pictured Merry with her students, and a smile creased his face.

If only Merry would listen to reason and understand why he wanted to help Lily.

Of course, he'd been wrong on his own part. He should have stayed and escorted her home. At least she made it home unharmed, but if she hadn't, the blame would have been on him.

Perhaps it was best for her to be angry and stay away from him. He couldn't take being around her much longer without revealing his emotions. Until he could prove to the people of Prairie Grove that he was a different man than he was five years ago, he would leave her alone and keep her reputation untarnished.

His gaze then caught the church steeple. It had been so long since he'd trusted God, so what was the point in it now? Pa believed in prayer, and that's what had helped him and Ma make the decision to help Lily. God listened to folks like his parents. He didn't have time for the likes of Clay.

A warm hand landed on his back. "By the look on your face, you're thinking heavy thoughts."

He turned to face his mother. "Yes, I was thinking about God. I deserved to be punished for what I did, but why did God let me get mixed up with Karl in the first place?"

"Son, God gave us free choice in what to do with our lives and the decisions we make. He wants us to be obedient and follow Him, but it has to be our choice to do so. You made a few wrong decisions when you were younger. If God had stopped you, He'd have taken away your free will and perhaps kept you from learning a valuable lesson. What you need to do is to learn from your mistakes, trust God to lead you in the right direction, and learn to follow Him."

"But what about things like the Henderson fire? Why would He leave little Jonathan without any family?"

"That I don't know, but He does have something in the future for Jonathan. That little boy will be all right as long as he has people like the Warners caring for him."

Of course Ma was right, but the fire shouldn't have happened in the first place. "Ma, you need to be praying for our plans to work for Lily. I can't believe that God would want her to stay in that place if she has real family nearby."

"He doesn't want her to stay there, and I've already been

praying for her. She has a lot of people who care about what happens to her, and I believe God will help us." She reached up to kiss his cheek. "Trust the Lord, Clay. He's never left you and has watched over you all these years."

Ma went back to help Pa with counting out the receipts. Clay gazed up at the gray sky. Yes, it was time for him to trust God and believe in His plans for all of them. Whatever lay ahead for Lily, Jonathan, and a relationship with Merry all depended on his reliance on God and the belief that everything would work out according to His will. The road back had been bumpy, but he was headed in the right direction. *Sorry it took so long, Lord, but I'm trusting You with Lily and my love for Merry.*

Chapter 19

THE TWO WEEKS since the box social had passed in a blur of activity along with much colder weather. Of course Clay had done a wonderful job of avoiding Merry since the supper, but at least he had saved her the embarrassment of having to apologize. Merry hoped she might see him tonight. Even with the rescue imminent, surely he'd stay long enough to watch Mayor Slater turn the switch that would light up the first-ever electrically lit Christmas tree in Prairie Grove.

When the mayor had announced his plan for the tree at the fall festival, everyone had cheered, but more than one had been skeptical until the mayor let them know Mr. Barlow had ordered a generator for the tree. An electric-lighted Christmas tree might be new to their town, but she'd heard stories of beautiful trees in the eastern and northern states. After all, electricity was coming to more and more cities, and Prairie Grove would be getting it soon as well. In just a few weeks they'd be entering the last year of this century, and it was time for more modern inventions to make their way to all parts of Kansas.

The bright reds and greens of the season always lifted Merry's heart. Something magical came with the Christmas season. Not only was it the time of the Savior's birth, but it was also a time when hearts turned to Him and love abounded. A cheery Christmas greeting seemed to bring a smile to faces, except maybe for a few like Dickens's Scrooge in *A Christmas Carol*.

The house would be festive and colorful when they all came back after the ceremony for dinner. Mama had invited Clay to join them for dessert and coffee, and his acceptance surprised but delighted her. Her nerves tingled with anticipation of his coming tonight, but doubt crept in to plague her as well. She couldn't help but think that Clay's avoiding her in recent days could only mean that he now cared for Lily.

A hand shook her shoulder. "Merry, can I go up and get my top and play with it?"

"Of course, Kenny." She laughed as he scampered up the stairs to his room. Papa had picked up the top for Kenny with the last of the boy's money on Wednesday. Since then Kenny played with it every chance he got.

Jonathan grabbed her around the knees. His round blue eyes shone with a mixture of joy and sadness. "I miss Ma and Pa."

Merry leaned over and hugged the little boy. "I know you miss them." Merry sat on the steps and drew the boy into her lap. "They're having Christmas with Jesus this year, and I bet they're talking about you and how glad they are that you're safe. You know something? As the youngest boy in our house, you get to put the baby Jesus in the manger on Christmas Eve."

"I do?" He laid his head against her shoulder. "Will Santa Claus bring me a new ma and pa?"

Merry's heart lurched. No word had come from Jonathan's aunt and uncle. If they didn't come forward, Jonathan would be eligible for adoption, but that most likely wouldn't happen before Christmas. "I'm sure he'll do his best, but toys and games are more along the lines of what Santa brings."

"Then I'll ask Jesus. He can do that. He can do anything." His solemn gaze met hers. "Ma says ask Jesus first."

Merry hugged him closer. "You do that." In the wonder and beauty of Christmas anything could happen. *Jesus, please help us find family for Jonathan. He's such a precious little boy. I wouldn't mind having one just like him.*

What would it be like to have a little boy with Clay? Merry shook her head to rid it of such thoughts. He barely spoke to her much less spent any time with her. Still, there was that kiss…had it meant anything? She still didn't know.

"Come on, Jonathan, let's finish decorating." She handed him a length of tinsel to hold while she wove it through the greenery now winding around the stairway banister.

When the stairway was finished, the clock in the entry hall chimed five times. She added the last bow and turned to the girls who were now sorting through decorations to put on the tree Papa and Henry would cut down later and bring inside. "Girls, it's time to get ready for the tree lighting tonight." Merry held out her hands for the twins.

Emmaline jumped up first. "I can't wait to hear the songs and see the tree all lighted."

Imogene smirked. "You only want to see Trenton, I bet."

"Do not. He can go off with the boys any time he wants."

She held her head high and marched up the stairs to her room. The twins giggled then followed.

In half an hour they were all ready, and Merry helped Mama and Grandma get all the children into the two carriages. No wagon tonight, they were traveling in grand style. Henry drove one carriage and Papa took the other. Merry admired the way Henry handled the horse with ease. In a few months he'd be fourteen, and he was already only a few inches shy of Papa's height. No wonder Phoebe and Maggie vied for his attention.

As they neared town, the lilt of Christmas carols filled the air. A group of ten formed a choir and roamed the streets caroling. Tinsel, bows, and flags adorned the posts along the boardwalks, and the flickering gas street lamps sported evergreen wreaths with red bows.

Yesterday, after school, Merry had watched the men erect the tree for the lighting tonight. It now stood proud and tall in the town square in front of the courthouse and town hall. The men had been busy today because all the lights had been added as well as tinsel and various ornaments. The girls' eyes grew wide with wonder at the sight.

Emmaline leaned over to get a better look. "Where did they ever find such a tree?"

"Mayor Slater had it brought in from some forest. Isn't it amazing?" She'd heard the men talking about it at church several weeks ago, but she had no idea it would be as big as this.

Henry parked his carriage beside Papa's and hopped down to secure the horse to the hitching post. Crowds of people mingled and strolled the streets in spite of the cold weather.

For Merry the touch of frost in the air only added to the holiday spirit.

She grasped the hands of the twins and followed Mama and Papa. Merry glanced around to make sure all the children stayed close. Getting lost would be very easy with the number of people around.

When Merry neared the tree, several people stepped out of the way. One man gestured toward the front. "They have a special section for children up front in that roped-off area."

She thanked them and guided her young charges to the area. Mama came up behind her with the boys. "This was certainly thoughtful of the mayor."

After making sure each one of the younger ones was situated, Mama placed her hands on the shoulders of Susie and Kenny. "Now, you two are the oldest. Keep an eye on the younger ones. I'll keep Jonathan with us. Stay put until Papa, Merry, or I come to get you. Understand?"

They both nodded and turned back to look up at the tree top. Merry returned to join Papa, who held Jonathan up so he could see better. She craned her neck to gaze at the top.

A hand grasped her arm, and she jerked around to find Clay next to her. Her knees turned to mush, and if he hadn't been holding her arm, she would have fallen right there at his feet.

"Beautiful tree, isn't it? I'm glad I'm home to see this very first one."

Merry smiled, but her words stuck in her throat. What should she say? Should she apologize for how she'd acted two weeks ago? Since that night at Holly Hill he'd avoided her like she had a dread disease, and now he acted as if nothing had happened. Feeling awkward and uncomfortable, she edged away from his grasp.

From her smile Merry must be glad to see him, but it didn't quite reach her eyes, which held a question in them when she pulled her arm away. Every bit of common sense declared his attraction to her to be a bad idea, but his heart had its own mind, and now here he was, close to her and smelling that sweet lavender she always wore.

Before he could speak to her, James tapped his shoulder. "Grace Ann and I are going to find Mr. and Mrs. Vaughn and keep them busy for the evening. Good luck, and God be with you."

"Thanks. We really need God's favor tonight."

Grace Ann hugged Merry. "Thank you and your family for helping us with this."

"We are glad to help. Grandma has everything ready at the house." The two women hugged again before James spotted Mr. and Mrs. Vaughn. After one last handshake with Clay, James and Grace Ann walked away.

Clay leaned down to speak to Merry. "As soon as the tree lights up, I'm leaving to go get Lily. Pray it will all work out." He glanced around. "Where is Jonathan?"

"There with Papa. He was afraid Jonathan might get lost or go off on his own." She grasped his arm. "Clay, this is a good thing you're doing, and I'm glad James and Grace Ann are helping you." The apology in her eyes told him everything he wanted to know. All was forgiven. She wouldn't hold it against him that he had neglected her after the box social.

Just then Jonathan spotted Clay at her side.

"Mr. Clay, Mr. Clay." Jonathan held out his arms to Clay.

Clay reached for the boy. "Do you mind, Mr. Warner? I'll be glad to hold him."

Mr. Warner handed him over. "Not a bit."

Jonathan clutched Clay's neck and grinned. "I can see the top. It's high."

"Yes, it is, and in a few minutes it will have hundreds of little electric lights to shine in the night." He'd left Pa only minutes ago with the generator, and everything checked out perfectly. "It won't be long now."

Mayor Slater held up his hands to quiet the crowd. The size of it had astounded Clay. The town had grown by leaps and bounds in the past five years.

"We're gathered here this evening for the first of what I hope will be many years of tree lighting. We are heading into a new century at the end of next year, and as long as I am mayor, Prairie Grove will be a town ready for all the modern conveniences that come our way. We will build a generating plant next year, and by the year 1900 all homes in Prairie Grove will have electricity and plumbing that comes right into your house, just like the ones in the big cities."

Everyone cheered and clapped. Leave it up to the mayor to make a political statement at a time of celebration. Still, from what Pa said, Slater was a good man and wanted only what was best for the town.

"The Christmas tree is a symbol of our season of joy over the birth of Jesus Christ. Along with the tree we have the nativity made for us by Charlie Norton and his workers at the furniture shop. Thank you, Charlie, for this beautiful reminder of why we are celebrating." He reached over and pulled away a large canvas that covered a stable, figures of Mary and Joseph, a manger with hay, and two shepherd figures.

The tallest figure was only three feet high, but even from this distance the attention to detail and color testified to a master craftsman at work. Clay clapped right along with the rest of the crowd.

Merry turned her gaze toward him. "It's even more beautiful than I imagined it would be when Charlie was appointed last summer to make it."

Jonathan stretched up to see better. "Where's baby Jesus?"

Merry patted his arm. "I think they'll wait and put him in on Christmas Eve like we do at home."

"OK." He settled back down in Clay's arms and leaned his head over so his mouth was right against Clay's ear. "Did you tell our secret?"

Clay darted a glance at Merry to make sure she hadn't overheard. Her eyes were still fastened on the mayor and his speaking. "No. I haven't told anyone. Did you?"

"Only Jesus."

"Oh, I see." Only Jesus? What did Jonathan think Jesus was going to do for him?

The countdown started by the mayor drew his attention. He chanted with the crowd, "Five, four, three, two, one."

Suddenly the tree came to life with spots of red, green, blue, and white. The crowd cheered and clapped, and Clay joined in with them. He'd never see anything quite like it in his life.

Jonathan clapped his hands. "It's bootiful."

Yes, it was beautiful. He glanced down at Merry. Almost

as beautiful as the young woman beside him. Tonight marked the true beginning of a season of magic. Here he stood beside Merry and holding Jonathan just like they were a family. What a gift that would be this Christmas.

Just as quickly as the idea came, it flew away. He had no business thinking of such things, especially now. This was the night he planned to rescue Lily. If that all worked out like he hoped, then maybe he could turn his attention to proving his worth to the townspeople—and winning the heart of Merry.

Clay handed Jonathan to Merry. "It's time for me to go. I'll see you back at your house." He turned a deaf ear to Jonathan's cries and pushed his way through the crowd to the street where Lily lived.

He no sooner stepped away from the crowd than Sheriff Devlin grabbed his arm. "Barlow, your old friend robbed another bank last week in Plainfield. That's getting close to us. You sure you don't know anything about where he's hiding?"

"No, I don't. I'd say he's getting rather bold to be coming this close." He may have seen Karl, but he didn't lie to the sheriff since he really didn't know where Karl had gone. And the threat from Karl loomed too large in his mind to risk telling the sheriff now.

"I see." The sheriff narrowed his eyes. "Where you headed off to?"

"I have an errand to run for Pa." Clay's breath caught in his throat. If the sheriff asked more questions, he'd have to come up with something. If only Lily would let him tell the sheriff what they'd planned. "Good night. I must be on my way."

He darted down the alley, but just before he turned the corner to the Vaughn house, he looked back over his shoulder and spotted the sheriff still standing at the corner, staring after him. He inhaled deeply and then let his breath out. This had to work. It just had to.

Chapter 20

CLAY TAPPED ON Lily's window, and she appeared immediately. Motioning for her to step back, he swiftly kicked a hole through the window then removed the shards.

Lily came forward. "I thought you'd never get here. I begged off going to town and said I wasn't feeling well."

"Did they believe you?"

"I think so, but they'll be back soon. We have to hurry." She climbed over the windowsill and pulled a carpet bag after her.

He grabbed the bag from her and led her away from the direction of the crowd. These alleys hadn't changed much since he'd been a boy playing hide-and-seek with his friends. Even in the dark he could find his way.

Noise from the revelers at the lighting ceremony echoed in the dark. Lily hung on to his arm. "They'll be celebrating for a while now." He stopped and peeked around the corner of the livery stable. Gas lamps and lanterns lit up Main Street with a brilliance almost as bright as day. The music of the choir singing carols reached their ears.

"Come on, we'll cross over here and go to the alley behind the store."

Pulling Lily behind him, he dashed across the street and into the darkness of another alley. Up the way he spotted the lamp Pa hung outside the back door.

When they reached the store, he tapped on the door to the storeroom. Ma opened it and held out her arms to Lily. "Come in here where it's warm. I have a pot of tea brewed, and that'll warm you up good."

"We don't have much time. Mr. and Mrs. Vaughn will be going home as soon as the crowd begins to thin out."

"The last time I saw them, they were enjoying themselves at one of the refreshment stands. Grace Ann and Jimmy will keep them occupied for a while. You at least need something warm to keep the cold away."

"All right, but we can't take too long."

Ma handed the girl a cup filled with hot tea. "This should help warm you up some."

Lily nodded and sipped her hot tea. "This is wonderful, Mrs. Barlow. What does it have in it?"

"Oh, a little honey and a bit of cinnamon. Supposed to be good for the throat."

"It's certainly soothing mine." She grinned up at Ma with the first big smile Clay had ever seen from her.

Ma sat down beside Lily. "Clay told me that you went to look for a cousin in Oklahoma."

"Yes. I got as far as Oklahoma City when I ran low on money."

Clay poured himself a cup of the hot tea. "That's when the Vaughns picked her up."

"So they didn't adopt you?"

"No, ma'am. They put me on a train with them and brought me here to Kansas."

Ma pursed her lips, letting them know how she disliked that comment. "Do you have any idea where your cousin might be living?"

"I'm not sure. My pa's brother died, and my cousins went to live with their mother's family somewhere in the western part of Texas. Sure would have been nice to live with them, but when I wrote to them, I learned they and my cousin, Carrie, had been killed in a wagon accident. I got a letter from the man running my uncle's ranch, and he said the last he'd heard my cousin had gone to Oklahoma Territory."

Clay shook his head. "That's a lot of territory out there, and much of it still belongs to the Indians. But if anyone can help you find them, Mr. Warner can. He just moved here from Oklahoma."

A shiver shook Lily's body, and her hands trembled as she set down her cup. "I never dreamed I'd find anyone who would believe my story and help me get away."

"God brought you to Prairie Grove because He knew people here would want to help you." Ma leaned over and wrapped her arms around Lily.

Lily's voice choked on her words. "I prayed and prayed, but God never did answer. I'd begun to give up hope until Mrs. Shanks was so kind to me."

"God answered your prayers at just the right time."

"Ma always talked about how much God loved us, and so

did Pa. We went to church all the time, and I loved the stories about Jesus and how He died for my sins. I believe now God was looking out for me even in all of this horrible mess."

The idea of God watching over Lily clutched at Clay's heart and confirmed his return to his faith. Everything would work out, but they still had to be careful. No sense inviting trouble. "I'm going to get the horses. We need to leave now." Clay set his cup and saucer on a shelf in the store room.

Pa stepped in through the door, his gaze quickly taking in the group. "The horses are here, ready to go, Clay. Frank Warner told me that Mrs. Collins stayed behind and is ready to meet you. He's keeping the family in town a little longer so she'll have time to get Lily hidden before they get home."

"Then we'd best hurry." Clay kissed Ma's cheek. "Thanks for everything, Ma. I couldn't do this without your support."

She hugged him hard. "Be careful, and we'll be praying for you all the way." Then she hugged Lily. "I pray we'll be able to find your cousin and get you back to family. But for now the Warners will take good care of you. I'm so sorry we had to do things this way."

Tears glistened in Lily's eyes. "I am too, but Mr. Vaughn would have sweet-talked his way out of any accusations I could have made against him. He'd just tell people I'm a spoiled young woman who doesn't like to be disciplined. I'd never get away without your help."

Clay donned his hat and buttoned up his coat. Pa shoved a gun and holster into his hands. "I know you quit wearing one, but you may need this tonight. Take it."

Clay grasped the handle and pulled it out to check the

barrel. All clean and shiny like new. "Thanks, Pa. I sure hope it'll be for show only."

A few minutes later he and Lily headed toward Holly Hill on horseback. "We'll go down this back way to the edge of town," Clay explained. "Once we're on the hill, we won't have to worry about anyone seeing us. The night will give us some cover, and if we stay to the old trail and off the road, we'll be OK. Stay close to me. We'll have to go slow because of the darkness."

Lily nodded and held the reins in a death grip as the tension and fear oozed from her. Clay wanted to get her to safety as quickly as possible.

Merry itched to get away from the crowds and hurry back home to see what was going on there. They had to stay away long enough for Grandma to get Lily up to Zach's old room, but what if something happened and Clay and Lily got caught?

She heard laughter and turned to see Mr. and Mrs. Vaughn with James and Grace Ann. James must have told one of his funny stories by the way the others were reacting. Good. That would keep them busy for a while.

A pair of arms grasped her around the legs. Jonathan held her like he thought she'd run away. "What's the matter, little fellow?"

"Where's Mr. Clay? I needs to see him."

"He had to go take care of some business, but you'll see him after a while. Remember, he's going to come by and have cake with us after we get home." Merry looked forward to that as much as Jonathan.

"Let's hurry and get home then."

"Soon, Jonathan, soon we'll go." She grabbed his hand. "But now let's go have some of that hot cocoa I see them serving over there."

After she got the beverage for Jonathan, the other boys all decided they wanted some too. By the time she had cups for all of them and had them seated so they wouldn't spill it, the choir had finished their carols and the crowd began to thin out.

Mama approached her. "I see you have the boys in hand, so I'll find Emmaline and the girls. We'll be leaving shortly to go home." She leaned close to Merry's ear. "Mr. Barlow just told us that Clay and Lily have left for Holly Hill." After a pat on Merry's arm, Mama disappeared back into the crowd.

A few minutes later Mama and Papa gathered them all to return home. Merry prayed there would be enough time for Clay to get Lily to Holly Hill and have her safely hidden. She saw no sign of them along the road, so they must have made it. Her heart skipped a beat both in fear and anticipation. As much as she wanted to see Clay, she couldn't bear it if he showed more interest in Lily than he did her.

No horses stood at the front hitching post, but then they could have walked. But if they had come by horseback, Clay would have taken them around to the stables rather than leave them out in plain sight anyway.

Merry rushed into the house when the carriage stopped, leaving her parents to sort out the children. Clay waited in the parlor and stood when she ran toward him.

"Did everything work out OK?" Merry asked. No time for greetings or formalities. The children would be coming any second.

"Yes, Lily is upstairs now. The room is very nice and will be a good place for her to hide."

Mama and Papa strode into the parlor with Jonathan in tow.

Clay picked him up and hugged him. "Hey, little fellow."

"Mr. Clay, you ran off." The little boy peered at Clay with wide eyes. His dark hair curled about his forehead, and at the moment he looked remarkably like Clay himself.

"I'm sorry, my little buddy, but I had something to do." He set Jonathan back on the floor. "Now, Grandma Collins has cake in the kitchen for you. Go get some, and I'll be there in a few minutes. I have to talk with Mr. and Mrs. Warner first." He turned Jonathan in the direction of the kitchen and patted his back to get him started.

Papa shook Clay's hand. "Good to see you. I take it this means all went well."

"Yes, sir, it did. Everything's all set."

"Good. Now let's go have some of that cake Grandma Collins baked this afternoon."

After they were all in the dining room, Merry helped Mama carry in the dishes and set them on the table. When she returned to the kitchen for the coffeepot, Grandma stopped her. "Lily's going to be fine. No one will know she's here. I left her eating a piece of cake a few minutes ago. We can both go up and check on her later."

Merry placed her hands on the countertop to steady her legs, which might give way at any second. Lily may be doing fine, but Merry wasn't. In the next day or so she'd know the truth. Either Clay cared for her, or she'd lost him to Lily.

She inhaled deeply, planted a smile on her lips, and strode

to the dining room, where everyone talked at once about the sight they'd witnessed a short time ago.

Jonathan had positioned himself between her and Clay again, which was fine with her. Heat rose in her cheeks as it usually did in Clay's presence. Papa bowed his head to bless the food. She closed her eyes, but she barely heard his words.

When Papa ended his prayer, Jonathan turned his head from Merry to Clay and back to Merry. The big smile he wore lit up his eyes with a sparkle that warmed the chill in her heart.

"I love you, Miss Merry." Then he turned to Clay. "I love you, Mr. Clay."

Clay leaned close to Jonathan. "I love you too, Jonathan Henderson." He glanced up at Merry, and his eyes sent a message that caused her heart to begin racing.

Jonathan grinned and pulled Clay's head closer. "Mr. Clay, 'member our secret?"

"Yes, I do." Once again he stared at Merry.

She blinked and dipped her head. What secret could he have with Jonathan? It must have to do with Christmas, a time when everyone had secrets.

Kenny's voice rose above the rest. "We're going to have snow for Christmas this year, and lots of it."

Grandma furrowed her brow. "Now how do you know that?"

"'Cause I prayed for it, and Jesus will answer with a big snowstorm." He looked around the table with confidence written all over his face.

"Snow's fun for you, but it's hard work for me and Papa. We have to shovel the paths to get to the barn and stables."

Henry let his opinion be heard with a frown and shake of his head.

Clay leaned toward Kenny. "Maybe we'll get just enough snow for you to play in but not enough to make work for Henry and your papa. I've already prepared the runners to make our wagon into a sleigh, and the jingle bell harness is hanging on a hook, just waiting for that snow."

The children clapped with glee at that suggestion. Even Henry offered a smile.

After the dessert Grandma led the children upstairs to their rooms so the adults could talk in the parlor. Merry hugged Jonathan and promised to be up later to check on him. Satisfied, he kissed her cheek, hugged Clay, then scampered up after Grandma.

The four adults seated themselves in the parlor, and Merry chose to sit across from Clay in order to observe him without turning her head. Clay explained what had happened and how he had brought Lily here.

Papa stood and paced in front of the window. "When we find out more about the girl, we can start looking for her family. I'm sure Mr. and Mrs. Vaughn are aware of her being gone by now."

"Probably. They kept the door to her room locked so she couldn't leave."

Mama's face paled at Clay's revelation. "That poor child kept locked up in her room. No wonder they didn't worry about her running away when they left her behind to attend church or go to town without her."

Merry's heart went out Lily. No one deserved to be treated like that. Grace Ann had been right to seek Clay's help.

Her gaze rested on him now as he talked with Papa. How she wanted to feel those lips against hers once more.

That dreaded heat filled her face again. To keep Mama from noticing, she lowered her head to gaze at her hands. How could she think such thoughts with Mama and Papa sitting right there by her? And how did she know that Clay would even want to kiss her again, anyway?

Chapter 21

CLAY RODE AWAY from Holly Hill with relief that Lily was now safely hidden there. By the time he returned to town, Mr. and Mrs. Vaughn would be looking for her. If they went to Sheriff Devlin, would they claim her to be kidnapped or to have run away? Didn't matter much which one since he planned to tell the sheriff the whole business in the next day or two anyway.

Clay surveyed the streets down below and jerked the reins of his horse. What he saw sent daggers of fear through heart. Three horsemen rounded the corner by the bank and disappeared into the space between the bank and the hotel next to it. Then the same men on horseback thundered up the street and out of sight

The truth hit Clay between the eyes with the force of a sledgehammer. Karl Laramie. He and his gang had robbed the bank. If he rode after them and tried to stop them, Karl would only say Clay was part of it all along. But if he went home now, he would have no excuse for not being at home, because he couldn't reveal his alibi for fear of putting Lily in danger. He had two choices, and both meant he'd be accused of a crime he didn't commit.

Voices shouted in the distance, and people began running from the hotel and homes and buildings. Then the sheriff ran from his office and said something to the other men gathered around. Five men jumped on their horses and followed the other group out of town. Pa rode with the posse.

Clay made a quick decision and headed his horse back to circle around and come into town from another direction. He'd grown up in these parts and knew every back road and trail that would get him back to town.

Even if he showed up now, he'd be under suspicion since he hadn't come from his house with Pa. That didn't matter right now. Lily was safe, and he could face whatever accusations came his way. If it meant getting arrested for the bank holdup in order to protect Lily, he would sit in jail until the truth could be revealed. The people who really mattered to him knew the truth, and that would get him through any hardship he had to bear. He had been to jail for doing the wrong thing, and it might actually feel good to be in jail for doing the right thing for once.

After Clay left, Merry headed up to the attic room while Mama and Grandma put the children to bed. Both curiosity and fear coursed through her veins, but the need to see Lily outweighed the fear.

Lily glanced up when Merry entered. She had been sitting in a rocking chair, looking at a book. She stood nervously. "You're the girl Clay talked about, the schoolteacher."

Merry swallowed hard and nodded. Clay had been discussing her with this woman? Woman? She was barely out of childhood. Merry's heart softened at the sight of Lily now sitting on the edge of the bed in the gown Grandma had provided. Her face, framed with dark brown hair, appeared soft and vulnerable. "How old are you, Lily?"

"I'm seventeen."

With her twenty-fourth birthday approaching in a few weeks, Merry looked at seventeen as being quite young. "I'm sorry we have to be so secretive, but the children may slip and say something about you without thinking."

"I understand, and I'll be as quiet as can be. I'm so thankful for people like you all. Not many would be willing to take such risks."

Merry crossed to the bed and pulled down the quilt. "You must be exhausted. I'll leave you to rest now. Mama will probably bring breakfast up to you as soon as I've herded the children off to church." If Grandma kept Jonathan busy, he would never know they had a guest, and with all the others at school most of the time, Lily could have a little more freedom during the day.

Lily climbed into bed. "I think I'll have the best sleep I've had in months. Good night."

"Good night."

Merry dimmed the gas lantern beside the bed. Then she closed the door behind her and went down to her room. As she prepared for bed, Clay's face filled her thoughts. *Please, Lord, let Clay care about me.* The prayer sounded selfish, but she couldn't help it. All evening he had been polite and friendly, but nothing more. Had the kiss at the school meant nothing?

She couldn't see any signs that he felt especially concerned about Lily—at least no more than anyone else—but neither did he show any special attention toward her.

After turning out the lamp beside the bed, she snuggled under the covers. Images of Clay and her with a family in their own home around a Christmas tree danced through her mind. Her whispered words broke the silence of the night. "Kiss me again, Clay. Kiss me."

People still shouted and milled about the streets. Lanterns and candles burned in every building he could see. After stabling his horse, Clay headed up the stairs.

When he came into the kitchen Ma jumped like she'd been shot. "Oh my, you scared me half to death. The bank's been robbed, and I'm all on edge." She ran to him and hugged him. "Thank the Lord you're safe. Is Lily all right?"

"Yes, she's with the Warners now, and they'll keep her hidden." Clay wrapped his arm about his mother's shoulders. "Everything went as planned."

"One of the sheriff's deputies was here looking for you. I didn't know what to do. I had to tell them you weren't here. When he asked me where you were, I said I didn't know. The look on his face then scared me. Did I do the right thing?"

He hugged her close to his chest. "Yes, you did the right thing. We have to keep Lily safe. The sheriff will probably come after me thinking I had something to do with the robbery, but that doesn't matter. Soon as we can, we'll tell Sheriff Devlin the whole story. Mr. and Mrs. Warner will tell them what we did." It had to work out OK, even if Karl insisted Clay had been with him.

After Ma went to her room, Clay sat at the dining table. He'd turned the lamps down low, but he wanted to wait for Pa to return and give a report. Clay would be willing to bet any amount of money that Karl and his gang wouldn't be found. They'd hole up somewhere and divide the loot among themselves. At least that's what they'd done when Clay was with them in the past. Meanwhile the citizens of Prairie Grove had lost what they saved in the bank.

When the clock in the parlor struck three, Pa opened the door and came into the room. He jerked back and blinked his eyes when he spotted Clay sitting in the semi-darkness. "What are you doing here? I figured you'd stay up at Holly Hill where you'd be safe and have an alibi."

"I didn't think about staying up there. I was on my way home when all the commotion at the bank started. Did the posse find any trace of Karl?"

"Not that I know of. I rode with them for quite a ways until the sheriff decided it would be best for me to come back to town with him. He left the others at a campsite for the night. Not sure they'll find anybody since the gang had a good head start. Just about the time people heard the horses thundering out of town, Mr. and Mrs. Vaughn were telling the sheriff that Lily was missing. The sheriff told them to look for Lily on their own because he had a bank robber to catch. That's about the time I got there, and the sheriff looked at me with hard eyes and said if he found out you had anything to do with this, you'd never get out of jail."

Clay shook his head. "I figured as much. But we can't tell

him where I really was, at least not yet. I'd rather go to jail and sit a few days until she's safe than to reveal what I did tonight."

Pa scratched his chin and sat down. "Well, now that might be best. You won't be suspected of helping Lily if you're thought to be involved in the bank robbery."

"I guess it's sort of like a double-edged sword. Whichever way we go, there's going to be trouble, and I'd rather that trouble be on me than on Lily or Holly Hill."

Before Pa could reply, someone pounded on the door. Pa strode to the door and opened it to find Sheriff Devlin and one of his deputies on the porch.

"May we come in, Stanley?"

Pa glanced at Clay then stepped back to let the sheriff in.

Sheriff Devlin headed straight for Clay. "Where were you tonight? I saw you leaving the tree lighting ceremony early. You were headed down an alley, but where did you go from there?"

"I came home." And he had, but only after he'd been delayed.

"You didn't come out to see what the noise was all about when the robbery occurred. Why is that?"

"I wasn't here then." Better to be truthful about that, but not where he'd gone.

"Can you tell me where you were?"

"No, I can't." And that was the truth too. If Devlin kept asking that type of question, no lies would be told.

Devlin produced a screwdriver Clay recognized as the one he'd used in the storeroom a few days ago. What was the sheriff doing with it?

"Found this in the bank. Has your pa's name on it. Now I know he wasn't there, but I don't know about you. So it looks to me like I have to take you in for questioning about the robbery."

Clay's heart sank. One of Karl's men must have taken it, but how had he gotten in without anyone knowing about it? Anger boiled inside Clay for the mess Karl had caused for his family. There was nothing he could do now but cooperate with the sheriff. "Yes, sir, I know that. I'll come with you if that's what you want."

"It is." He nodded to his deputy, who grasped Clay's arm. "I'm sorry about this, Stanley, but if I don't, you may have a mob on your hands. Some folks in this town will be quick to convict him."

"I understand. The truth will come out eventually no matter what the townspeople think."

From the corner of his eye, Clay spotted his mother standing in the doorway of the bedroom. The look of agony in her eyes hurt just as much now as it had five years ago when he'd been arrested the first time. How he wished he could turn back the clock and make those wasted years disappear.

He caught the glint of tears on Ma's cheeks. He hated doing this, but Ma and Pa both understood it was for the best in order to keep Lily safe. "Let's go, Sheriff. I'm tired and ready to bunk down no matter where it is."

Sheriff Devlin grasped Clay's arm and escorted him outside. No matter what else happened, it was now up to Merry and her family to take care of Lily. As long as he was in jail for the bank robbery, the Vaughns wouldn't suspect him of helping Lily escape, and they'd never think of looking for her at an orphans' home.

When the door closed behind them, Cora Barlow rushed to her husband. "Stanley, what are we going to do? We know he's innocent, but everyone else in town will believe he's guilty."

"We're going to pray for him and for Lily. Just think, God provided a distraction to keep the sheriff too busy to look into Lily's disappearance. Now we must trust that God'll be with Clay, and when the time is right, the truth will be told."

Cora's heart said the same thing, but it broke to think of her son in jail for something he had no part in. Trusting God in every situation had just grown a little harder.

Stanley wrapped his arms around her and held her close. "My love, God is with us. He hasn't abandoned us. He wants Lily to be free as much as we do, and He'll watch over our boy."

"I know that, but it's just so hard. How long will we have to wait until we can tell the truth about where he was?"

"I don't know. Frank Warner told me tonight that Louise planned to question the girl tomorrow about her family and that cousin she was trying to find." He tilted her head toward his and peered down at her. "The best part is that Clay has enough trust in us to let us help him. After what happened when he was arrested that last time, I was afraid he'd never trust me again."

"You only did what had to be done, and he understands that. He has changed a lot since he came home. I think the Lord's dealing with him too." She pushed away from Stanley's arms. "I'll never get to sleep now. Clay made coffee earlier. How about having some now along with a little of that pie left over from supper?" It'd be daybreak before they knew it, so there was no sense in going to bed now anyway.

"That sounds like a good idea. All the commotion of the past hours has made me a little hungry, and some of your apple pie will be just the thing to take care of it."

A few minutes later they sat at the kitchen table holding hands. Stanley grasped both of hers into his and held them tight. "Our boy's going to be all right, and Frank will find Lily's family. We just have to trust God and let Him handle it all."

Cora bowed her head and Stanley prayed. Her own prayer went up as well. *Lord, thank You that Clay's plan worked tonight, but please get it all straightened out before Clay can be tried and convicted again. Help Frank Warner find Lily's relative and take her to a safe place far away from the Vaughns. Protect her and the Warner family while she's at Holly Hill.*

Now if she'd simply let go of her fears and let the Lord take care of it, everything would work out. If not, this would be a very unhappy Christmas for them all.

Chapter 22

LOUISE WARNER PREPARED a dinner tray to take up to Lily. With Frank out with the posse and Merry in her room, Grandma made sure all the children were now occupied elsewhere for the afternoon. News of Clay's arrest had filled the church foyer this morning, and the children had talked of nothing else over dinner. She had reassured the youngest of her charges that it was all a mistake, that Mr. Clay would be proven innocent and would be with them for Christmas, but even as she spoke the words, doubt crept into her heart.

They needed to find out more about the girl and any family so they could find a place for her away from Holly Hill. That was the only way they'd finally be able to clear Clay's name. Mr. and Mrs. Vaughn had not been at church this morning, and one of the women said that they were terribly upset because their daughter had run away and no one was doing anything about it because of that bank robbery. That was one piece of good news, at least. As long as the Vaughns believed she'd run away, Louise would have time to get more information about Lily's family.

Her first instinct had been to run to the sheriff and tell him what was going on, but he'd left with the posse this morning to hunt for Karl Laramie and his gang. She'd have to trust Frank to know what to do and when.

She retrieved the jug of milk from the icebox and set it on the counter. For a moment she gripped the edges, anger boiling up inside. Her head still reeled from the horrible comments she had heard about Clay at church this morning. How could Christians be so cruel to their own fellow church members?

Several of the women, led by Mrs. Pennyfeather of course, had uttered most unkind words about Cora and Stanley as well. Neither one had been at church, and news of Clay's arrest had spread like wildfire.

Merry hurt too and was even now in her room, probably having a good cry. At least she knew the truth and could hold on to that. Louise sighed and poured milk into a glass. She and Lily would have their first good visit this afternoon, and maybe some new information would be forthcoming.

After checking the hallway for any stray boys or girls, Louise made her way to the attic stairway and up to Lily's room. She knocked on the door then entered to find Lily sitting up in bed reading a novel Merry had given her.

"Oh, Mrs. Warner, I'm so glad to see you. Do you have any news?"

Louise set the tray on the table near the bed. At breakfast she'd told the girl about the bank robbery and how it had delayed the search for Lily. But she had not yet told Lily about Clay's arrest. "The good news is that the sheriff and a posse are still out looking for Karl and his gang, so they have not been able to investigate your disappearance. The Vaughns were not in church this morning, but I heard they are upset because no one is available to help find you."

"You said that was the good news. Is there bad news?" Lily peered into her eyes.

Louise hadn't intended on telling the girl about Clay, but she was too perceptive. "I'm afraid there is a complication. Clay was arrested last night on suspicion of helping with the robbery."

Lily's mouth opened wide, and she shook her head. "He can't have helped rob the bank. He was with me or your family almost all evening."

"We know that, but to keep you safe he can't tell the sheriff where he was or what he was doing. Mr. and Mrs. Vaughn are telling everyone you ran away. That's good for now."

"I feel awful that he's in jail because he's protecting me. It's not fair."

"Sometimes things just aren't fair, but God will handle it all and the truth will be made known eventually." Louise reached down and stroked Lily's hair. They'd keep this young girl safe no matter what else happened.

"If we could only find my cousin, he might have some family that I could go to."

"Yes, let's start with that. We haven't had much chance to talk since you arrived, so now would be a good time as you eat." Louise handed the tray over to Lily then sat beside the bed in a cane-bottomed chair.

"Let's begin with your full name and the name of your

cousin." Any clue, no matter how small, would help, and having a name would get her even further.

"My full name is Lillian Rose Starnes. My cousin's name is Jake Starnes." She twisted the napkin in her hands and blinked her eyes.

Louise's heart jumped at the name. Jake Starnes! Could it be? "What do you know about Jake?" she asked.

"He was originally from Texas, but when his parents died, he went to live with another uncle. After his sister and aunt and uncle died in a wagon accident, he moved to Oklahoma."

"Lily!" Louise exclaimed. "I think I know exactly where to find your cousin. In Barton Creek, Oklahoma, where we lived until this past summer, a young man by the name of Jake Starnes married a young woman by the name of Lucy. And I think I heard that he lost his sister in a wagon accident."

Lily's eyes opened wide. "Are you sure? Could it be the same Jake who's my cousin?" Tears began a stream down her cheeks.

"How many Jake Starnes can there be in Oklahoma?" She fished in her pocket for a handkerchief and wiped Lily's cheeks.

Tears still swam in her eyes, but her smile spoke of the hope that Louise had given her. "It has to be him. How can we find him?"

"Well, it seems to me I have correspondence downstairs from them. When we decided to come back here and take over the home for my mother, Jake and Lucy were very generous and gave us a large sum of money to help keep our doors open."

Louise jumped up. "You finish your meal. I'm going down right now and find that letter they sent not long ago. I'll get Mr. Warner to send them a wire as soon as the telegraph office opens tomorrow." She bent over and hugged Lily. "With God's help and blessing, we'll have you with your cousin by Christmas."

Louise hurried down the stairs to the desk where she stored her correspondence. After searching the files, she finally found the letter from Lucy and Jake Starnes. This had to be Lily's cousin. All the pieces fit. This was the best news they could have had right now. The quicker they found Lily's family, the quicker they could get Clay out of jail.

Merry dried her eyes and sat on the side of her bed. If only she had some way to go down to see Clay. With Papa gone, she'd have to ask Mama, and she'd say no for certain. Maybe Grandma would go with her. After checking her face for signs of her crying jag, she smoothed back her hair and went in search of Grandma.

She found her in the kitchen. "Grandma, I want to go into town to see Clay at the jail. I won't be long, but I want to tell him that Lily is safe."

Grandma frowned. "That is not a good idea. The jail is a mean place. You don't belong there."

Merry started to argue, but Mama burst through the door before she could speak.

"Oh, Mother, I'm so glad I found you. And you too, Merry. I have some wonderful news."

Merry's heart jumped. "Is it about Clay or Lily?" Mama held a piece of paper in her hand and handed it to Grandma.

"It's about Lily, and it may mean we can clear Clay sooner." Mama's face beamed with delight at the news.

Merry grabbed the paper and saw the names listed. "You think Lily is related to Lucy and Jake Starnes? That's a stretch, isn't it?" Merry remembered Lucy Starnes, the young heiress from Boston who had been such a big help to Barton Creek after a tornado went through and destroyed a lot of the town.

Mama shook her head and clasped her hands to her chest. "It all fits. Lily's full name is Lillian Starnes, and her cousin's name is Jake. He's from Texas and went to Oklahoma after his sister and aunt and uncle were killed in a wagon accident. Isn't that the exact same thing that happened to the Jake Starnes we knew in Barton Creek?"

Merry gasped then hugged her mother. "Oh, Mama, this is the best news I've heard in a long time. I was just telling Grandma that I want to go down to the jail to visit Clay, and now I'll have something wonderful to tell him."

Mama's eyes opened wide. "You're going down to visit Clay in jail? You'll do no such thing. Have you lost your mind? You can't go down there. It's no place for a woman."

Merry's happiness dimmed, but only for a moment. "Mama, you or Grandma can go with me."

"I don't think so, young lady."

Grandma came to her rescue. "Now, Louise, I think if I ride down with her it will be fine. I don't think we'll get in to see Clay, but at least she'll know he's all right."

Merry hugged her grandmother's neck. "Oh, thank you, that would be perfect." She grabbed her cloak from the hall tree and wrapped it around her shoulders.

Mama shook her head. "It's still not right, but I can see we'll have no peace until she goes. I'll get Henry to hitch the horses to the carriage."

A few minutes later they were on their way with Grandma handling the reins. She might be over seventy, but she could still handle the horses.

Merry hooked her hand in the crook of her grandmother's arm. "I remember Lucy from when we were in Barton Creek. She's younger than I am, but when I came home from teacher's college in the summer last year, she was very friendly. Her friend, a part Indian girl, married Luke, the mercantile owner's son." What a time that had been with the town divided in their loyalties. God had worked all that out in a miraculous way, so He could also work out Clay's dilemma now.

"Yes, your mother wrote me all about that. She said something about a prairie fire and a woman's sister who came back after being kidnapped by Indians. God's hand was on that whole town last year. I believe that God's hand is on us now, and He's going to help us find Lily's family and get Clay out of jail."

When they had almost reached the center of town, a commotion arose in the streets. The sheriff and several other men rode in with three men on horseback. The men were tied to their saddles. The Laramie gang. It had to be.

Papa spotted them in the carriage and jumped down from his horse and ran to them. "What in thunder are you two doing here?"

Merry jumped down from the carriage and hugged her father. "I'm so glad to see you. Maybe now the sheriff will let Clay go since you brought in Karl's gang."

Before Papa could stop her, she burst into the sheriff's office as two deputies took the men back to the cells. Merry started to follow them.

Sheriff Devlin reached out to grab her arm. "Whoa there, Miss Warner. Where do you think you're going?"

"I want to see Clay. I have some news for him." She tried to pull her arm free, but the sheriff held tight and looked at Papa now standing behind her.

"That still doesn't mean you should be here. Frank, what are we going to do with this daughter of yours? She can't see Clay, especially now."

"She didn't know we'd bring in Karl and his men this soon." He grabbed Merry's arm. "It's time to go home."

Merry jerked away. "No, I have to tell Clay what we found out today."

"Not possible. There's too many of them back there now." Shouting voices came from the cell area, and the sheriff whirled around to investigate.

Merry didn't hesitate to follow. Papa caught her and restrained her before she could get near the cells, but the voices were loud and clear. She recognized Karl Laramie from her school days although now he looked more like a hardened man than the troublesome boy she'd known.

His voice rose above the others. "You can't get out of this one, Clay Barlow. You'll go back to prison."

"I'm innocent, Karl, and you know it. Tell them the truth so I can go free."

Karl's evil laugh sent chills through Merry's heart. How could one boy have become such an ugly man? She shivered and Papa gripped her arms.

"The truth is that you were our lookout and helped us to know just when to come into town and rob the bank." He laughed again and turned to his men. "Ain't that right, boys?"

"That's a lie and you know it, Karl Laramie!"

That evil laugh again. "Then prove it. Think they'll believe an ex-convict like you?"

Merry recognized the moment Clay noticed her presence. His face turned ashen, and he closed his eyes and shook his head.

Sheriff Devlin stood with his hands on his hips. "No one's going anywhere. We'll have the judge hear all the evidence and see about a trial. Now settle down before I have to knock some sense into you."

The sheriff looked at Papa and waved his hand back toward his office. "You two are supposed to be waiting there for me."

Papa pulled her back, but she held Clay's gaze, her eyes pleading for him to stay strong. His eyes only answered with a shame she wanted to wipe away. Then the door to the cells closed and separated her from him.

Alone in the front office, she clung to Papa and buried her face in his chest. "What are we going to do? What if the judge decides to have a trial right away before we can find Lily's family and get her out of here?"

"He won't be back for several days. I'll talk with him. He knows me well from my law days. It's going to be hard, but you have to have faith that all of this will be resolved by Christmas." He held her close and kissed the top of her head.

Papa could always make her feel so safe and loved, but this time the peaceful feelings his words usually brought would not come. Turmoil filled her heart, and her trust in God wavered on the brink of despair.

Chapter 23

YESTERDAY HAD BEEN a most miserable day. The comments and criticisms about Clay being involved with Karl Laramie again were bad enough, but the worst came when Karl had claimed Clay to be a part of the bank robbery right there in front of everybody. The mere idea of Clay going with Karl Laramie again was nonsense. They needed to tell the sheriff everything. But as long as Lily was here, they couldn't.

Merry blinked her eyes to keep the tears at bay. She had students to teach and a Christmas pageant to finish and present. Try as she might, her concentration lagged, and the children sensed it. In another week they'd be out of class for the holidays, and their attention tended to stray as well. Perhaps they were just as confused with what had happened over the weekend as she herself had been.

Papa had left early this morning to ride over to the next town to send a wire to Barton Creek. He didn't want to rouse suspicion by sending one from Prairie Grove with Lily's name in it. Not that he didn't trust the telegrapher, but he told Mama he'd rather ride a few miles extra than to be sorry later.

If Jake really did prove to be Lily's cousin, they could tell the sheriff, and Clay would be free. With so many credible people giving him an alibi, the sheriff was sure to believe them over Karl. She had to keep her faith in the truth strong.

The clock ticked to the noon hour, and Merry released her students for recess. The ones from in town scampered home to eat a hot meal on this cold day. Papa had brought the wagon down to take the children up to the home to eat. The Grainger children stayed with Merry at the school. They sat at their desks eating their lunch while Merry graded papers from the morning's work.

Jesse Grainger placed his trash in the can then stood by Merry's desk. "Miss Warner, Pa said he'd help rebuild the stable we'll need for the Christmas play at church. It's kinda dilapidated after last year."

Merry laid down her pen and gazed up at the boy, who seemed to have grown several inches since summer. "That's very kind of him, Jesse. We'll welcome all the help we can get."

Olivia Grainger came up to stand beside her brother. "My mother is making my angel costume. It's going to be so pretty."

"I'm sure it will, as well as the rest of them she's making. I'm glad she volunteered to do that for us after we found the ones from last year had mildewed." Sad to think, but most of the props and costumes from last year were in pretty bad shape. If not for the willingness of the parents to volunteer their time and efforts, there would be no Christmas program this year.

Jesse and Olivia returned to their seats and helped their younger brother and sister clean up their desks after eating. Merry concentrated on the pageant practice this afternoon.

She had chosen which parts the children would play, and it had been difficult to decide which ones would be best suited for Mary and Joseph. Phoebe had been her final choice. Emmaline may be disappointed, but her voice was best suited for the solo of the angel. Jesse, not Trenton, would be Joseph. She needed Trenton and Bert to be lead shepherd and lead wise man to help handle the younger boys, who would also be shepherds and kings.

Then the memory of the Thanksgiving program and Clay's kiss came back. The words on the papers before her began to swim before she realized her eyes had filled with tears. She grabbed the handkerchief in her pocket and dabbed at them. Clay sat in a jail cell for something he hadn't done, and she couldn't do a thing about it until Lily was safely out of town.

Merry bit her lip and frowned. It was all so unfair. Animosity for Lily rose in her chest. If it weren't for that girl and her problems, Clay wouldn't be sitting in jail right now. Finding compassion for Lily didn't make the list of things Merry wanted to do. Mama would scold if she knew Merry's thoughts, but she didn't care. What if they decided to try Clay before Christmas and Lily was still here?

Noah pulled on her sleeve. "Miss Warner, are you sad? You're not smiling."

Merry blinked her eyes and placed her hand over Noah's. "I'm sorry, I was thinking of something and it did make me sad, but everyone will be back from recess in a few minutes and we'll practice our Christmas play. Then we can all be happy."

"OK. I like to see you smile." He grinned up at her, revealing the empty space where he'd recently lost a tooth.

She had to have more control over her feelings than this.

The children must not see her sadness. Some of them were quite sensitive and noticed when things weren't quite right. Even Emmaline had offered her comfort yesterday after church. She was angry with the people who condemned Clay. Then little Jonathan had cried all afternoon because Clay wasn't coming for a visit.

Mama had reassured them all that everything would work out and Clay would be out of jail in time for Christmas. Merry could only pray that would be true.

Grandma had managed to take care of Lily yesterday without any of the younger children finding out, but Emmaline suspected something was going on. That girl was much too perceptive for her age, but then that would make her a wonderful wife and mother someday.

The sound of Papa's wagon bringing back the children from Holly Hill came from outside, and Merry hurried to ring the bell to bring the students in from noon recess. As they trooped into the room, she glanced at Papa still sitting in the wagon.

Papa smiled and tipped his hat. He mouthed the words, "Don't worry. It's all going to be OK."

Merry attempted a smile in return. *Please, dear Lord, make Papa's words come true.*

Clay lay on the cot in his cell trying to block out the conversation and stabs at his character coming from the other two cells. Devlin had been perceptive enough not to put any of Karl's gang in the cell with Clay.

Why did Merry have to be here last night to witness Karl's

accusing words? She should have been home with her mother. He sat up and propped his head in his hands. Now she knew the kind of place he'd been in the last five years. Why would she ever care for an ex-convict like him? Although her eyes had seemed to beg him not to give up hope, that could be simply that she felt sorry for him, nothing more.

"Son, you have a visitor." Sheriff Devlin unlocked the cell door.

"Reverend Tate? I didn't expect you to visit me here." Clay stood and shook the pastor's hand.

"I have some news for you and I wanted to pray with you. I don't believe you had anything to do with that bank robbery."

The burden on Clay's heart lifted a little. Somebody who didn't know the truth believed in him. Then the first words from the reverend sank in. "What's the news?" Fearing the worst, he slumped back on the cot.

"It's not good, but it involves the Henderson boy. I got a wire back this morning from Wichita. Seems his aunt and uncle do live there, but they can't take Jonathan because they already have four of their own and another on the way. They said if we couldn't find a home for him, they'd see if somebody up there wanted to adopt him."

The words gripped Clay's heart in a vise. The hope of a family for Jonathan died as the reverend went on to explain how they could post a notice about a child being available for adoption. Jonathan had enough tragedy in his young life without knowing his aunt and uncle couldn't take him in.

Reverend Tate rolled the brim of his hat in his hands. "I'm sorry. I know how much you care about that little boy. I was on my way up to see Frank and Louise and tell them what I'd heard. When I passed by here, I decided to come in and tell you."

"Thank you, Reverend. I appreciate your letting me know."

"Well, there's one more thing I need to know before I go." He stepped closer to Clay and lowered his voice. "A few weeks ago, James and Grace Ann Shanks came to me and told me some strange story about the Vaughn family. Do you know anything about that?"

Clay's heart jumped in his chest. He couldn't lie to the reverend, but would he believe the truth? He had to take that chance. "Yes, I do. I found out from Lily that Mr. and Mrs. Vaughn are not her real parents. They picked her up in Oklahoma City and brought her here. She was in Oklahoma looking for her cousin because her own family was gone."

The reverend frowned and tapped his chin as though to let the information sink into his mind. "Are you sure they didn't adopt her?"

"Yes. Lily is seventeen and old enough to be on her own." He didn't dare mention the abuse just yet. Reverend Tate first had to accept the fact that Lily was brought here and held against her will.

"I see. Mr. and Mrs. Vaughn think Lily may have run away Saturday night. Rather strange, don't you think?"

"No, sir. If she decided she'd had enough of being held captive, she very well could have run away." As long as people believed Lily had run away, she'd be safe at Holly Hill.

"That's quite possible." He placed a hand on Clay's shoulder. "Another thing I want to do before I leave is to pray with you." He cast a glance at the other cells and the men hanging on the bars. "And I'll include you men," he called.

Karl's laugh sent the other men into raucous laughter. "You go right ahead and do that, Reverend. Probably won't do much good, seeing as how we've already been convicted by the good folks in this town." More laughter followed his statement.

Reverend Tate didn't reply. He simply stepped closer to Clay, placed his hand on Clay's shoulder, and prayed. "Dear Lord, I lift this young man and the others up to You for Your mercy. I believe in Clay's innocence, and I pray that evidence will be revealed soon that will clear his name. Comfort him now and give the peace that only You can give Your children. In Your name I pray, amen."

Clay blinked his eyes to keep them from tearing up. "Thank you. I do feel better."

Karl's men only laughed louder.

The preacher took his leave, and the sheriff locked the cell door. He peered at Clay and spoke in hushed tones. "I wish I knew the truth of what went on Saturday night. I have a feeling you might have some role in Miss Vaughn's disappearance."

Clay said nothing, so the sheriff shook his head and left. Karl's nasty chuckle and a few choice words that stung even Clay's ears followed the sheriff back to his office. Then Karl leaned against the bars of his cell, his arms on the outside with his hands clasped together.

"You think that prayer of the preacher man is going to get you out of here? I warned you what would happen if you ignored my message, but you just wouldn't listen. I don't know how that posse caught us, but if we go down, you're going with us." He turned to the others. "Ain't that right, boys?"

Clay tuned out their agreeing words and concentrated on the news about Jonathan. His plight worried him more than that of Lily. Lily had been through a lot, but at her age she could handle trials much better than a four-year-old boy could.

The deputy came in with two men from the diner that provided meals for the prisoners. Clay's appetite had left him, but if he didn't eat, he'd feel worse later on. A bowl of stew and cornbread smelled good, so he ate what he could.

Later, after he'd napped a bit after lunch, the sheriff came back. "You have another visitor, but I can't let her back here with so many of you. She said to give you this letter, and you'd understand."

He held out a white envelope and Clay grabbed it from the man's hand. "Thank you. You're right, she doesn't need to be back here around these men."

"Gotcha a little love note there, Clay?" Karl crooned. "Bet it's from that pretty little schoolmarm...what's her name? Merry Warner, ain't it? I remember her from school. She's grown up to be a fine-looking woman. Ollie here got up close and personal with her a few weeks ago. Looks like you didn't heed our warning. Lucky nothing else happened."

Clay shot up from his cot and grabbed the bars. "Ollie was with Merry? What did you say to her?"

Ollie grinned, revealing his tobacco-stained teeth. "It was the night of that box thing at town hall. I grabbed her arm and told her to give you a message to do what we said. She was real cooperative after I warned her she'd be hurt otherwise."

Anger boiled over in Clay's stomach. His knuckles turned white as he gripped the iron bars. That's the night Merry walked home by herself. He should have been with her. No wonder she'd been so distraught, but she'd never said a word.

Through clenched teeth Clay warned Karl. "You'll never

get away with including me in your schemes. I'll be cleared when the truth comes out."

Karl sneered and pointed a finger straight at Clay. "The truth is, you're an ex-convict, and your pretty little school-marm's family won't let you near her after this, especially with her pa being a lawman himself."

"Shut up, Karl. Merry is too good for you to even speak her name." Clay breathed hard and deep to control his anger. He stepped away from the bars and turned his back on the other men.

The note the sheriff gave him crackled in his hand, and Clay sat back on his cot to read it. As he had hoped, it was from Merry.

We have a lead on Lily's cousin in Oklahoma. His name is Jake Starnes, and we actually knew him in Barton Creek. We're praying he will come and get Lily as soon as possible. We're all praying for you. Please believe you'll get out of this mess, and then the people here will see that you are the good man you were before you became so mixed up with Karl and his gang. I believe in you. Yours, Merry Warner

He sat holding the letter for a few minutes, letting the words sink into his heart. She didn't reject him, even though she'd seen him in a jail cell and knew all about his past. She believed in him! She saw him as a good man, not an ex-convict.

Hope and joy filled him. No more stealing kisses. No more avoiding her or hiding his feelings. Who cared what the town thought anymore. If Merry, her parents, his parents, and a few others believed in him, he could live with the Mrs.

Pennyfeathers of the world. When this was all over he'd let Merry know what was in his heart and court her properly, if she would have him.

And then there was Jonathan. He'd have to come up with some way to help that little boy through the holidays. He remembered the wish Jonathan has whispered as part of their secret. Making that wish come true would be his goal, and the sooner he could be released from this jail, the sooner he could go about making it happen.

Chapter 24

THERE WERE ONLY ten more days to Christmas, and one more day until school let out for the holiday break. The practice for the program to be presented on Christmas Eve at church went well that afternoon. All the children really enjoyed their parts.

Now home after a fun afternoon of practice and games, Merry helped the children finish decorating the Christmas tree in the parlor, but her heart wasn't in it like usual. Clay had been in jail almost five days now, and the judge wasn't due back in town until Monday. Her worry about Clay and Jonathan blurred all thoughts of having a good time. She tried to laugh and be happy, but the image of Clay in jail got in the way.

Papa would be back any time now from his trip to check for a telegram in the next town. He said he'd talk with the sheriff as soon as he received a message from Jake Starnes. She and Ma both had wanted to tell the sheriff about Jake right away, but Papa said to wait until he had a telegram confirming that Jake was willing to help.

Now Merry's patience wore thin. Lily had given no

indication in their conversations that Clay was more than a friend, but Merry couldn't shake the feeling that there could be more. Without coming out and asking point blank, she might never hear the truth.

Now with the news about Jonathan's family not being able to take him, her heart had lost all its joy. Jonathan cried every day because he couldn't see Clay, and he kept talking about a secret they had.

She hung the last ornament on the tree and stepped back to survey the finished product. It did look pretty, and the children had done a good job despite frequent stops to eat the popcorn left over from the garlands they made.

"Merry, Merry, look, it's snowing!" Kenny's voice carried across the room.

Merry hurried over to the window. Sure enough, large white flakes drifted down from the heavy gray clouds overhead. "Well, now, I guess we might have a white Christmas after all."

The boys immediately set up a clamor. "Can we go out and play in it? Please."

Mama entered with a tray filled with cups of steaming hot cocoa. "Let's have a cookie or two and cocoa first, then you can go out for a little while before it gets dark. There's not enough to do anything now, but it won't be long the way those flakes are coming down."

The boys scrambled to sit around the dining room table where Mama set the tray. The girls followed, giggling about anything and everything. What a pretty picture they made nibbling cookies and sipping cocoa.

Merry turned back to the window and gazed out at the

falling flakes. They were much larger and coming down faster now, and they clung to the frozen ground. Soon it would begin to accumulate, and then they could make snowmen and snowballs.

Someone tugged on her skirt, and she glanced down to see Jonathan by her side. "Miss Merry, I want to go see Mr. Clay."

Merry knelt beside him. "I'm sorry, Jonathan, but we can't do that. Children aren't allowed in the jail."

"But I gots to see him. He might forget our secret."

Her heart broke at the anxiety and fear in the boy's eyes. "I don't think he will. What is your secret? I can ask him for you."

His eyes opened wide and his mouth dropped open. Jonathan shook his head. "No. If I tell, it's not a secret no more."

She hugged him close. "OK. It is your secret, so you don't have to tell me, but I'll bet Mr. Clay hasn't forgotten it." Through the window she spotted her father riding up. "Papa's here. He'll be inside in a few minutes and can tell us more about Mr. Clay."

Jonathan returned to the dining room and grabbed a cookie. In a few minutes Papa came in, and the big grin on his face brought instant hope and joy to Merry's heart.

"Merry, Louise, I have great news." He motioned for them to come into the parlor. "You children stay right there. I have something I have to tell Mama, Merry, and Grandma."

Once in the parlor he closed the glass doors behind him. "Jake Starnes sent a wire from Barton Creek. He and his wife, Lucy, are on their way here. Jake is indeed Lily's cousin."

Mama hugged his neck. "That is wonderful news. When will they be here?"

"Saturday on the train from Barton Creek to Wichita. They'll stay over and go back on the Monday train down to Oklahoma."

"I must run up and tell Lily. This will be so wonderful for her." Mama left, and Grandma followed her.

"Oh, Papa, now we can tell Sheriff Devlin the truth and Clay will be free." Merry's heart danced with the joy that had eluded her for days. At last she could truly enjoy Christmas. Clay would even be out in time to help her with the Christmas pageant on Saturday at church. If she could have anything she wanted for Christmas, it would be the gift of Clay's release.

"I went over and told Cora and Stanley Barlow the news before I came home. They're just as excited about it as you are. They're going to visit Clay and show the telegram to the sheriff. I thought it would be better coming from them. It's time this town sees what kind of man Clay Barlow really is."

"Thank you for doing that. I know how worried his ma has been. This will give her the hope she needs for Clay." She headed for the door. "We promised the children a few minutes of play in the snow before it gets dark. I'll go take them out now."

She headed back to the parlor with a heart much lighter and happier than it had been in several weeks. Now if only they could come up with a way to grant Jonathan's Christmas wish.

Cora held tight to Stanley's arm as they made their way down to the jail. Snow swirled about them in flakes that clung to their coats and hats, but it could be forty below freezing and she wouldn't feel it. The warmth of Frank Warner's news filled her with enough heat to ward off any chill from the air.

Stanley stopped when they reached the sheriff's office. "We have to speak with Clay privately. When I was in yesterday, those robber friends of Karl wouldn't shut up. We kept our voices low, but we really couldn't say much in fear of their hearing us."

"What can Sheriff Devlin do about that?" She too wanted privacy, as this was her first time to visit him in jail. He'd insisted that she stay away, most likely because he didn't want her to be around those men.

"I'm not sure, but I'll talk with the sheriff and see what we can come up with."

She followed him through the door to where Sheriff Devlin sat going through a stack of papers that looked like wanted posters.

Stanley pulled Cora to his side. "Sheriff, we need a private moment with our son."

The sheriff leaned back in his chair. "How am I going to do that?"

"I don't know, but it's imperative that we do. We have news he must hear, but we don't want anyone else to hear it."

"I see." The sheriff stroked his chin a minute and stared at them. He must have seen the pleading in their eyes, for the next thing he did was to reach for the keys to the cell area. "I'll bring him out here, but only for a minute or two. Can't have that other bunch wanting the same privileges."

Stanley's hand squeezed hers. "We understand, and it won't take but a minute or so."

Cora held her breath while the sheriff unlocked the door and then returned a few seconds later with Clay in handcuffs. She ran to him and wrapped her arms around him. Her heart beat like a trip-hammer, but she held her son.

"I'll be back here in the cells. The door will be open, so don't try anything." He stared at them hard for a few seconds then went back to the cells.

Cora pulled back and took Clay's hand. "Pa has wonderful news for you. You'll be out of here as soon as we tell the sheriff what really went on last Saturday night."

Clay turned to Pa, hope dawning in his eyes. "What's happened?"

"We heard from Lily's cousin. He and his wife are coming up this Saturday to get her. They'll go back to Oklahoma on Monday morning's train."

Relief and joy filled Clay's face. "Are you sure? The judge came in today, and he's set the trial for Monday."

Pa pulled out a piece of paper. "Here's the wire that proves Jake Starnes is Lily's cousin. Frank Warner asked us to wait until the wire came so we'd have proof to convince the sheriff of Lily's story."

Before Clay could answer them, the sheriff stepped back into the office. "Time's up, folks. Sorry, but I have to put him back there." He motioned for Clay to come. "For what it's worth, I don't really believe you're guilty, but I can't do anything unless we can find some proof you're not."

Stanley glanced over at Clay, who nodded. "Sheriff, we have the proof to release our son. His ma and I have known the truth but couldn't reveal it until now."

Clay handed the telegram to Sheriff Devlin, who scanned it quickly. "What does this mean?" he asked.

Stanley grasped Cora's arm as he told the sheriff what they'd learned about Lily. Cora's heart beat so fast and hard she could barely catch her breath. The story sounded almost unbelievable, but she'd lived it, and every word Stanley uttered was the pure and simple truth.

When Stanley finished the story, Devlin shook his head. "It's about time someone told me what was going on. That story's far-fetched enough to be true, but I can't let him out until I speak with Lily myself. You say she's up at Holly Hill?"

"Yes, Louise Warner and Mrs. Collins are taking care of her. Please promise you won't say anything to the Vaughns until she's gone."

Devlin rubbed his chin and shook his head. "Not sure I can do that if they come asking for help again, but I can keep them away from her since they have no legal claims on her."

Stanley stood and grasped the sheriff's hand. "Thank you. Mrs. Barlow and I will sleep much better knowing Clay will be set free."

"He'll stay here until I can speak with Lily tomorrow. Then I'll stop by for a visit with Mr. and Mrs. Vaughn. We may have charges against them if Lily wants that."

"Thank you. That's all we can ask." Stanley gripped Cora's arm. "It's time for us to be going, and we hope this is the last time we have to visit him in jail."

After hugging Clay one last time, Cora bit her lip then

hastened to follow Stanley. On the boardwalk outside they met Mrs. Brooks coming from the bakery with several covered baskets.

"Mr. and Mrs. Warner, good evening. I'm just taking dinner in to our prisoners." She looked down at her baskets then back up to Cora and Stanley. "I made supper for the boys tonight, and I've got something special in here for Clay. I know how he always liked my nut bread at Christmas, so I put some in for him. And just so you know, I don't believe for a minute that he had anything to do with this whole thing."

Cora's lip quivered. "Thank you. It's good to know that some people in this town believe in him. We'll get through this. His innocence will be proven."

"I hope so. Now I'd better get this inside before it freezes here in the cold." She grinned. "It'll be nice to have snow for Christmas. Good night."

She stepped around them and into the sheriff's office. Cora snuggled close to Stanley. "Let's get home where it's warm. I made some berry cobbler from those berries I canned last summer, and I'm thinking it will taste good with a cup of hot coffee."

"You're speaking my language, my dear. Now that the situation with Clay is nearly resolved, I could stand a little something to eat."

Cora's head filled with all the things she wanted to do for Clay when he was released—like preparing for the family's best Christmas in years.

Clay accepted the basket from Mrs. Brooks and sat back on his cot to enjoy his meal. For the first time since his arrest, his hope bloomed full. Merry's note had given him a glimpse of it, but Pa's message had sealed it. Maybe those prayers were working after all.

Soon as he could get out of this place, he'd start working toward making Jonathan's Christmas a merry one too. That little boy deserved a good, happy time after what he'd been through. The words of Jonathan's request came back to him. If that little boy wanted Clay to be his pa, then that's what he'd work toward. Of course he needed a ma too, and if all went as Clay would like for it to go, Merry would be that for Jonathan.

Merry loved Jonathan as much as he did, but did she love the boy enough to be his ma? For that matter, did she even love Clay at all? From what he'd sensed when he'd been with her, she did care, but it would take a heap more than caring for her to consent to be his wife.

Clay ate the fried chicken with his mouth watering for more. When he finished, he put the plate and utensils back in the basket and spotted a wrapped packet in the basket. He opened it and found his favorite nut bread from Mrs. Brooks. She'd remembered after all these years. He sank his teeth into the thick slab and savored the nutty pecan flavor.

Karl and his men finished their eating, and Karl hollered out, "What are you eating there, Clay? We didn't get no dessert like that."

Clay wanted to laud it over Karl but decided he was one man that didn't need to be riled any more than he was.

"It's just bread, Karl. Nothing fancy." Clay stuffed the last bite into his mouth and wished for some of Ma's hot coffee to wash it down. He put the dishes and utensils back into his basket and covered it with the piece of cloth.

Karl and the others settled down to a game of cards, the three of them mumbling among themselves. Clay stood and gazed out through the bars to the back alley that was now almost covered with snow. At least the stove back here kept the cells somewhat warm. He returned to the cot and lay down.

With his hands behind his head, he stared up at the ceiling for a minute or two then closed his eyes. *Lord, I haven't talked to You much in the past seven years, but I feel the need to do so now. Please give the Starnes a safe journey, and let them be Lily's kin. She needs to be with her own family. Thank You for people like those at Holly Hill and for Ma and Pa. Thank You for taking care of me. I've been so wrong all these years...*

He stopped and considered his next request. If God answered prayer, he might as well pray for what he'd really like to have. *And Lord, if it's OK with You, I sure would like it if Merry loved me enough to be my wife.*

There, he'd said it. He loved her with all his heart, and if he could have one gift for Christmas, it would be her love in return.

Chapter 25

ERRY STOOD ON the top step to the school and watched the children whoop and holler as the school day ended and the holidays began. Snowballs flew fast and furious as the boys played in the school yard. Pa waited for the Holly Hill children with the wagon. She waved at him and wrapped her coat tighter about her shoulders.

He jumped down from the wagon and headed toward her, leading her mare. "Brought you a ride home so you wouldn't have to walk so far. I figured you wouldn't be ready to leave with the children, so here's Duchess for your ride home. We'll have some news for you when you get there."

They must have heard from Jake Starnes again. "Thanks, Papa. I do have some things to finish up here. I also thought I'd drop by to visit with Mr. and Mrs. Barlow for a few minutes."

"All right." A twinkle sparkled in his eye. "We'll see you at home, but be careful. Looks like these clouds might hold more snow for us."

"I will, and if it's snowing when I leave here, I'll come straight on home." After he left, she caressed the nose of her horse. "I won't keep you waiting out here too long," she promised Duchess. Even though Papa had covered the mare's back with a heavy blanket, Merry didn't intend to subject the horse to the freezing temperatures very long.

She hurried back inside and began collecting what she would need the next two weeks and shoved them into her satchel. The students had free time with no assignments, but the teacher always had papers to grade and lessons to prepare. She placed the upper-grade essays in her satchel then closed it with a snap.

With the stove put out as the children left, the room already had a chill to it. No need to stay there any longer than necessary. She glanced around the room to make sure the children had left nothing they would need in the next two weeks before reaching for her hat and gloves. The scarf Grandma had knitted sure came in handy today. She wrapped the woolen piece around her neck then pulled on her gloves.

Outside she mounted her horse and turned up the street toward the middle of town. The snow hadn't started yet, so she headed for the Barlow's store. How she wished she could stop in at the jail and see Clay, but the sheriff wouldn't allow it, and no amount of argument on her side could change his mind. A visit with his parents would have to suffice.

She hitched Duchess to the post outside the store and hurried inside to the warmth of the stove there. "Good afternoon, Mr. Barlow. The stove sure feels good." She'd only been outside for a few minutes, but the cold had penetrated her cloak to her bones.

"What are you doing out in this? You ought to be home

where it's nice and warm." He came around the counter to greet her.

"I'm on my way there, but I wanted to stop and see you and Mrs. Barlow for a few minutes."

"The missus is upstairs." He strode to the door and turned the sign over to indicate he was closed. "I was fixing to close anyway. We haven't had any customers in the last hour, and with more snow threatening, there probably won't be more. Come on upstairs. Mrs. Barlow will have some hot tea for you if you like." He motioned for her to go upstairs.

"That would be wonderful. I much prefer tea to coffee."

When they stepped into the parlor, Mr. Barlow called for his wife. "Cora, we have a visitor."

Mrs. Barlow hurried from the bedroom and stopped short when she saw Merry. "Oh, my, dear, what are you doing out in this weather? You should be home already."

"I told her the same thing, but she insisted on visiting with us." Mr. Barlow pulled out a chair at the dining table. "I told her that you'd have a cup of tea for her too."

"Oh, that I do. Just a minute." She reached over for the kettle of hot water sitting on the back burner of the stove and began preparing the tea.

Merry removed her hat and scarf and laid them aside along with her cloak. Both Mr. and Mrs. Barlow appeared to be in good moods. The visit with Clay must have gone well. "I stopped by to find out how it went yesterday when you told Clay the news about the Starnes coming for Lily."

Mrs. Barlow set a cup of tea in front of Merry as well as a plate of shortbread cookies. "He was so happy and as excited with the news as we were." She grinned and nodded to her husband. "But that's not all that happened. Tell her, Stanley."

As Mr. Barlow revealed the fact that the sheriff now knew about Lily and had even planned to visit with her today, Merry's heart began to thud in her chest. Clay would be free, most likely later today. That must be the surprise Papa mentioned.

Merry clapped her hands as Mr. Barlow concluded. "That's the most wonderful thing I've heard in weeks. Oh, this Christmas is going to be the best one yet."

Then the memory of her attack dimmed the joy. In all the confusion of the past two weeks, she'd forgotten about it. "Mr. and Mrs. Barlow, something else happened that I haven't told anyone about. The Saturday night of the box social, I was on my way home when a man grabbed me and held me. He said for me to tell Clay he'd better do what he'd been told, or people he loved would be hurt. He said it was a warning for Clay."

Mrs. Barlow gasped and her hands covered her mouth. Mr. Barlow's fist hit the table. "I knew it. Karl was scheming all along to get Clay mixed up with his thieving ways. I found a note in Clay's room, but I had no idea what it could mean. Now I do." He stood and grabbed his hat. "I bet if I tell the sheriff this and show him that note, it'll take some air out of Karl's accusations, and he'll let Clay go and not wait for the judge. I'm going over there right now."

Both Merry and Mrs. Barlow jumped up. Mrs. Barlow grabbed her husband's arm. "Do you really think so?"

"Leave it to me. I'll take care of it." With that he buttoned up his coat, jammed his hat on his head, and almost ran out the door.

Mrs. Barlow plopped back in her chair, her hand fanning

her face. "Oh, my, I do hope the sheriff will listen and believe the note."

"I'm sure he will. Sheriff Devlin is fair, and he already seems to believe your story about Lily."

"I pray you're right." She leaned on the table and peered at Merry. "You care a great deal about him, don't you?"

"Yes, ma'am, I do. To be honest, I love him. I've loved him ever since we were sixteen years old and he kissed me behind the church." Heat flooded Merry's face. Why had she said that? She'd never told anyone, not even her best friend, about that kiss.

Mrs. Barlow smiled and reached across for Merry's hand. "That's good, my child. I couldn't choose anyone better for our son than a girl like you. I'm so thankful the Lord saw fit to bring your family back to Prairie Grove so you could be here when he returned."

"I don't know about that, but it seems as if Clay isn't all that happy I'm here. He's nice to me some of the time, and then other times he avoids me or tells me we can't be friends. He says he doesn't want to hurt my reputation because Mr. Pennyfeather might tell the school board they have to let me go if I'm friends with him. And now there's Lily in his life."

Not that she really cared what the school board thought anymore. If her teaching skills and the love of her students didn't mean anything to the school board, then she was better off not teaching. But the thought of Clay caring for Lily did hurt.

"I don't think you have to worry about Lily. Clay wanted to help her out and that's all." She softened her eyes and smiled. "You know what his behavior tells me? He cares a great deal about you, but out of concern for your reputation, he has not been able to fully express those feelings."

"Do you really think so?" Hope blossomed full force in her heart for a future with the man she loved. If Clay could be released from jail tonight, all would be perfect.

Clay stood by the window of the cell, counting the hours until he could hear good news and be released. He'd learned to block out most of what Karl and his men said, but their barbs could still hurt on occasion. He couldn't wait to prove them wrong. He'd prayed again this morning for patience to hold out until the truth could be revealed.

"Clay, you have a visitor." The sheriff unlocked the cell door and opened it. "I'm taking you to my office, where we need to talk."

Karl gripped the bars of his cell and shouted, "Why does he get to go out and be free and have visitors? We have rights too."

"Shut up, Karl. If and when you have a visitor, I might consider it, but not likely." He handcuffed Clay then led him to the outer office.

Pa jumped to his feet when Clay appeared. "Son, we have some news that I've shared with the sheriff. I found a note in your room that explains a lot."

Found the note? The one Karl had left on the outside stairway. That alone wasn't enough to clear him, but hope still crept into his heart.

"Sit down so we can discuss this." The sheriff pulled another chair up to his desk and motioned for Clay to sit.

"Now, your pa showed me this note, and he told me about something that happened with Miss Warner that might be of interest as well."

A vise clamped Clay's heart. He must be talking about the night Ollie said he waylaid her and talked with her.

Pa propped his elbows on the chair arms. "It seems that the night of the box supper, one of Karl's men stopped Merry on her way home and gave her a warning to give to you. He told her to tell you that if you didn't cooperate with Karl, people you cared about would be hurt. Merry was upset and afraid to tell her parents. Then all the confusion of the next two weeks shoved it from her mind until this afternoon when she stopped by to visit Ma and me."

Anger boiled in Clay as he remembered the night of the box supper. So Ollie's story was true. Clay clenched his hands into fists at his side. Just one good punch at that ugly face, that's all he wanted…one good punch. Merry could well have been hurt by that man. Clay would never forgive himself for inadvertently putting her in harm's way.

"That's the same night Karl grabbed me in the alley and warned me of the same thing. I found the note when I came home that night. I had no idea what Karl was up to." The sheriff started to speak. Clay held up his cuffed hands. "I know, I know. I should have told you I'd heard from Karl and about the note, but I was too worried about what he might do to Ma and Pa and Merry if I did. For that I'm sorry. You might have been able to catch Karl before he robbed the bank."

"It sure would have made things a sight easier if we'd known Karl was still hiding out in these parts. As it is, we recovered the money, so the bank's OK. The problem is what

I'm going to do with you now that this has come to light. If I let you go, the people in town will be riled up, and Karl will keep insisting you helped him."

Clay leaned forward. "What did you learn from Lily today?"

"She supports your story, and with the telegram from her cousin in Oklahoma, I have to believe it isn't something she made up to get away from the Vaughns."

"Then let my son go, Sheriff. He's innocent."

"I know that and you know that, but the people in town don't and won't take any explanations from me or you. If he can stay here until Monday when the judge comes, then his release will be official, and no one can do anything about it. They may complain, but that's all they can do."

He leaned back in his chair. "If I let you go now, what would you plan to do?"

"Get on with helping Lily get out of town and making sure nothing happens to any of us before then." Clay held his breath waiting for the sheriff to make his decision.

A hint of a smile crossed Devlin's face. "I tell you what I'll do. I'll let you go free and tell people new evidence has been found that will prove your innocence. If they want to know what, I'll tell them they'll have to wait until the trial."

Pa stood and leaned over to pump the sheriff's hand. "Thank you. My son here believed you'd see the situation and help us."

"Just don't make me sorry for my decision." He unlocked the handcuffs. "I'll get your stuff, and you can get on out of here."

Clay rubbed his wrists, his mind whirling with things that

needed to be done. His first destination would be Holly Hill. He had to see Merry and Lily. Then a whiff of his own essence caused him to stop and think. Make that first stop at home for a good bath and a shave. No sense showing up at Holly Hill smelling like a polecat that'd just been riled.

When the sheriff returned, the curses from Karl and his men followed Clay. "Come on, Pa, let's get out of here. I've heard enough from those three to last a lifetime."

He shoved on his hat and pulled up the collar of his coat. When he and Pa stepped out into the cold, Clay breathed deeply. Freedom had never smelled so good.

Chapter 26

ACK FROM HER visit at the Barlows, Merry hurried inside the house with new snow beginning to fall around her. This would make for a great Christmas, but a lot of work for Papa and Henry.

Jonathan greeted her with a big hug around her legs before she could even remove her cloak. "Hello, my little buddy. Let me take off my cloak and gloves, and then I'll pick you up."

He stepped back with a solemn expression in his eyes that melted Merry's heart. She dropped her cloak and hat on the hall bench and gathered the child up in her arms. "What's troubling you, Jonathan?"

He blinked his eyes and his lip quivered. "Mr. Clay. I has to see him."

Merry stood, holding him in her arms. "I know you do, but it's impossible for you to see him now. Look, we're having more snow outside. Maybe Papa can put the runners on the wagon and we can go for a sleigh ride. Won't that be fun?"

Jonathan didn't say anything but shook his head against her shoulder. She carried him into the kitchen where Mama and Grandma prepared supper. "Do you need me to do anything for dinner? I want to spend time with Jonathan. He could use some cheering up."

Mama stopped chopping carrots and peered at the boy. "He's been looking forward to your coming home all afternoon. Go on and sit with him a while. We can handle things here. Ask Emmaline and Susie to come in and set the table."

On her way back to the parlor Papa came through the door. "I took care of your horse for you. Henry and I are outfitting the wagon so we can use it as a sleigh to get into town tomorrow to meet Jake and Lucy's train. After supper we have more good news for you."

"Thank you, Papa." Then she grinned and whirled around with Jonathan. "I already know your news. The Barlows told me." She lifted Jonathan's chin so she looked him in the eye. "See, Papa is fixing us up a sleigh, and we'll go riding in it tomorrow."

"I even put bells on the harness so they'll jingle when we're riding. You'll like that." Papa cupped his hand around Jonathan's head and leaned over to kiss him. "It'll be a lot of fun." He glanced up at Merry. "I'm glad they told you about Clay, but he probably won't be released until the judge arrives on Monday."

Merry reached up and kissed her father's cheek. "Thank you, but I wouldn't be too sure about that." Jonathan snuggled against her neck. "I'm going to take him into the parlor and read a bit to him. He misses Clay."

"That'll all be over soon, and Clay will be here to visit. Maybe you can keep him entertained until then."

Merry nodded and went into the parlor where Emmaline

and Susie read while the twins played with their dolls. "Emmaline, Mama needs you and Susie to come help set the table. I'm going to read to Jonathan, so I'll watch the twins. Where are the boys?"

Emmaline marked the place in her book and puffed out her breath in a mild protest. Guilt filled Merry as she realized Emmaline had set the table and helped with supper every night this past week because Merry had other things to do. She'd have to make it up to her sister during the Christmas break.

"They all went out to the barn with Henry. He said Papa was going to put runners on the wagon, so they wanted to watch." She laid her book aside. "Come on, Susie, I guess we have work to do."

After they left, Merry sat down with Jonathan on the sofa. "Is there a special book you want me to read?"

"Uh-uh, tell me about Baby Jesus." He clung tight to her arms.

Merry snuggled him close to her chest. "That's always a good story. Now let me see. Where shall we start?"

She held the boy close and told the story of Baby Jesus. No matter how many times she heard or recited the events of that holy night, she'd never grow tired of it. As she came to a close with the shepherds' visit, Jonathan tilted his head back and stared at her.

"What is it? Didn't I tell it right?" Something in his dark eyes didn't sit right with her.

His mouth puckered up, and he frowned like he was in deep thought. Then his words burst forth. "Will you be my ma, Miss Merry?"

Merry's heart lurched in her chest. He'd hinted at such a thing before, but now he'd come right out and asked. How could she answer him? She had no right to be his mother unless she could adopt him, and without a husband, that wasn't likely to happen.

"I'd like to be your ma too, but that's not possible right now. You know what, I bet there's a wonderful young couple out there somewhere who would just love to have you as their little boy."

"Don't want them. I want you." He folded his arms across his chest and stuck out his bottom lip.

Now what could she say? She needed a whole lot of Mama's and Grandma's wisdom right now. She cuddled him again and swallowed hard. "We'll have to wait and see what Jesus works out for us."

After supper Merry helped clean up the kitchen while Grandma sat with Jonathan and the boys. When she told her mother what had happened earlier, Mama dried her hands and led Merry to the kitchen table.

"We need to talk about this, Merry. Jonathan has become way too attached to you. I've seen it happening, but I didn't really know what to do about it. Maybe in the future it'll be best if Grandma and I take over his care."

"He misses Clay so much. If Clay comes around to see him after all this jail stuff is over, then maybe Jonathan will feel better and not depend on me so much." She wanted to see Clay as much as Jonathan, but for very different reasons. With both of them here, they could give Jonathan a little more attention. Between the two of them, maybe a smile could be brought back to the little boy's face.

Papa called from the dining room. "Merry, you have a visitor out here." His voice sounded like something amused him.

Who in the world could be visiting in this snow? She dried her hands and untied her apron. Her mother did the same and followed her from the kitchen.

When Merry reached the entry hall, she stopped dead in her tracks, her hands flying to her mouth. Clay!

The look on Merry's face sent Clay's heart somersaulting, and joy rose in his soul. "Yes, I'm here, and it's a long story."

She rushed toward him as though she would fling her arms about his neck, but she stopped just inches short of him and blinked her eyes. "I can't believe you're free. I hoped you would be after your pa gave the sheriff the note you'd found and told him my story too."

Clay frowned. "That's something we need to discuss, Merry. You should have told me or your parents about that right away. Ollie bragged about it in jail." He clenched his fists at his side to keep from grabbing her around the waist. The anger he'd held because she'd kept the attack secret melted at the look of remorse on her face.

Mrs. Warner did explode in anger. "Merry Warner, what is he talking about? You got attacked and didn't say anything?" She turned to Mr. Warner. "Did you know anything about this?"

He looked as stunned and angry as Clay had been. "No, I didn't. Seems we're going to have to have a little talk. What exactly happened?"

"I'm so sorry. I was more angry than scared, and then all

that other happened, and it got shoved out of my mind. He just grabbed my arm and gave me the warning to give to Clay, and I never did. If I had, then you could have been more careful. Please forgive me."

Mrs. Warner hugged her tight against her chest, but fire still burned in Mr. Warner's eyes and the look he sent Clay's way burned its way into his soul.

After Mrs. Warner finished scolding Merry, she turned to Clay. "You better make sure nothing like this ever happens again."

"Believe me, I will." He'd welcome the chance to watch over her and keep her safe.

Merry blinked her eyes and shook her head. What that meant he couldn't tell. He'd never understand some of the things women did.

Clay glanced about the room. The boys must be upstairs, but the girls sat in the parlor playing a game of pick-up sticks with Henry. Clay lowered his voice. "May I go up to see Lily?"

Merry's eyes clouded, and she shook her head. "Now's not a good time. The boys might hear you, and Jonathan will come apart when he sees you."

Jonathan. Of course he had to see the little boy first.

Emmaline sidled up to Merry. "Is Lily that girl you have up in the attic room?"

Merry gasped. "How…how did you know that?"

"Henry saw her when she first came, and then I saw you take a tray up to the attic room."

"But you never said a word."

A frown crept across Emmaline's face. "We can keep a secret just as well as some other people around here." Then she grinned. "We figured it had to be pretty important for you to go to that much trouble to keep it a secret."

Merry placed her hands on Emmaline's shoulders. "Yes, it is very important that we keep her presence a secret. We don't want some people in town to know she's here and try to take her away."

"You mean Mr. Vaughn? I don't like him. He scares me."

This girl was far more perceptive than either he or Merry had given her credit for. They'd have to fill her in on most of the details to keep her curiosity from leaking information.

Mr. Warner reached for Emmaline's hand. "Lily is in danger from the Vaughns. They're not her real parents, and we think we've found her family. They're coming tomorrow to see her."

Merry added, "So you see how important it is for all of you to keep absolutely quiet about her being here until her family can take her home. We have to protect her."

The twins and Susie had joined the group, and Merry included all of them and Henry in her warning. Clay looked at each of them as Merry explained the situation with Lily. How wonderful it would be to have a family like this. Ma and Pa were great, but having this many family members around would be fun. He had liked being an only child, but often he'd wished for brothers and sisters to play and share life with.

A commotion sounded at the top of the stairs, and a little boy scrambled down with his arms held high. At the bottom he made a running leap right into Clay's arms. "Mr. Clay, Mr. Clay, you came. I prayed you would." He placed his mouth close to Clay's ear. "'Member our secret?"

Clay squeezed his eyes shut as tears threatened to spill out.

"You bet I do. How could I forget something as good as that?" Holding that little boy was as natural as breathing, and until this moment Clay hadn't fully realized how much he loved the bundle of energy now squirming in his arms.

Jonathan slipped from Clay's arm but clung to his hand. There'd be no seeing Lily until this young man went to bed. Mrs. Collins and Mrs. Warner rounded up the children.

"Come into the kitchen with Grandma and me. We'll have us a bedtime snack." Mrs. Warner winked at Merry and picked up Jonathan despite his protests.

When the troupe had gone into the kitchen, Mr. Warner nodded toward the other room. "Let's go into the parlor where we can talk."

Clay would much prefer being alone with Merry, but her father's presence right now was a good thing. No telling what his tongue might blurt out if her father didn't sit right across from him.

He settled back into a chair and crossed one foot over his knee. "Now tell us how you came to be free."

Clay explained what had happened. "Sheriff Devlin is going to wait until the trial on Monday and after the train has left for Oklahoma to tell the real story of that night. Right now he's just going to tell people he has some new evidence he can't discuss until the judge gets here."

"Do you think it will work?" Merry's fingers kneaded the folds of her skirt, worry filling her eyes.

"Yes, I do. Karl and his gang weren't too happy about my being let go, but the sheriff just told them to pipe down." At least that was the gist of it. He wasn't about to tell her the language Devlin had really used, but judging from the amused look in Mr. Warner's eyes, he already knew.

Merry slumped back against the sofa. "This is just amazing. I still can't believe you're actually sitting here across from me. This is the best thing that could have happened for Jonathan. He's cried every day and night to see you."

That news wrenched his heart. "I'm so sorry. I love that little boy. He has a way of working into a person's heart like nothing I ever saw." *Except for you, Miss Merry Warner.*

"I know. He's done that to all of us. It's so sad that his aunt and uncle can't take him, but I'm glad he has us to love him."

By us did she mean the two of them or her family? Probably her family, but he'd be included. "I hope we can make this the best Christmas possible for him without his family, although he seems to fit in as part of this big family."

Mr. Warner stood and reached out to shake Clay's hand. "He does, and he will until somebody comes to claim him or he grows up and leaves us. Now I'm going to join the children for that snack. If you'll excuse me."

Excited chatter burst through from the kitchen when he entered.

"Sounds like they're having a good time."

Merry twisted her hands again in her lap and gazed toward the closed kitchen door. "Yes, with it being a Friday and the beginning of the holiday, they'll probably be up later than usual."

"May I wait around until they're all in bed and then see Lily?" He really wanted to check on her and let her know he hadn't forgotten about her. Of course she knew he'd been in jail, but still he needed to see her.

"I suppose that will be all right."

Her words agreed, but Clay spotted doubt in her eyes. She tugged at her skirt and twisted her fingers around a fold. Light dawned in his head. She was jealous of his interest in Lily. He had to do something to squelch that idea.

Merry sent him a sidelong glance, probably wondering about his silence. "I can get you some coffee and a piece of Mama's custard pie if you'd like."

He crossed the room and took her hands into his and waited until she raised her head to look him in the eyes. "That will be fine, but right now all I want to do is be with you. After this is all over, I have so much that needs to be said."

Her eyes brightened, and a sparkle that had been missing before now shone there. "You want to be with me?" She moved her hands to hold tight to his. "That's all I want, and I have much that needs to be said to you too." A smile turned up one corner of her mouth.

Clay's heart filled with hope. Two, maybe three days, and he could speak what was truly on his heart. Monday now seemed an eternity away.

Chapter 27

ON SATURDAY MERRY joined her parents to greet the train bringing Jake and Lucy Starnes to Prairie Grove. While they waited for them to arrive, Merry remembered last night. What a momentous day it had turned out to be. First her visit with the Barlows, Clay's surprise arrival, and then Clay's hinting that he planned to say more to her at the right time.

The best part had been to see Jonathan with Clay. Clay's gentleness with the little boy warmed her heart and increased her love for them both. And when she finally took Clay to visit Lily, their behavior together laid her final fears to rest. Lily was nothing but grateful, and Clay's compassion and concern for her proved what an honorable man he had become. Any woman would be proud to be seen with Clay Barlow, and if God chose to answer her prayers, she would be that woman.

The shrill blast from the train broke through the morning air, and the engine chugged into the station followed by a baggage car and one passenger car. When Lucy and Jake stepped off the train, she recognized them immediately, but her attention went straight to the young man stepping down behind them.

She and her mother yelled "Zach!" at the same time and ran forward. Mama wrapped her arms around the tall cowboy. "I'm so glad you made it home. I was afraid none of you would make it with all the snow we've had."

He reached out for Merry and drew her to his side. "The snow's not so heavy down Oklahoma way, so we had no trouble at all."

Lucy Starnes grasped her husband's arm and grinned. "We tried to get him to let us tell you he was coming with us, but he wanted to surprise you."

"Well, he certainly did that. We weren't expecting him until Christmas Eve." Mama hung on to Zach like he might run off and disappear any minute.

Having Zach home early would make this next week go a lot faster and be a lot livelier. She turned to greet Lucy Starnes. The young woman was even more beautiful than Merry remembered from last summer. Her raven hair was piled on her head in a style that supported her deep maroon hat with ease. Jake was as handsome as ever and looked the part of a rancher with his boots, western coat, string tie, and Stetson hat. His blue eyes, identical to Lily's, sealed the fact of their kinship.

Mama took charge. "Let's get out of this cold and up to Holly Hill. Lily will be excited to see you. She's been beside herself with joy since we told her you were coming."

Another couple stepped off the train. They were a handsome pair and strangers. Somebody else must be expecting visitors for Christmas. She heard them ask for directions to the hotel. Strange. If they were visiting family, someone should be there to meet them. Oh, well, they were none of her concern. She turned back to hear what Jake said to her parents.

"I have some news about our family that I hope will make her even happier that we've come for her." True concern laced his voice and calmed Merry's concerns about his feelings toward his cousin.

Clay came up to greet them and introduced himself to Jake Starnes. "So you're the one I can thank for rescuing my cousin?" Jake asked.

"Yes, and I was glad to do it, and I'd do it again," Clay replied. The two men shook hands. A look passed between them, and Merry could only imagine the meaning behind it. Jake may be a few years younger, but he stood eye to eye with Clay with shoulders as broad.

The two men retrieved baggage from the cart and carried it to the carriage Papa and Mama had driven into town. Papa had attached the curtains to the sides to give more protection from the cold. Jake helped Lucy on board then Mama. He turned to assist her, but Clay intervened.

"Mr. and Mrs. Warner, would you mind if Merry rode up to Holly Hill with me? That is, if it's all right with her."

Papa's grin almost split his face in half. There was no doubt about how he felt about Clay, which only gave her more hope as to the future she could have with him if he'd quit being so evasive. Half an hour alone last night and all he'd really said was that they needed to talk. She had some things to say to him, but until he let her know exactly where he stood, she'd have to keep quiet.

"Go right ahead, Merry. We'll meet you up at the house. We'll all have a fine visit."

Zach eyed her with that familiar teasing expression on his face. "Hmm, I think I've missed something here." He winked then climbed into the carriage with the ladies.

Papa and Jake joined him, and the carriage rolled away from town and up to Holly Hill. Clay grasped her elbow. "If you'll follow me to the livery, I have a buggy waiting for us."

She walked by his side, her long skirt swishing in the snow. Her hem would be damp when they reached home, but she could be covered in snow herself and not feel a bit of cold. Her heart and soul were that warm with Clay beside her.

Not many people were out in the streets on this snowy Saturday morning. Most of those who came into town for supplies went into the businesses and took care of their needs where it was warm. No visiting and loitering in the streets today.

Neither of them spoke as they reached the livery and Clay brought over the buggy that had been outfitted with sled runners. He'd hitched his own horse to it, and Merry patted his nose before letting Clay assist her up onto the seat. He strode around and climbed up beside her. Why couldn't she think of anything to say? Plenty of words had come to her in her daydreams of being with him.

He turned his dark brown eyes to hers with a gaze she could have drunk from all day. "I'm glad your brother was able to come home early. Your ma sure was glad to see him."

"He said in his letters that he planned to stay until the first week of January. The boys will certainly have fun with him."

Her brother was the last thing she wanted to talk about, but nothing else would come to mind.

When they reached the edge of town, Clay reached over for her hand. "When this is all over, we're going to have that talk I mentioned before. There are a few things we need to settle between us, but we must wait until I'm officially cleared by the judge of any involvement in the bank robbery. Maybe then the people of this town will see me for who I am today and not who I was five years ago."

"I know they will. They have to. Look at how many people love you and support you now. Women like Mrs. Pennyfeather and Mrs. Hickman don't really count. We had special prayer for you at church. Reverend Tate has faith in you." It had given her great joy and comfort to hear the reverend's prayer on Sunday for Clay. It had taken some of the sting out of the unkind words from others.

"I'm thankful for his belief in me. I realized how God has been working in my life to take me where He wants me to go and be the man I should have been before I got mixed up with Karl."

"That's all in the past now. Let's think ahead to the future and what a wonderful Christmas this is going to be." And the only thing to make it even better would be to hear him say he loved her.

They approached Holly Hill, and once again the beautiful home now decorated with green garlands and red bows across the front filled his heart with a longing for a home of his own. The shiny ornaments on the tree sparkled through the window, and the movement of the people beyond those great windows spoke of reunion and hope.

He hitched the sleigh to the post and helped Merry down. If all went as he'd prayed and hoped, he'd ask her to marry him Christmas Eve. If she said yes, it would be the best day of his life.

They hurried up to the house and inside to find everyone laughing and talking in the parlor. He helped Merry off with her cloak just in time to feel little arms circle his legs. "Now I wonder who could be trying to tackle me." He glanced down. "Well, I do declare, it's a little elf. Are you here to help Santa?"

Mrs. Warner had dressed Jonathan in red and green for the season, and with his bright red cheeks and impish eyes, he did look like he belonged with Santa Claus. "No, Mr. Clay, it's me, Jonathan."

"Oh, I see it is. You had me fooled there for a minute." He reached down and picked up the boy and held him in the air. Jonathan giggled and reached for Clay's neck. He snuggled the boy against him and glanced at Merry. The love coming from her eyes gave promise of a bright, new relationship.

He carried Jonathan into the parlor where Mrs. Warner had trays of hot chocolate and cookies waiting. Lily had come down. She was dressed in one of Merry's dresses that had been altered to fit, and her hair was arranged in an attractive style, making her look quite grown up.

She sat now with her cousin and his wife. They certainly made a handsome couple, and from his experience with piece goods and women's apparel, the gown Lucy Starnes wore showed expensive tastes and background. Clay approached them now, but he hesitated to break into their reunion.

Lily reached out for his hand. "And I have this wonderful man to thank for rescuing me. He had it all so well planned." Her bright blue eyes sparkled with happiness.

Jake turned to Clay. "Yes, we met Clay at the station. Again I must thank you for all the trouble you went through."

"Like I said, I was glad to do it. The situation she was in was deplorable, and I'm hoping the sheriff will be able to do something about it before long." When people found out just how bad things were and why Lily had left, maybe there would be more incentive to make laws against child labor and hurting children. The Vaughns certainly would not be welcome in town after this. Their moving would be good riddance.

Merry joined them, sitting beside Clay. Jake grinned over at Lily. "Miss Warner, I was just telling her that when I received your wire, I began doing a little research on my own and found our grandmother. I thought she had died long ago and never even thought to look for her until now. Found out that she lives here in Kansas. She's meeting us Monday and will go back to Barton Creek with us for Christmas."

Merry reached over and hugged Lily. "Now that's really good news. I'm so happy for you."

Lily fairly bounced with excitement. "Isn't it wonderful? To think I'll actually have real family for the first time in a long time." Then her eyes darkened. "I only wish my baby sister could be here too. She's with a good family in Texas, so I guess I can be happy about that."

Mrs. Starnes reached over and grasped Lily's hand. "If we can find out where, then maybe we take you down for a visit and make contact with her again."

"Oh, that would be wonderful, Lucy." Tears welled in Lily's eyes. "I still can't believe all this is happening."

Someone knocked on the front door, and Mrs. Warner hastened to open it. A few moments later she led a young couple into the room. Merry gasped beside him. "It's the couple I saw at the station. What are they doing here?"

Mrs. Warner raised her hands. "Everyone, we have some very special guests with us. This is Mr. and Mrs. Thornton from Guthrie, Oklahoma."

Murmurs and questions circled the room. Merry stood and approached the couple. "I'm Merry Warner. I saw you at the station and heard you ask about the hotel. Are you staying long?"

Mrs. Thornton glanced up at her husband, who said, "That depends on what we have to do." He cleared his throat. "Mr. and Mrs. Warner, may we speak with you in private?"

Papa stepped forward. "Of course, we can go into the office." He led the couple to his office, and Mama followed.

Merry returned to sit beside him, concern written all over her face. "What's the matter? You look worried."

"What if they've come for Jonathan?"

Fear grabbed Clay's throat, and he couldn't swallow. Come for Jonathan? But his relatives said they didn't want him. Had they changed their minds? Not possible. From their nice clothes and staying in the hotel, this couple didn't look like they were in need. Jonathan's uncle had said they couldn't afford to take him in because of their own large family.

His curiosity was piqued as much as Merry's but without the concern she had. "I don't think so. They're not anything like Reverend Tate described as his folks."

"I hope not." Merry bit her lip and stared at the office door.

Lily frowned. "Is Jonathan the little boy that hung onto Clay until Mrs. Collins took him?"

"Yes, his parents and brother and sister died in a fire a few months back. Clay comforted him and brought him up here, and Clay's been his hero ever since."

Mrs. Warner stepped back into the room. She motioned for the twins to come to her. She led them back to the office and closed the door.

Merry gripped his arm. "They're here to adopt the twins. Oh, that would be wonderful for the girls." Then her eyes misted over. "I'll miss their bright smiles and personalities. They're so precious, but they deserve to have a mother and father who love and take care of them. Mama and Papa and all of us love them, but it's not the same."

Lucy looked to her husband, and he nodded. "Merry, I planned to tell your mother later, but we have some money we want to leave with you for Christmas. I know that your love is a great gift for them, but we want them to have some special things for Christmas."

"Thank you, Lucy. You are so generous. I'm sure Mama and Papa will appreciate whatever help you can give."

"You're doing a great work here, and one that's sorely needed. God will bless your home and give you more opportunities to help children in the days ahead. We plan to make a donation twice a year so you'll have whatever you need to keep things running smoothly."

Clay's mind could barely wrap around what this young couple wanted to do. Younger than he was, they showed more maturity than people much older. Then a question darted across his mind and pierced his heart. Merry made such a difference in the lives of these children and those in her classroom. Would it be wrong to take her away from them?

Chapter 28

AFTER A HARROWING week of charges against Clay
dropped, the adoption of the twins, departure of Lily
with her cousins, and getting ready for the Christmas pageant
on Christmas Eve, Merry wanted to crawl into bed and sleep,
but today was Christmas Eve, and the play was tonight.

Emmaline had rehearsed her solo yesterday with Merry,
and it had been nearly perfect. Bert, Henry, and Kenny had
swelled with pride when she selected them as the wise men.
Robert, Noah, and the other boys were happy to be shepherds.
Jesse had seemed pleased to be chosen as the narrator too.

Without the twins, she came up short of two angels, but
she still had three girls to back up Emmaline, and four angels
would be enough. Merry finished with her hair and smoothed
down the sides of her new red skirt with a bright red and green
sash. Mama had made it as a surprise for tonight and given it
to her this afternoon.

Merry blinked her eyes and puffed out her breath before
pulling on the heavy shoes she'd need walking in the snow.
The only thing that hadn't happened this week was her talk

and time with Clay. They'd both been so busy with getting things ready for Christmas that there had been no time to be together.

Papa waited for her downstairs. "There you are. If you want to get to church early enough to make sure everything is ready, we have to leave now. Remember, I need to come back and pick up everyone else."

"Yes, Papa, I remember." She grabbed her heavy wool cloak and fastened it around her shoulders. "I'm ready to go."

"Good." He turned and strode through the door with Merry following. This would be one of the best Christmas Eve services ever. The twins had found a home with a wonderful couple who promised to bring the girls back for a visit in the spring. Then letters had arrived only yesterday inquiring about adopting boys. Someone was sure to want little Jonathan.

When they were settled in the carriage, she asked, "Papa, do you think those other two couples will want to adopt Jonathan? I hope that maybe one of them will want to take Robert and Kenny. I don't want to see them split up."

"Now, you know we won't let that happen. Just like the twins, siblings must be adopted together. And one of them may very well want to take Jonathan. His aunt and uncle gave us the go ahead for that, so we'll have to let him go. You do realize that, don't you?"

"Yes, but I'll miss him so much, and so will Clay." Those two had bonded like no others she'd seen in the past. She loved the little boy herself, and if circumstances were different, she would adopt him.

"The twins were sad to leave, but I think they were also happy to be going with Mr. and Mrs. Thornton. They certainly were a nice couple. And isn't it wonderful that Lily and Jake's grandmother came to spend Christmas with them?"

"Yes, it seems the Lord had plans all in place for everyone. He wants what's best for all of His children." He reached across for her hand. "I've seen how Clay looks at you and how love fills your eyes when you're with him. If it's in God's plan for you two to be together, then it will happen. Just be patient."

She hadn't done a very good job of hiding her feelings. Even Emmaline said something about it. "It's hard to be patient. That week he was in jail was the longest one of my life. I was so afraid he'd be convicted before the truth could be revealed."

Pa shook his head. "No, as a former lawman, I wouldn't have let it go that far. But it all worked out for the best." He lifted a hand and pointed. "There's Reverend Tate waiting for you at the church. You go on and get done what you need to do, and I'll go back to get the family."

Merry leaned over and kissed his cheek. "Thank you for everything. I couldn't ask for a better Papa than you are." She jumped down from the carriage and hurried to meet Reverend Tate.

Clay finished helping Ma with the supper cleanup then went to shave again before going to the church. The week before Christmas had been extra busy in the store with so many orders coming in and having to be delivered. Most came in to get their items, but some out on the ranches and farms had theirs delivered. Clay had spent most of his week on the delivery wagon.

Tonight he had to find time to speak with Merry. There

was so much he wanted to say to her. He had a special gift picked out for her and a wagonload of gifts donated at the store for the children at Holly Hill. He'd miss Imogene and Eileen, but they were with a good family and would have a great Christmas. Pa had given Mr. Thornton the two gifts the townspeople had collected for the girls, so they'd have something from Prairie Grove too.

He kissed his mother good-bye. "Wish me luck tonight, Ma. If she says yes to my question, this will be the happiest Christmas of my life."

"I'll be praying for you, son, and we'll be over to the church directly."

Clay whistled as he bounded down the outside stairway. The Christmas tree glowed bright and happy from the town square, and the decorations put out by the merchants sparkled in the light from the gas lamps along the streets. What a pretty sight it all made, and one he'd missed for so long, but no more. He was home to stay.

When he reached the church, he found Merry with several church members making sure the stage was all arranged and ready. "Hi, I'm here, ready to help."

Merry's eyes shone bright with happiness when she turned to greet him. "Everything's all set. Soon as the children are here, we'll get them in the dressing rooms and ready to come on when Reverend Tate calls for them."

"We're here, Miss Warner." Mr. and Mrs. Morris walked through the doors followed by the Grainger clan. Both men greeted Clay and expressed their approval of what he'd done for Lily. The women didn't say anything, but their smiles of acceptance said more than words ever could. God had been good to him this past week, and even for the past five years. It'd just taken that long for him to realize it.

He stood around talking and mingling with the members of the congregation. Not a one had an unkind word to say. They all praised him and thanked him for his bravery. He wasn't so sure about the bravery, but the thanks he'd take any day. In addition, Mr. and Mrs. Vaughn had done what he'd predicted. They up and left town before Lily could press charges, and no one knew where they'd gone.

One of the best events of the week had been the arrival of James and Grace Ann's baby girl, whom they named Emily Rose. If plans went the way he wanted them to go, maybe he and Merry would be celebrating a birth of their own a few Christmases from now.

Reverend Tate grasped his hand. "Clay, I can't begin to tell you how proud we are of you. I'm so thankful Karl Laramie and his gang have finally been captured and sent to prison. It did my heart good to see that marshal and his deputy take them away on Thursday."

"It's sad to think they've gone all this time robbing and stealing and hurting people. I just wish I'd been smart enough to stop it earlier." Five years of his life wasted, but now, with God's help, he planned to make up for them. The Scriptures promised that God would return what the locusts had eaten, and he would take God up on that offer.

The reverend placed his hand on Clay's shoulder and peered up at him. "I'm so sorry I didn't listen to James and his wife when they first told me about Lily. We could have taken care of her without all the trouble you went to. I'm glad the three of you persisted and rescued her from that couple."

"I think it all worked out exactly the way God planned it. We're all better people for the experience." Even if no one else believed that, Clay did with all his heart.

Reverend Tate raised an eyebrow. "Now, Clay, I've seen you with Miss Warner. She's a mighty fine teacher, and we sure would hate to lose her, but if what I see passing between you is real, then I want you to know you have my blessing and Mrs. Tate's."

"Thank you, Reverend, that means a lot to me. Just pray all goes well tonight."

The preacher's grin split his face. "I think you mean about more than the play and services tonight. You can count on it." The reverend pumped Clay's hand then turned away with a wink to greet other guests.

The play went off without a hitch, and Emmaline's solo was the highlight of the evening. That young lady would be a beautiful young woman someday. She reminded him of Merry when they were that age.

After the children's presentation, they joined their parents for the remainder of the candlelight service. Merry sat beside him, and just the warmth of her next to him sent emotions through him that he had never before experienced. God had given him a second chance with this woman, and he prayed he wouldn't make a mess of what he wanted to say.

When the final hymn, "Silent Night," had been sung and the candles extinguished, Reverend Tate prayed then wished them all a merry Christmas. Mr. and Mrs. Warner had invited him and his parents to Holly Hill for a Christmas Eve party. Jonathan ran up to him and lifted his arms to be picked up.

"Hey there, Jonathan. I'm glad to see you." He held the

boy high for a moment and let him giggle then lowered him. "You ready for the party?"

"Yes." Jonathan squeezed Clay's cheeks. "You gonna be there?"

"I am indeed. Wouldn't miss seeing you have fun for anything." That was the truth, and Clay hugged the boy. If all went well, Jonathan would be even more excited tomorrow.

He had asked Merry to ride in the sleigh with him up to Holly Hill, and perhaps he'd have a few minutes alone with her. She stepped to his side and grinned at Jonathan.

"I see you found your friend. Mama's looking for you to go back to the party."

Jonathan locked his arms around Clay's neck. "I'm going with Mr. Clay. You go with Mama and Papa."

"Well now, Jonathan, don't you think Miss Merry can ride with us?"

The boy stared at first one then the other and screwed up his mouth. Finally he laughed. "Miss Merry, come with us."

Clay let his breath go in relief, and Merry tweaked Jonathan's nose. "All right, I'll tell Mama and Papa we're going with Mr. Clay. I'll meet you at the buggy."

A few minutes later they boarded the buggy and made their way to Holly Hill with bells jingling on the horse's collar. Jonathan chattered all the way there, the excitement of the night spilling over and infecting everyone with joy.

At the home Mrs. Warner greeted them with hot mulled cider for the adults and hot chocolate for the children. They sang carols around the piano, and Mr. Warner read the Christmas story from the huge family Bible. Clay's gaze circled the room. So many happy, smiling children, a tree glowing with candles, holly leaves and berries everywhere, and the story of Christmas ringing in the air created a memory he wouldn't soon forget.

God had brought him a long way this year, and Clay appreciated his freedom more than he ever dreamed he would. Still, the thing that would make this evening perfect would have to wait just a while longer.

Zach approached him when Merry went off to refill Jonathan's cup. "I was sorry to hear you'd gotten mixed up with Karl, so it's good to see that you've turned your life around. Especially now that it seems you've got your eye on my sister."

"I'm hoping to make Merry a permanent part of my life if she'll have me. And if you approve." Zach had been Merry's protector all those years ago, and now his approval meant more to Clay than he cared to admit.

Zach grinned. "I do approve, but I warn you, if you ever treat her badly or do anything to hurt her, you'll have not only Pa but also me to contend with, and that won't be pretty, believe me."

"You have my word I will treat her well." And that was one promise he intended to keep.

Later Merry sat beside him, and Jonathan sat in his lap. As the little boy nodded off to sleep against his chest, love rose in Clay's heart so that he thought it would burst. This was what he wanted, and he envisioned the years in the future with a family of his own.

Mrs. Warner came and picked up Jonathan. "I think it's time for this one and some others I see around here to go upstairs to bed. It'll be Christmas morning before you know it, and the tree will be filled with wonderful surprises."

Jonathan blinked his eyes and peered over at Clay. "'Member our secret." Then his head fell back on Mrs. Warner's shoulder. A few protests arose from the others, but they all trooped up the stairs to their rooms.

Clay stood with Merry while his parents said good night to Mr. Warner and Mrs. Collins. In a few minutes he'd have Merry to himself. His palms dampened with perspiration, and the words he'd intended to say flew away and left his mind a blank slate.

Mr. Warner and Mrs. Collins said good night and headed up to help with the children. Clay turned to Merry and took her hand. "Now we can have our talk."

Her eyes misted over. "I've missed you so this week. I can't believe everything that's happened in such a short time. So many lives have been changed."

"And I want to change a few more." His heart pounded so hard he figured to break a rib any second. He guided her over to the sofa and sat down, still holding her hand.

"Years ago I saw what a pretty girl you were and how nice you were to everyone. I liked you then, but you moved away and I got mixed up with Karl. I figured I'd never see you again. And then when I saw you that first day back, those old feelings returned and wouldn't let go."

He stopped and paused for breath. He'd have to be careful to make the rest of what he wanted to say mean what he wanted it to. "I've seen what a great teacher you are and how much the children love you. They're lucky to have you. I don't want to take you away from them."

Merry gasped and yanked her hand from his. "What? I thought…never mind what I thought."

She started to stand, but he pulled her back down. "That didn't come out right." He waited until Merry raised her gaze back to his. "What I mean is, I don't want to take you away, but I will if you'll consent to marrying me. I love you and want to be your husband and have a family right here in Prairie Grove."

This time her eyes opened wide, and a smile lit up her face. "Yes, oh, yes." Her arms went around his neck. "I love you too, and I would like nothing better than to settle here with you."

He placed his hands on the sides of her head and brought it close to his. "That's the best thing I've heard all night." Then their lips met again, and all the love they'd bottled up for the past weeks burst forth. As she pressed against him and the kiss deepened, he could think only of the wonders that lay ahead with this woman by his side.

Jonathan's secret. Clay pulled Merry's face away from his but still held her. "There's one more thing, but it will have to wait until morning."

"Clay Barlow, that's so sneaky. How do you expect me to sleep tonight with that kind of statement hanging over me?" She leaned back from him with her hands on her hips. Her face wore a frown, but her eyes danced with merriment.

"Just like the children upstairs are sleeping in anticipation of all those gifts Pa and your father brought in earlier and put under the tree." Except the one he planned for her couldn't be gift wrapped. "With that I'll say good night and wish you pleasant dreams." He brushed her lips with his once again. If he didn't leave now, he may never leave at all.

Chapter 29

On Christmas morning Clay awakened before dawn. He had much to do in order to get to Holly Hill before the children awakened. His parents had been invited up to share the morning with the children, and after his parents heard about what he planned to ask Merry, their enthusiasm for the morning grew.

Ma already had coffee brewing. The aroma spurred Clay to dress in a hurry to join her in the kitchen. He poured himself a cup of coffee. "Where's Pa?"

"He's down in the store looking for something special for Merry to welcome her to our family." She poured herself a cup and joined him at the table. "I have something I want you to give her."

If Clay had to guess, he'd pick his grandmother's cameo brooch as the gift. It had come to Ma as the oldest daughter, and she'd said it would pass on to him one day to give his wife. What a wonderful gift that would be.

Pa appeared at the top of the stairs. "I found that music box I ordered last month. I'm glad it didn't sell, because it's perfect for Merry." He strode to the table and set the glass-topped box on the table. He opened the lid, and the melody of a waltz by Strauss tinkled forth.

"She'll love it. Thank you, Pa." Clay pictured Merry's face when she opened such a treasure. "Speaking of which, we better get on our way to beat those children awake." Breakfast would wait until after the gifts this morning.

A few minutes later Ma returned all bundled up and ready for the ride to Holly Hill. She handed him a black velvet box. "This is for Merry."

Clay opened the box to find the brooch as well as a pearl ring. He blinked his eyes and hugged his mother. "I didn't expect both."

"One is for Christmas, and the other for her birthday. Both your grandmothers left these for you."

"She'll love them. I'll give her the ring for Christmas then announce our plans to marry." He kissed her cheek. "Thank you."

Ma's eyes misted with tears and she said nothing, only smiled. Then they hurried down to the wagon now fitted with sleigh runners and headed for Holly Hill, the bells on their horse jingling all the way.

Anticipation for the morning ahead warmed his heart and soul. His pulse quickened just as it had so many times when he'd awakened on Christmas morning in excitement for what gifts he'd find. Only this time he would be giving the gifts, and that made him want to shout for joy.

Merry awakened before dawn and stretched. Just as she turned over to snuggle back under the covers, she remembered this morning was Christmas. Throwing back the covers, she shivered in the cold then swung her feet from the bed. Her toes searched for and found her slippers. Christmas at Holly Hill had always been special when she was growing up, but now it had even more meaning to her.

She started to pull her wrapper around to tie then flung it aside. Clay would be here with his parents. Nightclothes would not do this morning. Noise from across the hall meant the boys were waking up. She'd have to hurry to beat them downstairs. Of course they wouldn't even get dressed and would run down in their pajamas.

Emmaline's voice carried from the hall. "You'd better come on, Merry. We're going to get there before you do."

Merry buttoned her blouse and then hurried out just in time to see six little heads running down the stairway with Emmaline following. Their squeals of delight echoed to the entryway as they discovered packages with their names under the tree. Ma and Pa had already bought each one a gift when Lucy and Jake Starnes gave her a goodly sum of money to purchase more. Those had been added to what the town had collected, so each child had an abundance of gifts this Christmas. Not like some she remembered from her childhood when one gift had been a wonderful surprise.

She entered the parlor to find the boys all holding gifts. Zach even held a few for himself. "Wow. This is certainly different from some Christmases I remember."

Merry hugged her brother. "It's the best one I've ever had."

Zach tilted his head then lifted her chin with his finger. "Hmm, is that the light of love I see in those pretty green eyes this morning?"

"It just might be, big brother." She turned toward the tree, and a grin crossed her face at the eight faces waiting expectantly for Mama and Papa to appear. They would wait to open their gifts until everyone had arrived in the parlor. Kenny and Henry counted theirs aloud while the girls fingered the bows adorning the packages.

Jonathan pulled on her skirt. "Where's Mr. Clay?"

"He'll be here in a minute." A knock sounded on the door. "I bet that's him now."

The little boy flew across the room and yanked open the door. "It is! It is, Mr. Clay."

A few seconds later Clay entered the room with Jonathan in his arms. "Well, looks like it's time to open some gifts." He set Jonathan on the floor and turned to greet Merry's brother.

Zach grabbed his hand and winked. "If you did what I figured you'd do last night, then welcome to the family."

"Thanks. I'm glad we have your approval. I remember a time when you might have socked me one."

The two shook hands, and Merry's heart wanted to burst with the joy of not only the season but also Clay's newly declared love.

Grandma, Mama, and Papa came in with Mr. and Mrs. Barlow. Once greetings were expressed, they sat down, and the children tore into their packages. Wooden trains, animated penny banks, whirligigs, tops, dolls, and games filled the children with glee. After the adults had exchanged a few items,

Mr. Barlow handed Merry a box decorated with a large red bow.

Even the children quieted down as Merry opened the package. She removed the cherry wood music box, and tears misted her eyes at its beauty. When the melody filled the room, the tears fell. "Thank you so much. It's beautiful."

The girls came to inspect the box and see how it worked. As Merry showed them, Grandma and Mrs. Barlow picked up the paper and ribbon to dispose of it.

Clay stepped to her side. "And I have something for you too. Actually two more things for you. One is a question, and the other is a gift."

What in the world could the question be? He'd already proposed last night. This must be what he'd hinted at last night. First he handed her a small black velvet box. "This is my gift to you, and I want you to wear it as a symbol of our love. It belonged to my grandmother, then my mother, and now it is yours."

She opened the box and tears filled her eyes again. She'd never been this weepy on Christmas before, but then she'd never accepted a marriage proposal either. Her fingers caressed the pearl ring. "It's beautiful. I'll treasure it always."

"Here, let me put it put it on." He slipped the ring onto her finger. It went on smooth as silk, and he kissed her cheek.

Then he turned and called for everyone's attention. When quiet settled over the room, he made his announcement. "Last night, Merry consented to be my wife."

Emmaline squealed. "You're getting married?"

Merry laughed. "That's right, and all of you will be a part of it."

Everyone gathered around to offer hugs, congratulations, and exclamations over the ring. Finally Mama stepped back and clapped her hands. "It's time to get this cleaned up and eat that breakfast waiting for us."

A few groans sounded, but the aroma of cinnamon rolls from the kitchen got them busy. Clay pulled Merry aside.

"Now for the question part. You said you'd marry me last night, and that was the best gift you could give me, but there's a little boy here who wanted a gift that only you and I can give him. If you notice, he's sitting over there by the tree, but he's not playing with his things like the others are. I think he's waiting for something else."

Jonathan's facial expression was not that of a happy child with an armload of gifts. He stared up at the tree as though he expected something else to happen. Then the meaning of Clay's words hit her. She whirled around to stare at him. "You mean a mother and a father."

At his nod, Merry threw her arms around Clay's neck. "Yes, let's tell him now."

Clay called out to Jonathan, who jumped up and ran to him. "Did you 'member, Mr. Clay?"

"Yes, and Miss Merry and I want to be your parents just like you asked me." Clay picked up Jonathan and held him in one arm with his other arm around Merry. Jonathan reached out and wrapped one arm around Merry's neck and the other around Clay's.

"Now you're my ma and pa."

The room had grown quiet when Clay had called to Jonathan. Grandma Collins and Mrs. Barlow stood with their arms crossed, big grins on their faces and tears in their eyes.

They were joined by Mama and Papa and Mr. Barlow. The children also gathered around them with expressions of delight.

Mama clapped her hands again. "Well, now, I say it's time we all have a good breakfast and make some plans for a wedding."

Zach clapped Clay on the back. "Good show. Guess I'll have to get used to being an uncle right away."

"That you will, big brother." Joy and love filled Merry's heart to the bursting point.

Jonathan pushed away from Clay. "Put me down. I has to do something."

Clay set him on the floor, and the boy ran to the front window. He pulled back the curtain and pressed against the glass with his eyes looking toward heaven. "Thank You, Jesus, for a new ma and pa. That's the bestest gift of all."

Tears ran down Merry's cheeks again, but she didn't care since they were tears of pure joy. "This is one Christmas I'll never forget. You are one wonderful man, Clayton Barlow, and I love you more than you could ever know." Then her lips met his with a promise of more to come in the days ahead. In such a short time her future had grown even brighter than she could ever have dreamed. It was a perfect Holly Hill Christmas.

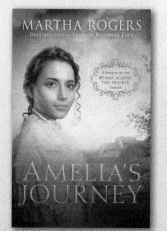